Some glittering reviews for the GEEK GiRL books:

"Charming, flawed, wise and true… Geek Girl has transformed funny fiction in a way unseen since the mighty Louise Rennison"
The Bookseller

"Funny, original and this year's must-read for teenage girls"
The Sun

"A must-read!"
The Guardian

"Delightfully quirky"
Teen Now

"Uproarious misadventures"
Publishers Weekly

"A timeless classic that will be remembered forever"
LoveReading4Kids

The **GEEK GiRL** *series in reading order*

For teenage me.
High-five.

FOREVER GEEK

HOLLY SMALE

HarperCollins *Children's Books*

First published in Great Britain by
HarperCollins *Children's Books* in 2017
HarperCollins *Children's Books* is a division of HarperCollins*Publishers* Ltd,
HarperCollins Publishers
1 London Bridge Street
London SE1 9GF

The HarperCollins website address is:
www.harpercollins.co.uk
1

PAPERBACK ISBN 978–0–00–796820-6

Holly Smale asserts the moral right to be identified as the author of the work.

Typeset in Frutiger 11.5/18 by Palimpsest Book Production Ltd, Falkirk, Stirlingshire
Printed and bound in England by CPI Group (UK) Ltd, Croydon CR0 4YY

luck [lʌk] noun

1 The chance occurrence of situations or events favourable or unfavourable to a person's interests
2 A person's apparent tendency to have good or ill fortune
3 An expression of good wishes
4 To prosper or succeed

ORIGIN fifteenth century, from early Middle Dutch *gheluc* – "happiness or good fortune"

1

My name is Harriet Manners, and I am lucky.

I know I'm lucky because:

1. I'm right next to a window, even though seats are randomly allocated so my chances were only one in four.

2. My Wi-Fi is working perfectly, which means I can let everyone at home know I'm sitting next to a window.

3. And send them a list of points detailing how amazingly lucky I am... Much like this one.

4. I've just watched *seven* documentaries back to back, thus deepening my understanding of aeroplanes, orcas, mating rituals of the flamingo, Russian space stations, the Yucatán Peninsula, parrots and Christian Dior.

5. I actually enjoyed the last option, even though it was definitely not voluntary.

6. So far this morning, I have already been to Hong Kong.

Since waking up today, I have ridden a glass cable car across Tung Chung Bay to a giant statue of Buddha, taken photos of the South China Sea and educated tourists in the immediate vicinity about the political tension caused by the Chinese government trying to claim the region for itself.

(A couple of Americans tried to tip me ten dollars for my knowledge, although the official park guides didn't seem quite as impressed.)

And it gets even *better*.

In the last twenty-four hours I have crossed thirteen countries and three oceans, travelled 9,865 miles and eaten three and a half doughnuts (two of mine and one and a half of Bunty's).

With the aid of a map and satellite navigation, I have tried to spot the 960 bridges in Berlin, stared in wonderment at the 62 per cent of Austria covered in the Alps, watched the dark sands of the Karakum Desert in Turkmenistan and the shimmering lakes of Sakartvelo (also known as Georgia).

I have identified Clear Air Turbulence over France.

But the *main* reason I know I'm lucky is because of whose head is currently resting on my shoulder.

I'll give you a couple of clues: she has dark, wavy hair.

Her eyes are gently closed, and her nose is twitching like an adorable baby rabbit. Her feet are crossed at the ankles, her arms are flopped loosely across her stomach and her mouth is slightly open.

Every now and then our seats jiggle and she mutters, her head moves a bit to the side, her eyes open and –

"Harriet, *will you please stop watching me sleep*?"

Delighted, I beam at my Best Friend.

Natalie Grey: Sartorial Genius, Temper-Loser, Truth-Sayer and the non-kissing soulmate of my sixteen-year-old life. And – as of yesterday morning – my intimate travel-adventure companion. The Samwise to my Frodo; the Robin to my Batman; like Tom and Jerry, except without all the firecrackers, hammers and attempts to poison each other.

The widely loved salt to my less popular pepper.

"Nat!" I say happily, handing her the half of doughnut I saved specially. "You're awake!"

She blinks, sits up stiffly and gazes blearily around the plane. "Harriet, it's been a twenty-four-hour journey interrupted by an unexplained walk up a mountain to see a big fat stone man," she says, yawning widely and rearranging her ponytail. "Honestly, I'm as surprised by this news as you are."

"It was Siddhartha Gautama," I inform her. "And he was made out of bronze and quite slim compared to some other representations of the father of Buddhism."

Then we both lean forward to look curiously at Bunty, propped up on the seat next to us. My nomadic grandmother has a pale pink velvet cushion wrapped round her neck and a blue silk tasselled scarf tied round her eyes, and she's snoring so loudly the tiny child in front of us keeps popping up over the seat and asking if she's "broken".

Nat takes the doughnut-half and grins.

"So how much longer have we got?" she says more perkily, leaning over me to stare at the approaching clouds. "Are we nearly there yet? Give me the precise facts, Harriet Manners-style."

The seat-belt light pings and my beam widens.

"Twenty-eight minutes, three hundred and one miles," I say, obediently clicking myself into place then pushing rule-breaking Nat back into her seat and doing the same to her. "Or twenty-eight thousand feet."

There's a small plane shudder and my ears pop.

"Twenty-seven thousand feet," I amend in excitement, watching the screen in front of me. "Twenty-six thousand..."

"Twenty-five…" Nat laughs.

"Twenty-four, twenty-three…"

"Twenty-two."

And – with a squeak – we high-five each other loudly.

Because this is the *biggest* reason I know I'm lucky.

The word *gravity* comes from the Latin *gravis*, which means *heavy,* and the force of Earth's gravity on us at all times is a constant 9.80665 m/s^2. Gravity holds the universe together: it pulls stars, galaxies, planets and subatomic particles towards each other, anchors us to the floor and keeps us grounded.

But science and the screen in front of me can say what they like: gravity has nothing on me any more.

We may be going Down Under, but I'm on top of the world.

Because as the clouds finally clear and the blue ocean expands beneath us, I look down at the home-made badges pinned to our T-shirts:

OZ – THE LUCKY COUNTRY

This is going to be the holiday of a lifetime.

Australia, *here we come.*

2

So while we get on with the landing preparations – seats forward, tables up and so forth – you'll probably want to know what's been going on since you last saw me, right?

That's what we normally do here.

I update you on the ups and downs of my life, interesting developments, a few particularly fascinating facts that I've found out in the interim period (like the fact that anthropologists can track human migration by examining earwax or that Lithuania has an annual crawling race for babies).

And you listen very politely, even though you didn't actually ask me how I was in the first place.

Well, this time I'm afraid there's not much to say.

There really isn't that much that can happen in four days. Especially when a large chunk of that period has been spent sitting on a fuzzy aeroplane seat with inadequate leg room, watching documentaries

and devouring guidebooks about Australia before enthusiastically sharing the information.

Apparently there are more stars in the night sky than there are words that have ever been spoken by every human who has ever lived, but after the last few days of sitting next to me I think Bunty, Nat and our exhausted flight attendant would question that statement.

I have certainly narrowed the gap.

What I *can* tell you, however, is the following:

My maverick father started back at the advertising agency that fired him last year and immediately set about trying to get fired again, and my baby sister Tabby said her very first word (which made me an incredibly proud big sister, even though "manana" would never be allowed in a game of Scrabble).

Wilbur is back to being Supreme Agent Extraordinaire, and the last time I saw him he was spraying himself all over with rainbow glitter while calling it "unicorn deodorant".

Toby is now in an official *Romantic Twosome* with Rin, who has moved temporarily into my bedroom while she models in London and dresses our cat Victor up like an extravagant Disney princess. (Statistically, cat owners are thirty per cent less likely to suffer a heart attack than those without a pet. Nobody has looked into the statistics vice versa.)

My stepmother, Annabel, spent the entire preparatory period writing down Emergency Numbers, then Back-up Emergency Numbers, then Reserve Back-up Emergency Numbers, then laminating them all in case they get wet in a famously dry country.

"Just…" she said, thrusting shiny KEEP WITH YOU AT ALL TIMES sheets of A4 into the back pocket of my already stuffed suitcase, "make sure you take care of each other, OK?"

Bunty and I rolled our eyes at each other from across my bed.

"Bels, darling." My grandmother smiled fondly. "The universe holds us carefully in its warm, cupped hands, like a small child with a tiny fluffy bunny. You don't need to worry so much."

Annabel immediately swivelled her eyes towards me.

"Sure," I agreed with a shrug, even though I'm sixteen years old and a fully fledged sixth-former: I think I know how to take care of myself.

And last but not least, I said goodbye to Jasper.

My…

Well, I'm not entirely sure *what* he is, to be honest.

My handsome, sarcastic, More-Than-Friend-But-Not-Quite-Boyfriend of four days: firmly occupying the space where you kiss and hold hands but haven't signed a formal relationship agreement in pen yet.

Although I've drafted one up in pencil, obviously.

It's important to stay prepared for the next step of romance at all times.

"I'll be ten hours ahead," I explained to him. We were curled up on the sofa, watching a *Planet Earth* episode about 400-metre-deep caves in Mexico while Annabel, Bunty and Dad talked quietly in the kitchen, presumably about how best to control me abroad.

"I know, Harriet."

"That means when it's eight am in England, it's six pm in Australia. And when it's midday for you, it'll be ten pm for me. And when it's seven pm here it'll be—"

"Five am," Jasper said, narrowing one bright blue and one brown eye at the printout I'd just given him. "I have basic mathematical skills of my own, but thanks for the calculations."

I fixed him with a stern expression.

"You *say* that, Jasper King, but accuracy is *everything* when large distances are involved. So our scheduled phone calls are in blue, webcam calls are in pink, emails are in green and texts are purple. You may want to stick the A2 version on the cafe wall."

His thick eyebrows shot up. "Or we could just play it by ear?"

"Well, of *course*," I agreed, rolling my eyes and gesturing at another section. "Ad hoc and breezy romance options are in orange: here, here and *here*."

At which point Jasper shook his head and kissed me.

And that's about it.

Team JINTH was transformed into Team JRNTH with a quick swipe of a marker pen, exam preparation was packed into my suitcase, and I've efficiently put my whole world in order so I can leave it neatly behind for two weeks.

I'm now ready to pioneer the unfamiliar, like Harriet Adams who travelled South America, Asia and the South Pacific in the early 1900s and wrote for *National Geographic* magazine.

Or Harriet the tortoise, who was transported from England to Australia, where she passed peacefully away.

Which hopefully won't happen here.

At least... it'll be *mostly* unfamiliar, anyway.

"Harriet," Nat says in a low voice as the plane lands with a jolt and Bunty wakes up with a loud snort. "Do we need to talk?"

I blink at my best friend in surprise. "We've been doing that for the last forty-eight hours, haven't we?"

She had an airbed on my floor the night before we left: I made the most of the situation.

"*You* have," Nat laughs. "Solidly. But I meant about...

you know. *Where* we are. Or, more specifically –" she studies me carefully – "*who might also be here.*"

Because there's a reason why I know all about the gap between England and Australia. I understand how messy conversations can get between two countries because there's experience behind that knowledge too.

And if I'm keen to stick to a definite schedule of communication, we all know there's undeniable logic involved.

This is *not* my first long-distance romance.

"Nope," I say firmly, standing up and grabbing my satchel. "This is a clean slate, Nat. A brand-new adventure for both of us."

And it starts right *now*.

3

Anyway, here are some great facts about Australia:

1. It's the sixth-largest country in the world, covering over 7.6 million square kilometres.
2. Which makes it thirty-two times bigger than the UK.
3. The population is only 24 million: less than half of England.
4. It has 200 different languages.
5. And three times more sheep than people.
6. There are only on average 2.66 humans per km/sq.

You know what all this means?

It means that if you *happen* to have an Australian ex-boyfriend, and he *happens* to currently live in Australia, and you *happen* to also be there for a fortnight, the chances of bumping into him are so small they're not even worth worrying about.

Especially if he doesn't know you're in the same country

because you haven't spoken a word to each other in seven months.

They're minuscule. Ridiculous. Tiny.

There's *literally* three times more chance of being jumped on by one of Australia's sixty million kangaroos or being bitten by a particularly aggressive sheep.

So I'm not concerned or anxious about my new location in the slightest.

I just wish I could say the same for Nat.

"But, Harriet," she says as we wobble off the plane on aching legs, Bunty yawning and stretching in front of us like a jingling pink cat. "Shouldn't we at least *prepare* an... Emergency Ex-boyfriend Contingency Plan or something? Make a... pie chart or a... scatter graph? Just in case?"

Those are ridiculous suggestions, frankly.

We'd clearly need a flow chart: the other two options would be absolutely useless for this particular purpose.

"We don't need anything," I say reassuringly, patting her arm and trying to dredge up my newfound breezy attitude. "Life's more about going with the flow, isn't it? Embracing wherever fortune leads you. Gracefully gliding over the waves of chance and luck, like a bottlenose dolphin."

"Or an alpaca," Bunty says cheerfully from some

distance in front of us. "You wouldn't *believe* what they can do on a surfboard."

Nat lifts her eyebrows, then looks pointedly at my old, beaten-up school satchel. "OK... Are you telling me you've got *no* plans for the next two weeks? At *all*?"

I stick my nose in the air. "Yup."

"You're planning on *winging it* the whole time? Just *seeing what happens*? *Flying by the seat of your pants* for fourteen days? Without *strategy*? *Completely plan-less?*"

A warm fizz is starting at the bottom of my stomach.

You may remember that last week there was rather a lot of drama caused by my relentless controlling, demanding and organising; by my inability to just let things *happen*.

And Nat was right at the front of the I Told You So queue.

So I promised her I'd work on being more laid-back and free-flowing moving forward.

"Exactly." My nose gets a bit higher. "I have learnt my lesson, Natalie. I understand that life doesn't always do what I want it to do, when I want it to, and sometimes I have to stop trying to force it. In the last few days I have *grown* and *developed*."

Then I try to walk faster so I can catch up with Bunty.

"Sure," Nat laughs, keeping pace with me easily on

her long legs. "So what's in your satchel, Harriet? It looks kind of *heavy*."

"Australian dollars," I say, walking a bit faster. "Did you know they were the first country to introduce plastic money? Plastic money weighs more than paper, you know."

"Can I see it?"

"What?" I speed up a little more. "No. This is my *private property.*"

"I mean," Nat grins, "it's almost as if there's something in that bag you *are hiding from me.*"

I'm now jogging and my best friend is effortlessly striding next to me, thanks to her natural levels of athleticism and lower body strength and my complete and utter lack of them.

In 1996, three neuroscientists were probing the brain of a macaque monkey when they stumbled across a cluster of cells in the premotor cortex: the part responsible for planning movements. They found that the cells fired not only when the monkey performed an action, but when the monkey saw the same action performed by someone else. Then they investigated humans, and found that "mirror neurons" can include sensation and emotion too.

Which basically means that we are *scientifically* capable of reading the minds of the people around us.

I really wish Nat would stop doing it right now.

It is *super* invasive.

"Did you know," I say, clutching my bag tightly and dipping to the left, "that Roman legionaries carried satchels called *loculi*. Isn't that interesting?"

"Random Distraction Facts won't work on me," Nat laughs, dipping smoothly after me. "I've known you *way* too long."

See what I mean? *Meddlesome.*

I hop to the right. "Why are you so obsessed with me?"

"Give me your bag."

"No."

"Give it to me."

"NO!" I dodge the other way, then take a few steps backwards, stumbling into a disgruntled fellow passenger.

Nat abruptly does a sharp twist on the spot.

And before I can react, she's tackled me into a firm headlock, undone my satchel and pulled out something heavy and bright.

"Ha!" she shouts, waving it in the air. "Busted!"

"Oh, what *pretty* colours!" Bunty says from where she's been calmly watching us scrummage at the side of the corridor. "And what neat calligraphy skills, Harriet, darling! How *clever* you are."

You know what it is, don't you?

Of course you do: we haven't known each other for years for nothing. It's a rainbow-highlighted folder with HARRIET'S TOP SECRET EPIC AUSTRALIAN FORTNIGHT OF FUN "DOWN UNDER" PLAN written across it in big purple and pink letters.

With *Attached Detailed Strategy* written underneath in silver.

And *(Don't Show Nat – I Am Breezy Now)* in gold.

Sometimes I really hate having a kindred spirit who knows me inside and out.

There's just no privacy at all.

"Even dolphins need echolocation guidance now and then," I mutter crossly, head still clamped under Nat's forearm like the ghost of Anne Boleyn. "Waves can be *extremely* disorientating."

"Idiot," Nat laughs, pinching my nose with her fingers.

Then she lets go and starts walking towards baggage reclaim with my no-longer-secret folder held against her stomach.

"Natalie!" I shout after her. "What are you going to do with that?"

Honestly, it took me ages. I had to hole-punch and put everything together in the bathroom so Nat wouldn't see that I'd regressed to being an epic organisational wizard all over again.

"We've only got two weeks to tick it all off, you total Control Freak," Nat yells over her shoulder. "So I reckon we'd better get cracking."

4

Are you ready for a particularly awesome new fact?

In the middle of the human ear are three tiny bones, each smaller than a grain of rice. They're called the *ossicular chain,* and they're the only part of the body that never changes as you get older.

That's what I think true friendship is.

It's realising that while many parts of you are going to grow and develop over the years, others are going to stay exactly the same and there's nothing you can do about it.

Accepting that tiny bits of somebody are what make them who they are, and that they'll always be there: even if they're inconvenient or unattractive or sometimes extremely irritating.

No matter how deeply they've been buried or hidden.

But loving them intensely anyway.

Which is handy, because I *really* thought Nat would go off the deep end when she realised I'd planned out the entire two-week vacation in close detail.

Then laminated a schedule, in case it got wet.

"Watch *La bohème* at Sydney Opera House," Nat reads as we stand by the luggage area. "Inform Nat that its 15,500 light bulbs are changed every year, then tell her about the chicken."

She glances up at me with a frown.

"In the eighties a live chicken walked off the stage during a performance of *Boris Godunov*," I say, scanning the bags. "And landed on a cellist."

"Oh, I *remember* that," Bunty laughs, nodding. "Feathers everywhere. There's been a net over the orchestra pit ever since."

"Throw axes in St Peters?" Nat says, glancing down again.

"There's a warehouse where you can pay fifty dollars to do so," I explain, watching the conveyor belt carefully. "I feel like it's a useful life skill to develop."

"Sure," Nat laughs. "If we lived in *Game of Thrones*."

"You can never be too prepared for unexpected dragons," I mutter, still searching for my luggage.

Nat got her black suitcase more than ten minutes ago, Bunty carried her scruffy floral patchwork bag on the plane with her and I'm kind of impatient to get going. There are 4,775 square miles of Sydney and we have just one fortnight to see them all.

That's 341 square miles a day, or more than fourteen an hour.

According to my calculations, we'll have to move faster than three Eastern Grey Squirrels.

"There's also Mrs Macquarie's Chair," I add distractedly. "Made out of stone and carved by convicts who—"

A loud commotion is coming from the baggage entrance.

Sugar cookies.

It appears that my enormous yellow suitcase has started a pile-up: boxes and bags are wedged behind it and there's a screeching noise coming from the conveyor-belt wheels.

"Blimey," somebody laughs. "Anybody missing a dead body or the kitchen sink?"

Flushing, I leap forward to free my suitcase.

"There are half a million bacteria in every square inch of a kitchen sink," I mumble, grabbing the top handle. "I really don't think they would let one through customs."

Then I put all of my admittedly limited strength into trying to lift the yellow monster off the conveyor belt. "Umm," I grunt as it shifts forward and I start being dragged along next to it. "Guys?"

Still tugging, I'm dragged a few more metres. "Guys?"

The average fully grown human has approximately 640

muscles, and it's at moments like this I really wish I'd spent a little more time on those in my arms and a lot less on the ones in my mouth.

Strangers are beginning to dive out of the way as I'm jerked rapidly along the floor like an obsessive dog refusing to let go of its chew-toy.

My cheeks are starting to flame; my eyes to prickle.

Hello, familiar signs of public humiliation.

"Guys?" I bleat for the third time, desperately clambering on top of my stupidly large suitcase with one foot hopping along the ground like an amputee kangaroo. "Can I get a bit of help over here, please?"

"Madam," a security guard says sharply from across the room as I raise my hopping foot and perch on my suitcase. "Get off the conveyor belt. This isn't a fairground ride."

I already know that. The world's oldest fairground ride dates back to the 1870s and was a very regal little merry-go-round with painted horses, i.e. somewhere comfortable to sit.

Finally, just when I think this is my life – I'm going to go through the flappy plastic doors at the end and disappear forever like Veruca Salt in *Charlie and the Chocolate Factory* – a sympathetic stranger hits the emergency STOP button.

In the meantime, two of the people I love most in the

world are collapsed in a tear-stained heap on the floor. They're laughing so hard that Bunty's headscarf has slipped over one eye and Nat's glossy ponytail has fallen out completely.

Apparently in Japan you can rent new friends: maybe I should look at how much pocket money I have.

These two are literally *useless*.

"If I'd known this was a suitcase rodeo," Nat snorts, finally standing up and helping me off, then grabbing the other side of my gigantic suitcase, "I'd have brought my cowboy boots."

"Sorry, darling," Bunty laughs. "But I *did* tell you to pack light. What happened to the lovely new backpack I bought you?"

It's on the floor of my bedroom, where it belongs, given that it's candy-floss pink and there are no compartments in it for novels, homework, a laptop, emergency planning supplies, staple guns, hole-punchers or a miniature printer.

I mean, you just don't know when you're going to need to change your documents at the last minute abroad, do you? They may not have the same size hole-punchers in Australia.

"What's even *in* here, anyway?" Nat asks as we finally manage to lug the ginormous suitcase on to the floor with a loud *crash*.

"Literally everything," I admit in a small voice.

OK. I get it. Maybe I should have tried to wing this holiday a little bit after all.

5

So I think it's about time this vacation started in earnest.

As I haul sixteen years' worth of belongings across the Sydney arrival lounge, I can feel the sunshine; bursting in bright waves through the windows. Piercing the glass ceilings; baking the outside of the building like a huge loaf of bread; bouncing off the glowing brown and freckled cheeks of the people around us.

Australia is officially the world's oldest, driest and flattest inhabited continent. It has the highest solar irradiance of any country, over 3,000 hours of sunshine a year and enough sunlight per square kilometre to power the entire country by solar energy alone.

It also has the highest incidence of skin cancer anywhere on the planet.

This is *literally* the sunniest place on Earth.

It was raining hard when we left England, and Jasper emailed me a photo of himself a few hours ago: freezing

cold in the corner of the cafe with raindrops running down his face.

What did I tell you? *Lucky.*

"Wow," Nat sighs as we push through the airport doors and a vivid cobalt sky opens up in front of us. "Harriet, have I told you recently how much I love you modelling? Like, I *love* it. You should do it forever. Maybe in the Maldives next."

Then she slips on her gold sunglasses, pulls them down her nose and winks at a really good-looking blond boy to our right.

He walks straight into the glass door.

Much like the sun, Nat's undiluted effect on boys has always been overwhelming, disorientating and potentially physically damaging.

"Poppets," Bunty says, leaning against a wall and smiling as we start giggling. "I need a few minutes to tap back into the universe and relocate, or the Aussie Karmic Spirits won't know where I am. Why don't you take this and I'll meet you there?"

She reaches into what I assumed were rips in her long, floaty orange dress but are actually pockets, and pulls out a rusty key tied with string to a scrap of bark with this scratched into it:

MAGICAL KOOKABURRA SHANTY CABIN
Bondi Beach
Sydney

There are droopy pink feathers attached to the wood and what appear to be stars etched on it with biro.

"Take any taxi you like, lovelies," she adds, handing us a shabby floral purse. "I'll be just behind you."

Nat and I look at the address again, then at each other.

I don't need my *Oxford English Dictionary* to translate *shanty cabin*. The kookaburra is a native Australian bird: the world's largest kingfisher, which – unlike other birds of the same family – hunts non-aquatic prey like snakes, frogs, insects, mice and rats.

I'm guessing there's lots of the above at this "shanty cabin" too.

And possibly, judging by the hand-drawn stars, no roof either.

In fact, knowing my grandmother, we're going to be sleeping on a rough, splintery wood floor, covered in hessian sacks, surrounded by hundreds of lovingly nicknamed pests.

Which doesn't particularly bother me – although Australia *does* have more deadly spiders than anywhere else on the planet – but it's going to *massively* bother Nat.

For once, I might just keep my knowledge to myself.

"*Magic*," Nat reads with another delighted grin at me. "Coooool."

I don't have the heart to tell her that this means there's no electricity and her mobile phone will have to work via "happy vibes" and "high energy auras".

Still – we're in *Australia*!

Hopping with excitement, we grab our suitcases and wheel them towards a shiny white taxi.

Then I pause and turn round.

Bunty's shielding her eyes against the harsh sunlight and searching for something in the patchwork bag strung across her front. Her pink, fluffy hair is backlit by sunshine, and sparkle is flickering from the sequins on her purple flip-flops, the orange beads on her dress, the blue glitter on her scarf, the amethyst rings on her fingers.

She looks like a flamingo dressed for its first prom.

Impulsively, I run back. "Thank you," I say gratefully, throwing my arms around her. "I know we wouldn't have been allowed to come here without you."

My parents may have gently relaxed the reins and resigned themselves to the jet-setting demands of my fashion career, but agreeing to two sixteen-year-olds hanging out together, unchaperoned, on the other side of the world?

They're more flexible; not clinically *insane*.

Bunty hugs me, then taps her hands on my shoulders. "Don't be a silly-billy," she says, nudging me towards Nat. "I'm just thrilled to share a little bit of the world with my granddaughter. Now, off you go."

6

You know those moments when life feels like a film?

The world is ordinary and everyday, then – with an unexpected *pop* – suddenly it's not. Colours are brighter and air is lighter and you somehow know you're exactly where you're supposed to be, doing exactly what you're supposed to be doing, with exactly who you're supposed to be doing it with.

And for a second you detach and frame it in your mind.

Capturing the scene; saving every detail so you can play it back when something is happening in real life that you don't know how to close your eyes to or turn off.

Well, this is one of those moments.

And as the taxi sails through the clean, broad streets of Sydney – as we open the car windows and stick our heads out so that our hair whips upwards like Sulphur Crested Cockatoo feathers – Nat feels it too.

I know, because she's wearing the ridiculous duck-face

pout she claims she doesn't have, but which she's been using every single time she puts on sunglasses since she was nine years old.

And – with a bang – I can suddenly feel the happiness radiating from us both like summer.

"*G'day*, Sydney!" my best friend yells jubilantly at the sunlit streets. "Aren't you a little *ripper*?"

"*Strewth*," I shout, laughing. "Sydney, you are *bonzer*."

"*Reckon!*" Nat bellows, black hair streaming behind her.

"*Deffo!*" I roar.

"*Fair dinkum*," Nat screams at a passing dog, "put some *snags on the barbie*!"

I knew my *Ace Australian Catchphrases and Words!!* book would come in handy at some point: despite being clichéd and culturally insensitive and inexplicably fronted by a photo of an outdoor wooden toilet.

"British, are you?" the taxi driver smiles wryly, turning up the radio so we have a suitably glorious soundtrack for our ride. "Never have guessed."

Grinning, Nat and I turn to each other: hair floating, imaginary camera whirring, fictional director giving us a big thumbs-up.

There are only 27,375 days in the average lifetime.

That's 657,000 hours, or just under forty million minutes. Two and a half billion seconds each, if we're very lucky.

And we don't get to keep all of them.

Thanks to the finite capacity of human long-term memory, we only get a limited selection of choice moments to play over and over again: whenever we like, for the rest of our lives.

But these are the moments that last forever.

Twenty minutes and a lot of singing (Nat) and incoherent warbling (me – because I don't know any words to songs) later, the taxi pulls into a dappled street lined with gnarled trees and bright flowers I don't recognise.

There are 24,000 native plants in Australia, and I intend to learn about as many as I can, as fast as physically possible.

Especially the ten per cent that make cyanide.

It's a really good idea to improve your knowledge of botany in an environment where trees and shrubs can literally poison you.

"Nat," I say as the car stops next to a high, straggly and knotted wooden fence and we pay and clamber out with our suitcases. "Umm, I think I need to prepare you."

Then I pause, reach into my suitcase and give Nat a mosquito spray, a fly net, antibacterial hand wipes, a pack of matches and an inflatable cushion.

Sometimes actions speak louder than words.

"Harriet," Nat laughs as we cautiously approach a

rotting door with our rusty key. "Bunty just spent twenty-four hours sleeping or putting half-eaten plane food in her knapsack. I'm fully aware that for the next fortnight we won't be exactly living in the lap of I—"

The door swings open with a click and there's a silence.

The kind of silence you could surf all the way home on, should you be interested in wave-riding silences.

"—uxury," I finish for her.

Because there's no other way to put it.

We're looking at the most expensive apartment either of us has ever seen in our lives.

7

Honestly, I have no idea what Bunty does for a living.

(Or did. She must be retired now.)

But – as Nat and I stand stock-still like the fauns in Narnia, frozen into stone in the doorway – it occurs to me that at some point I probably should have asked.

Worldwide, women earn a combined eighteen trillion US dollars a year (approximately 24 per cent less than men), yet – thanks to running most of the world's households – spend twenty-eight trillion between them.

My grandmother must be *singlehandedly* skewing these statistics.

Gleaming in front of us is a huge, beautiful room. There are polished oak floors and high walls reaching up to a cavernous, cream-painted arched ceiling, and giant windows edged with transparent muslin curtains, glowing with warm yellow sunshine.

On one side is an enormous, tufted velvet green sofa scattered with silk pillows of every imaginable hue; under

it are delicately embroidered rugs; propped around the floor are books and carvings and vivid paintings.

The air is filled with the intoxicatingly deep fragrance of flowers and incense and potpourri and just-lit candles.

To the other side is an intricately carved mahogany kitchen, and from the high ceiling hang dozens of tiny crystal lights suspended like stars. Just visible to the left – through an arched door – are two wood-panelled bedrooms with the biggest four-poster beds I've ever seen: one hung with pale yellow fabric, the other with green, surrounded by fresh white flowers interwoven with hundreds of tiny sparkling lights.

Directly in front of us are huge sliding doors, opening on to a sparkling emerald infinity swimming pool dropping into nothing with a musical splash, surrounded by giant beanbags and multicoloured lanterns.

And behind it all is the Tasman Sea.

Glittering and immense and throwing prismatic rainbows through the crystals strung from every possible hook.

I know Annabel has told me that money isn't important: that there are more precious things in life and that cash can't buy happiness yada yada yada.

But it *must* be able to rent it for a little while.

* * *

"Oh!" Nat whimpers happily, running forward with her hands stretched out like a toddler seeing a Labrador puppy. "Oh. Oh. *Oh.*"

She presses a button and a wall panel slides open to reveal a free-standing green marble bath with clawed gold feet and a spectacular view of a huge, rambling garden, complete with cinema screen and miniature teepee.

"Oh!" Nat opens an enormous walk-in closet.

"Oh!" Nat claps and every light in the house turns on. "Oh!" she says, clapping again to turn them off. "Oh!"

I laugh as the house starts flashing with Nat's joy.

Then I watch my best friend scamper ecstatically around the apartment, rubbing herself against everything like our cat Victor when he's expecting food.

The last place Nat stayed in abroad was a ramshackle farmhouse in the South of France with a boy wearing green Lycra cycling shorts: she really deserves this.

Finally, she lobs herself on to the bed in a starfish shape – clicking the radio on and off by snapping her fingers – and I wander outside towards the sea.

There's a small path winding over a tiny stone bridge to a little wooden hut with a single white bed, a basic table and a large window facing the ocean. Unlit candles and flowers are scattered along the windowsill, and there's a tiny shelf full of hippy books about rainbows and crystals.

"Nat!" I yell in excitement, running my hands over a battered copy of *The Daisy-Chain Guide To Living Your Most Petal-Filled Life*, lying on the middle of the bed. "I found the fairy shed!"

"I'm afraid Natalie's discovered the vintage copies of *Vogue*," a familiar voice says behind me. "So we may not see her again for quite some time."

I spin round. Bunty is standing on the centre of the bridge, shimmering like a female Merlin. And standing next to her – with arms crossed tightly – is a severe-faced woman with a sharp crop, a neat, plain blue T-shirt, black trousers and little black trainers.

They're so mismatched it's a bit like seeing a parrot hanging out with a starling.

"This is the very *special* granddaughter I was telling you about," Bunty says to the stranger as I ogle shamelessly at her. "And this is Moonstone Dream, darling. She's going to keep me company while you two young whippersnappers live life to the maximum and so on."

I blink at the woman again. *Moonstone Dream?*

A study of 3,000 parents recently found that one in five parents regret the name they gave their child.

I'm going to guess that hers are two of them.

"Indeed," Moonstone nods curtly: conversation over.

"But… where *are* we?" I say, turning to look at the huge villa again. "Whose is this house, Bunty?"

"I've rented it from an old friend," she beams. "It's a magical place, where you can bathe in warm rainwater and cook using the heat of the morning rays and grow vegetables out of your own poop."

"Really? Is there an instruction manual somewhere?"

Bunty laughs. "It's an environmentally friendly, organic, sustainable house, which means we'll leave no trace, sweetheart. When we go the universe won't even know we've been here."

"OH MY GOD, THERE'S A BOWL OF CHOCOLATE TRUFFLES IN THE BATHROOM!" Nat screams.

"Although it'll probably guess," my grandmother smiles.

With a tinkle of bells, Bunty picks up the *Daisy-Chain* book, pats it a few times and puts it inside her bag. "This is my room," she says firmly. "It's nearer the ocean and I like lots of tidal energy so I can synchronise my body with the moon."

Umm, scientifically in what way could you possibly…

Nope, not even going to ask.

"Is there Wi-Fi?" I say instead, grabbing my brand-new phone out of my bag. "Or is that… organic and sustainably sourced too?"

"Exactly, darling. All you have to do is climb to the top of that hill, hold your mobile device up to the moon at high tide and wait for the call of a migrating nightingale."

I look up in horror. At the last count there were ten billion Wi-Fi devices shipped worldwide. Is my grandmother actually telling me we don't have *any* of them? In which case *who* is taking ours?

I bet it's Toby somehow.

"Really?"

"No," Bunty laughs, holding out a little bit of crumpled paper with "DREAMCATCHER1234" written on it.

Within five seconds a message pops up on the screen.

HARRIET??? ARE YOU THERE? Jxx

My stomach gives a little swoop of excitement.

And also guilt: I'm running forty minutes behind schedule, and it's *my* schedule.

Quickly, I type out the promised "immediately on landing" text to my parents.

The eagle has landed safely on The Other Side! Harriet x

I get two back straight away:

Haha, who are you kidding – I'm the eagle, you're a little fluffy pigeon. Dad x

And I'm the phoenix so I win. Annabel

You have to be eighteen to legally divorce your parents in the UK.

Just over a year to go...

"Sorry," I say to my grandmother as my phone abruptly starts ringing and Jasper's name pops up in a flash of light. "I think I need to take this call."

"Go for it, darling," Bunty beams, waving me away affectionately. "You must always grab your moments."

8

The housefly has one of the fastest wingbeats on the planet.

It's so fast that the wings actually produce music: creating the instantly recognisable fly-hum of a middle octave pitch of F. At three hundred and fifty-four beats per second, their wings become totally invisible to the human eye.

And as I run down polished stone steps towards the beautiful ocean, I think I kind of know how that fly feels. As if my entire body is vibrating and humming and singing all over.

This is going to be the best two weeks *ever.*

I'm so excited, it feels like I'm about to lift off the ground.

"Hello?" I blurt, hitting the green button. "Hello, Jasper? Are you there?"

In front of me are countless shimmering blue waves.

But not quite so many radio ones, judging by the black fuzziness of the phone screen in my hand.

"Hello?" I give it a shake. "Jasper?"

Finally the image clears and my Not-Quite Boyfriend appears in profile. All I can see is one bright blue eye, a straight nose with a few freckles scattered across it and a quiff of bronze hair sticking up at the front, like a gold Triceratops horn.

Unsurprisingly, he's already scowling.

It's a commonly held misconception that it takes more muscles to frown than it does to smile, but in fact it's actually the other way round: looking grumpy actually requires eleven muscles, while an expression of happiness needs twelve.

I like to think of Jasper as just being facially economical.

"No!" he's calling crossly to the side. "Dad, I'm *on my break*." He frowns harder as somebody in the background yells back. "Yes, *another* one." More yelling. "Fine, take it out of my inheritance."

Then he turns to me with an eye-roll.

"Dad seems to think we're the Starbucks dynasty or something," he says flatly. "He actually made me move my portfolio away from the side of the coffee-maker, as if I don't have exams and university and a *life* to prepare for."

I grin. "Remind your dad that world-famous composer

Philip Glass simultaneously worked as a plumber. So it's perfectly possible to combine skills efficiently."

"Bet Philip Glass didn't have to empty a dishwasher three times every hour," Jasper grumps. Then he leans forward. "So how was the journey?" He holds up JASPER AND HARRIET'S ROMANTIC COMMUNICATION CHART. "Also, can I just point out that thanks to the delay we're currently in the *pink zone*, which I believe is Me Time?"

My whole face abruptly flushes to match it.

It seemed like a good idea to allocate "quality moments to ourselves", as recommended by various online relationship articles. Apparently it strengthens the bond between brand-new couples by protecting our independence at an early stage and making sure we don't get bored of each other too quickly.

Although now I'm kind of questioning taking that advice quite so literally.

It probably didn't need its own colour code.

"I'm sorry I'm late. It took a while to get our bags, then we had a long taxi drive, then we got distracted by the pool…"

"Whoa – you've got a *pool*?"

"I strongly advise against getting in it," a voice says from off-screen. "Statistically, seventy per cent of people do not shower before swimming and twenty per cent of adults admit to urinating in public pools."

49

Jasper raises his dark eyebrows, then slowly spins the phone.

"Hi, Toby." I smile before it's even refocused.

"Good evening, Harriet," Toby salutes. He's wearing a bright red T-shirt with a picture of Mr Spock on it. "For you. For us, it's obviously good morning, thanks to the rotation of the Earth."

"*Ohayo gozaimasu!*" a voice chirps from next to him. "Which is literal meaning *it is early* but is also super-polite hello in Japan."

Jasper turns the phone a little further round.

Rin is sitting close to Toby, wearing a red vest with a picture of Captain Kirk on it. "Looking at me!" she says triumphantly, pointing to her top. "I am star hiking too!"

"Trekking," Toby corrects fondly.

"*Hai,*" Rin laughs, nodding. "We are matching perfectly and walking far together in space. Walk walk walk."

"It's more of an orbiting, really," Toby objects. "But I guess Starfleet Officers on a vessel are simultaneously on foot so that's an excellent point."

The screen subtly tilts so I can see they're holding hands.

Cyanoacrylate (aka Super Glue) is unsticky on its own, but as soon as it comes into contact with water ions in the air it undergoes anionic polymerisation: forming polymer chains and creating a mesh that joins surfaces together and becomes almost impossible to remove.

Something tells me Rin and Toby are stuck for good.

"*Anyway*," Jasper says, turning the screen back to him. "What's it like Down Under? Have you unleashed your scheduling skills on the unsuspecting Aussies yet?"

"It's amazing," I say, ignoring his sarcasm and holding the phone up so he can see the sea. "Plus Nat and I have the whole day tomorrow to explore Sydney before work starts properly."

"Ooh," Jasper breathes, eyes suddenly lighting up. "Do me a favour – will you go to the Art Gallery of New South Wales? They've got some amazing Aboriginal paintings – their use of colour is *extraordinary.*"

Well, that does sound intriguing from a historical perspective but... It's not on the Plan, and while my interest in art has been whetted slightly by Jasper's enthusiasm, it's still *way* down my list of Things I Genuinely Like And Will Make Time For.

But he probably doesn't need to know that right now.

Google says not this soon, anyway.

"Absolutely." I nod, making a mental note to download images of the exhibition off the internet. "We'll head there first thing."

"*Arigato gozaimasu* for the Victor cat!" Rin calls out, poking her rosy face into the screen. "Which is meaning *thank you* but in literal *it is rare and precious.* And Victor, he is!"

"Especially when wearing his tiny tiara," Jasper says darkly. "He's as precious as it gets."

I laugh, suddenly wishing I could be there in the cafe as well as here.

As much as I obviously respect scientists, I really wish they'd work faster on time travel and body-cloning: being in one place at a time is so restricting.

"*Jasper!*" a voice yells from nearby. "Break's over! We've got customers!"

"Kill me," Jasper sighs, standing up.

"So when's our next appointment?" I ask, pulling out my laminated chart and scanning it for green blocks. "Tomorrow at one?"

"I can't," Jasper grimaces. "New work shift. Make it nine-thirty?"

And this kind of required flexibility is *exactly* why I needed the hand-held printer. "OK, so that's seven-thirty my time," I say, tucking the schedule back into my pocket. "And, umm... Make sure you eat some biscuits for me!"

"Huh?" Jasper frowns, distracted by more yelling. "They don't have biscuits Down Under?"

I flush. That was my code way of alluding to the burnt biscuits he makes me, thus attempting to be subtly romantic as many seemingly reputable dating advice websites would suggest.

"Ah, yes." I cough in embarrassment. "Maybe I'll try a supermarket. So… umm. See you tomorrow?"

"Sure," Jasper says, tying his stripy apron back on. "I'll aim for a bit more privacy next time."

"Goodbye, Harry-chan!" Rin beams, waving.

"*Sayonara*, Harriet!" Toby calls. "*Ganbatte!*"

And the phone goes dead.

9

So, do you know what I really love about plans?

Everything.

Literally everything about plans is awesome. I love coming up with them, and I love writing them down. I love laminating them and hole-punching them and double-underlining them; I love bullet-pointing them and giving them their own little hierarchy.

I love showing them to other people, so they can fully appreciate their objective beauty, and also – let's be honest – my subjective organisational skills.

And I *really* love ticking them off.

In fact, I love ticking them off so much I've been known to write *Tick Off Plans* on my lists, just so I can tick that off too.

Which means – as I get up the next morning, bright-eyed, bushy-tailed and (thanks to carefully ensuring that I adjust to the time difference over four days) not even vaguely jet-lagged – all the signs point towards today being *brilliant*.

I've just got to get Natalie Grey out of bed first.

"Nat?" I whisper at the corner of the mattress where she's flung: arms akimbo and pillow-dried hair spread across her face.

We spent our very first evening in Australia splashing around in the infinity pool and watching *Home and Away* on the giant outdoor cinema screen. Since then – after she passed out like a damp starfish on the bed – I've genuinely seen oak tree trunks with more mobility.

"*Nat!*" I shake her right shoulder briskly.

"Natalie?" With my middle finger, I tap her forehead.

Then I abruptly pull the pillow out from under her so her head hits the bed with a *thud*. "Natalie Grey. Wake up now."

Her eyes flicker, then she starts snoring again.

A wood frog hibernates for the winter by stopping its own heart, freezing its own lungs and allowing ice crystals to form in its blood until it's essentially deceased.

Right now I'm kind of tempted to put my head on my best friend's chest and check she hasn't done the same thing.

Instead I stick one of Bunty's stray feathers up her nose.

"Mnnneeeurggh," Nat mumbles aggressively, shoving me away and wrapping an arm tightly over her face. "Leamelonemsleep."

"But it's ten am," I point out patiently. "Ten-fourteen, if you want to be precise. Half the morning is gone already."

"Dontcare," she mutters from under her elbow. "Goway."

"And we're in *Australia*," I remind her, bouncing up and down on her bed encouragingly. "On an *adventure*. Our Best Friend escapade. A once-in-a-lifetime Kindred Spirits caper."

"Mmmnneeurgh," she mumbles, turning over and sticking her head firmly under the duvet. "Canwaitnotherhourgotjetlag. Soannoying."

Apparently koala bears sleep more than any other animal: twenty-two hours every day, which means 91.7 per cent of their average lifespan. Scientists obviously didn't include Nat in their studies, because as soon as the holidays hit she can out-snooze any marsupial on the planet.

Destroying other people's carefully made plans in the process.

And yet *I'm* the one who's irritating?

"We've got *Things to Do*," I say as brightly as I can, sliding my folder of carefully researched plans under the duvet. "If we want to get anything ticked off today, we'll have to get moving."

"*You* do it," she says in a muffled voice, pushing the

folder straight back out again. "Go to bookshops or whatever and come get me after lunch."

OK: *bookshops or whatever*? Napoleon's of Sydney Military Bookshop is entirely military- and history-based and has World War Two *action figures*: I'd like to see anyone not enjoy that thoroughly.

Maybe it's time to break out the big guns.

Obviously I *had* intended for today to be a surprise, but it's quite difficult to spread joy to other people when they insist on being unconscious.

Leaving Nat snuffling, I run to the walk-in closet and unzip my giant suitcase. Carefully, I pull out some of its many plastic-covered contents: neatly packaged with Rin and Wilbur's help. As quietly as possible, I unwrap one of them.

Then I tug my pyjamas off, slip it on and sashay up to the bed.

"Maybe we should *a dress* this situation one more time," I say, prodding Nat again. "Or it may start to look *shift-y.*"

She groans loudly. "What?"

"I mean," I say, grabbing another item from its package, "I wouldn't want to *skirt* around the issue or get the *cold shoulder.* It would be really hard to *top* this kind of opportunity."

Another groan.

"You could always tell me to *shoo*," I say, starting to grin in anticipation. "Or maybe… *shoes*. Hahaha."

There's a short silence.

And – truthfully – a small chance I may have overegged that particular linguistic pudding.

"Harriet," Nat says, finally emerging from the duvet with nigh-on vertical hair. "I don't know what the hell you're talking about but you sound bonkers even for y—"

She stops and blinks at me slowly.

"What do you think?" I beam, doing a little ballerina spin and ending in an elaborate curtsy. "Like it?"

"Is that *my dress*?" Nat looks in shock at the striped, knee-length black and white number. "More specifically, is that my A-level coursework?"

"Yup," I say, hopping from foot to foot, unable to contain myself any longer. "It certainly is."

"That's the jacket I designed for the show last term," she says blankly, pointing at my embroidered grey top half. "And they're the shoes I customised."

"I know." I beam at my red feet. They're inherited vintage Prada and to say her mum went bonkers would be the understatement of the century. "They fit me perfectly."

"But I don't understand…" Nat sits up with a confused frown, pillow creases on her forehead. "What are they doing in Australia?"

"I brought all of it," I say triumphantly, grabbing a huge pile of packages from my suitcase and throwing them on to the bed next to her. "Every single thing you've ever made. Team JRNTH helped me get it together before we left."

Then I take a step backwards and gesture at the heap like a magician dramatically revealing a fluffy white rabbit.

My best friend stares mutely: at the beautiful, shiny collection of everything she's done for the last seven months at college. Red silks and orange cottons and blue velvets; brown leathers and stripy knits. Personally designed, hand-sewn and lovingly, carefully, furiously laboured over.

Everything Nat's given up her life for this year.

Sacrificing parties and sleepovers and picnics and films and potential boyfriends and properly straightened hair because she's been working so hard and with such dedication there's been no time for any of it.

And she thought nobody had noticed, but I did.

"So that's why your suitcase was so heavy?" Nat says finally, looking at me with wide eyes.

I nod with another grin.

"But..." She looks round the room. "*Why?*"

"Because this is the *primary* Australian plan," I say, pulling out a secret piece of paper, stored in my wallet. "We're going to get your fashion blog up and running again, Nat. We're going to launch your social media accounts. And I'm going to model your amazing, wonderful clothes so everybody can see them."

Then I show her the bullet-point list that is headed with:

MAKE NAT A FASHION ICON

Apparently girls cry on average 5.3 times per month, but to the best of my knowledge Nat has done it three times in eleven years.

It looks like she's about to up that ratio.

"Harriet," she says in a quiet voice. "Your plan is *me*?"

And as she abruptly drags me on to the bed in the hardest cuddle of my life, I can feel myself filling from top to toe with a warm, happy, best-friend glow.

Because that's the thing I love *most* about plans.

Now and then, you get to put somebody else at the top of your list.

10

Suffice to say, Nat's not sleepy any more.

The copepod is a one-millimetre crustacean that lives in the ocean, and is capable of accelerating to five hundred body lengths per second. In fact, it has the strongest legs in the world.

Judging by the speed with which Nat leaps out of bed and runs to the closet, she's trying to compete this morning.

"I'm going to need the white Mary Janes," she shouts as she runs back in with her empty suitcase bouncing behind her. "The high-waist cream trousers with black blouse. The blue leather dress with pockets, the striped shirt, the black fedora and the gold necklace and—"

The rest of her demands are lost in the pile as her head disappears. "Belts!" she yells, suddenly popping up like a manic meerkat. "Eyeliner! Bracelets!"

Then she disappears again.

"Give her some food, darling," Bunty whispers to me as she and Moonstone appear with a tray of toast and eggs and two glasses of orange juice. "Or trust me: she's going to fall asleep in the rosemary bed of the Royal Botanic Gardens and smell like artisan pizza for a week."

So I spend the next fifteen minutes perched on the edge of the bed, trying to feed Fashion Cyclone Nat in tiny, encouraging mouthfuls like she's an over-stimulated hamster.

Finally, she emerges from the chaos: cheeks flushed, hair dishevelled, creative levels dangerously peaking. It's a good thing she's going to be *behind* the camera today because I don't think anyone wants to order clothes from a girl with eggshell in her fringe.

"I'm going to need a unique username," Nat fires out, yanking her overstuffed suitcase towards a taxi waiting outside. "A new website an updated blog a Twitter account Instagram tumblr a new biography isthecameraonmyphonegoodenoughdoyouthink? Haveyou—"

Humans can emit a maximum of fourteen sounds a second but I think my best friend is starting to test that theory.

"Nat," I say, putting a hand on her arm again. "Breathe."

Grinning, I tap my phone, hold it up and show her a

beautiful silver and white website with *NGrey Designs* etched on the front in curly writing. Then I open a few apps and show her a brand-new network of social media platforms.

"Toby did it while we were on the plane," I explain. "Jasper wrote the content and Rin... umm, sent lots of photos of baby goats wearing wigs."

Nat peers at the screen, then laughs loudly. "Let me guess," she says, pointing at the image under her name. "That bit was you."

Underneath *NGrey Designs* is a silver pair of scissors.

The kind you can make dresses, cut thread or shape fabric with. Or steal from the art room and use to chop off the ponytail of your best friend's arch-nemesis.

And across the bottom it says in tiny silver writing:

Natalie Grey: Always at the Cutting Edge.

"Obviously," I grin as we climb into the taxi. "Fame, glory and success, here we come."

Honestly, my plan for today is not particularly complicated. It goes like this:

- *Visit Sydney's most recognisable landmarks.*
- *Wear Nat's best designs.*

- *Pose for effortlessly trendy and hip photographs.*
- *Post photographs online.*
- *Nat becomes a household name.*

And OK, I'm not totally sure of the social media *timeline* – I've only got four friends so group text does just fine for me – but I'm sure it won't take long.

I mean, there's a cat on YouTube with a baseball cap, leaning on a record and pretending to DJ, and that's got three and a half million views.

History has proven that this plan *absolutely* works.

Within an hour it's going perfectly.

Nat has carefully styled my hair in a scruffy, fluffy top-knot, and then applied mascara and hot-pink gloss to my face.

I've changed into an elegant blue jacket and trousers covered in white herons taking flight, made out of a silk kimono I brought back for her from Tokyo last year.

And I'm sitting casually on the kerb.

Chilling out in a downbeat, laid-back and Australian kind of way. Easy, informal, imperturbable. *Insouciant.* Which is kind of ironic, because normally when I sit on the pavement I'm having some kind of panic attack.

"Nice!" Nat says, holding her iPhone up a bit higher. "Can you lean back a bit more, H? On your elbows?"

I lean back a bit more. "A bit less?" I lean back a bit less. "Poke your chin forward?" I poke. "Slant your head to one side?" I slant. "The other way." I slant again. "No, the *other* other way. More? Even more? Over your shoulder?"

I hold my hand up to block the fiercely hot sunshine beaming down on me.

I've been professionally modelling for nearly seventeen months and my jobs have included *Vogue*, Baylee and Yuka Ito, but apparently Nat Grey is the most demanding client I've ever had.

"Owls can rotate their heads by two hundred and seventy degrees," I say sharply. "Natalie, do I look like an owl to you?"

"Well, you *do* have unnaturally large, round eyes. And that bird documentary you made me watch last year said they eat whole mice and then barf up the skeleton. I've definitely seen you do that with a chocolate wrapper."

"It was the *foil*. And it was *Christmas*. The lighting was insufficient for me to see it in time."

"With eyes that size I sincerely doubt it."

We stick our tongues out at each other.

"Just let me make sure the background is visible," Nat says, bending down and taking another photo. "Or this whole location is kind of pointless."

We both turn to look at the view behind me.

The huge silver arch of the world's largest steel bridge: curving delicately over bright blue, shimmering water, filled with busy, graceful boats and yachts.

"Sydney Harbour Bridge contains 52,800 tonnes of steel," I tell Nat, turning to face her and trying to look casual and laid-back again. "And 79 per cent of that was imported from England."

"OK," Nat says as she takes a photo.

"They've found 586 species of fish in the harbour itself. That's more than in the English Channel."

"Mmmm," Nat murmurs, taking another one.

"It was tested by ninety-six different locomotives."

"I'm trying to focus, Harriet, so will you please stop talking?"

Sometimes my best friend totally underestimates the importance of fish, trains and one of the world's most recyclable metals.

"Now what?" Nat says, glancing up after the final frame. "What's the next bit of the plan?"

Jumping up, I run over and throw my arm across her shoulder so we can stare at the screen together. I'm not entirely sure what she's done with the filter but I look kind of green.

Like an alien or an avocado.

Although 95 per cent of avocados on sale today are descended from one tree grown by a Milwaukee postman in 1926, which is a brilliantly unique heritage, so maybe it's intentional.

"I'm in charge of all your social media," I say decisively. "Toby and I spent nine hours researching every aspect so I know *exactly* what I'm doing. You just focus on the creative side of the business."

Toby and I couldn't decide if my title should be Social Media Controller, Networking Chief Executive or Communications President. I'll let Nat know when I've made up my mind.

Nat nods in visible relief. "Great, because we haven't studied online marketing yet: they're saving it for next term."

I smile knowingly: I've already got her syllabus printed out and stuck on my bedroom wall beside mine.

"This is *it*," I say in delight, uploading the first photo and quickly adding a few nuggets of essential information underneath. "We can do this, Nat. Our very first Official NGrey Designs Post. Are you ready?"

"Ready!" she squeaks.

"On your marks!"

"Get set…" she beams happily.

"*GO*," I shout, clicking a button.

And – just like that – a brand-new Fashion Icon is born.

==

We rocket around Sydney for the rest of the day.

Or – if I'm being a little more specific – we walk as fast as physically possible.

After all, official modelling kicks in tomorrow so Nat and I need to squeeze as much productivity and fun out of our special day together as we can.

And also pizza.

Lots and lots and lots of pizza.

"Done!" Nat cries, taking a photo of me wearing green denim shorts, a white ruffled blouse and gold flip-flops: casually standing next to the wooden slatted wharves of Sydney Harbour.

Then she hands the phone over to her social media guru.

Did you know that Sydney Harbour contains over 500 gigalitres of water? WOW! I write in the caption, adding a few heart-eye emojis.

"Done!" Nat says after a short boat trip under the bridge: me, windswept in an embroidered lilac jumpsuit and black sunglasses.

Just one of 20,000 boats in Sydney, which is more than 52 per square kilometre! I add below it, with three little yacht emojis.

"Done!" she declares after we've captured me nonchalantly strolling down the streets of The Rocks: a picturesque neighbourhood of red-brick buildings, churches and tree-lined avenues, formed almost immediately after Captain Cook "discovered" Australia in 1770 and claimed it for the British.

Despite this land mass having had its own Aboriginal population for well over 60,000 years.

So I add that into the caption too.

Together, we run up and down the grey granite steps outside Sydney Opera House: me wearing a gold skirt and yellow blouse, with the world-famous semicircular white sails of the building soaring into the cobalt sky behind us.

This building is inspired by the peel of an orange :) I write.

Then I Google it, kick myself and edit with *Although that is "apocryphal" which means a story with dubious factual sources so don't quote me on it! Haha. :) :)*

"Make sure you put all the relevant information

underneath," Nat reminds me for the fourteenth time.

I mean, as if I hadn't done that already.

Exhausted by our efforts, we take a quick break to eat pizza and drink lemonade in the Botanic Gardens.

Then we head towards the centre of Sydney, taking photos all the way: past Queen Victoria Building (*an 1898 former produce market restored in 1986*), through the ornate, balconied and glass-ceilinged Strand Arcade (*genuinely Victorian!*), and down tree-lined Martin Place (*the site of annual Anzac Day war remembrance services*).

"Put the guidebook down, Harriet," Nat says gently as she hands me a flamingo-print dress. "We need to *focus*."

Which shows how much she knows.

I've memorised most of it anyway, so *ha*.

Finally we make our way to the top of Sydney Tower: an elegant, thousand-foot spire topped with a shining, round, gold turret. Nat takes a quick photo of me in silver shorts and black jumper and I upload it.

420 windows, 56 cables made of 235 high-tensile wires which, if laid end to end, could stretch from Sydney to New Zealand!!!! NO WAY! :) :) :)

Then – handing Nat's phone back, workday finally over – I turn to stare at the view. And, slowly, the rest of my extremely relevant information begins draining out of me.

It's *incredibly* beautiful.

The air is silent and warm, and three solo clouds hang in a darkening lavender sky: pink and purple in the haze. Below us the waters of Sydney are shimmering like blue ribbons, the jagged parks are deepening to jade and the edge of the horizon is glowing orange.

Below us the lights of Sydney are switching on one by one, and above us stars are popping out.

Around us are views stretching eighty kilometres in every direction. Turning one way, I can see the Blue Mountains just visible in profile like a stegosaurus back; spinning the other, I can follow the Pacific Ocean up the east coast of Australia towards Queensland.

And I can't help wondering – for just a second – if somebody else I know is watching this sunset.

Whether they're facing the same way too.

"Nat," I say, finally tearing my eyes away. "Aren't we lucky? Isn't this the most magical view you've ever s—"

My best friend's head is lowered and her eyes are glued to her phone.

"Nat? Are you OK?"

"Harriet," she says, glancing up. "What on earth have you been writing under these photos?"

I blink. "All the relevant information, just like you told me."

"I *meant* fabrics, cuts and inspirations," she says in

exasperation. "*Fashion* stuff. *Not* 'one in eight people living in Sydney is over sixty-five years old'!"

Oh.

Oooohhhh.

"You should always keep your social media fresh and entertaining," I say defensively. "It said so in the guidelines."

"Well, I've got two followers," she says bluntly, holding up the screen to me. "One of them is a colon detox centre and the other has posted eight times, offering me a job earning five thousand dollars a week from home."

"See?!" I exclaim in delight. "That's so much money, Nat!"

"It's not a job offer, Harriet," Nat sighs. "It's *spam*. We've been working our socks off *all day*, you've uploaded *twenty-six* photos and the only people we're talking to are poo and junk."

I stare at her as she flicks through each account and holds them up to me, dismay growing.

She's right: there's no activity at all.

Not a single heart or star or favourite: not a comment, not a mention. Other than *Did you know that a Sydney cafe broke the record for the world's biggest burger and it was 95.5kg?* by @TobyAwesomePilgrim, it's an electronic wasteland.

With the exception of her blog, where somebody has written "ugly dont like her carot hare bad nose gross" under one of the photos of me. Which is a) written by someone who can't spell *carrot* or *hair* and b) aimed at my looks and not Nat's designs, so we should try to stay positive.

But even with the soft pink glow of an Australian sunset on her face, my best friend still looks crushed.

And a sharp twist of guilt corkscrews my stomach.

This was *my* big idea.

Nat would never have put her creations on the internet so hastily without my masterminding. Which means any failure she feels is down to me too.

Not a consequence I'd considered before literally this precise moment.

I need to start thinking plans through to the end.

"It's early days," I say brightly, patting her shoulder. "And I've got *lots* more social media tricks up my sleeve, don't worry. This is just Stage One."

Her eyebrows lift hopefully. "Really?"

"*Absolutely,*" I say confidently, trying to think back through the nine hours of research.

"OK," Nat says, taking a deep breath and putting the phone in her pocket. "It's your plan, so it's your call."

"Yup," I nod. "It's my plan so it's—"

We each get a new stomach lining every three or four

days, and I think I just physically felt my old one peeling off and dropping to the floor.

It's my call.

Ah, bat poop.

I totally forgot about Jasper.

12

OK, *forgot* is the wrong word.

I *pretermitted* to hear the alarm I set in time for our call this evening, which is a fifteenth-century word from the Latin origin *praetermittere,* meaning *to neglect or let pass* and is therefore a totally different thing.

And not at all a synonym for the same verb.

"Sugar cookies," I mutter, grabbing my phone out of my satchel. "Sugar cookies, bat poop, frog bum."

I hate saying *I told you so* – especially to myself – but this is exactly why itineraries, schedules and timetables are so important.

Otherwise fun just completely takes over.

"Whoa," Nat laughs as I start waving my glossy mobile frantically like a maraca. "Frog bum? Language, dude."

"They've recently discovered that when red-eyed tree frogs fight each other they shake their bums," I tell her, turning my phone upside down. "It's actually a deceptively violent statement."

Finally, a Wi-Fi signal appears.

Within seconds, a plethora of messages have popped up in a flurry of little beeps.

7:29pm

Yo! I'm here! Found a quiet spot in the kitchen cupboard – should be able to talk uninterrupted! Jasper xx

7:43pm

Are you there? Did I get the times wrong? Maybe I needed that chart after all haha. ;) J xx

8:01pm

Sorry I couldn't say goodbye properly yesterday – it was awkward in front of the others and with Dad yelling. You're not mad, right? Jxx

8:28pm

Ok, guess you're either mad or you've been held up with THE FASHION. Got to work now but speak tomorrow. Jx

With a flush of guilt, I look at the time stamps.

An *hour*. Jasper was sitting in a damp cupboard surrounded by smelly cloths, detergent and mops for nearly an entire hour, waiting to talk to me.

And yes, climbing into furniture may be something I historically do more often than I probably should, but it's not behaviour I want to force on others.

I ring back but it's too late: it goes straight to voicemail.

"Bat bat bat poop," I mutter, slamming my phone back in my sachel and scowling at the beautiful view. The sun went down a while ago and the lights of the Sydney sky are clear and bright, but I'm feeling far too guilty to count them properly.

"It's only one call," Nat reminds me, turning me round by the shoulders and leading me towards the lift. "Jasper will understand that we were busy."

"I *told* you I needed my satchel on me at all times," I say crossly. "But you just *had* to take it off me because it wasn't *fashionable* enough for your shots."

"No, it was because it still has the word GEEK written on it in red marker pen," Nat laughs, pointing at the scratched-up front pocket. "Or C-E-H, which must be a new insult developed since I left school."

The corner of my mouth reluctantly twitches. "It actually stands for Certified Elephant Herder, Natalie, so *you wish*."

"Or maybe Crazy Ewok Hoarder."

"Casual Egghead Hooligan."

"Fits you perfectly," Nat snorts in agreement. "I love

77

you, Harriet Manners, but you're such a total and utter CEH."

We laugh as the lift starts dropping down towards Sydney.

Nat's right: there's no point getting worked up about one missed phone call. I can ring Jasper in the morning when he's finished work.

As long as the cafe shuts before ten am, obviously, or I'll be fast asleep.

This rotating Earth thing is a *real* spanner in the works.

The metal doors open and – at the very moment they ping – my phone starts vibrating again. Feeling a jolt of relief I lean down to grab it while Nat steps out and then get promptly hit on the bottom by the lift doors. I slam forward a few steps and drop my brand-new phone hard on the unforgiving stone floor.

There's a loud crack.

No.

No no no. No no no no no *no no NO NO*.

There's a crack all the way across the screen, the light's off and spider-web-shatters are covering the middle. Apparently one in three phones will break within their first ten weeks, and mine is now officially included in that statistic.

On the upside, at least it's still ringing.

"Hello?" I blurt desperately, stabbing a finger at bits

until something connects. "Jasper, are you there? I'm sorry. Again. I'm *such* an idiot."

There's a loud crackle.

"We – *crackle* – always – *crackle crackle,*" a voice says faintly with a distant fizz. "*Crackle* you're in Oz *crackle crackle.*"

"Hello?" I say again, shaking the phone in growing confusion. Jasper always refers to Australia as Down Under. "Can you hear me?"

"Can't *crackle crackle crackle* I missed you *crackle.*"

And my stomach abruptly plunges as if I'm in the lift again: plummeting seventeen floors (or one thousand feet, or twelve thousand inches) towards the pavement.

Because it's a male voice but it's not my nearly-boyfriend and I have literally no idea who I'm talking to.

All I know for certain is *they missed me*.

13

Apparently, it would take 1.2 million mosquitos, each sucking once, to completely drain the average human of blood. Maybe they were really quiet ones, because I don't seem to have any blood left now.

Panic is starting to rise like a flood.

"What... *crackle crackle* if you *crackle crackle* come and *crackle crackle crackle* in Sydney."

It's definitely not Dad, because he's been banned from making personal calls at his new job. Or Toby, because he would never, ever tell me he misses me in case it gives me "the wrong idea" and makes me "try to French kiss him again".

My stomach abruptly makes another even sharper dive.

Which means...

No. It couldn't be. No way. He doesn't know I'm here. *Does he?*

"H-hello?" I say, heart lodged firmly behind my tongue. "Who is this? What did you just say?"

"*Crackle*… where… *crackle crackle* not what *crackle*."

I glance at Nat, whose eyes are open wide. *Who is it?* she mouths.

I don't know, I mouth back. *A guy.*

Oh my God, Nat whispers, taking an urgent step towards me with her hand held out protectively. *I knew it.*

We stare at each other as the phone keeps crackling.

What do I do, Nat?

I don't know!

NATALIE, WHAT DO I DO?

I DON'T KNOW.

And – before I can even register what's happening – Nat has grabbed the phone out of my hand and lobbed it hard against the floor.

Smash.

14

Scientists have discovered that black holes are so massive that they severely warp the fabric of space-time (the three spatial dimensions and time combined in four-dimensional continuum).

As a result, you'd essentially be trapped inside one forever.

Apparently I've just fallen into one, because as Nat and I stare at my brand-new and completely smashed phone, in bits on the floor, it feels like every single second is stretching out infinitely.

Until there's nothing but silence and time.

Nothing but silence, and time, and darkness, and staring at the ground forever and ever and—

There's a loud beep, and we both jump.

"*No way*," Nat whispers as we both bend down towards it. "*How?* How is it doing that?"

"Maybe it's haunted," I whisper back in horror, eyes wide. "Maybe it's *alive.*"

There's another beep, and we both squeak.

"Oh," Nat says, putting her hand in her bag. "Wait. That was mine."

She pulls her mobile out.

Hello Mini Me. Harriet's parents tell me that you've both arrived safely. Thanks for the update darling. Mum xx

I'm being sarcastic, just in case you couldn't tell. Mum xx

"Whoops," Nat says guiltily. "I totally forgot to call her. God, parents can be so passive-aggressive sometimes."

Then we stare at each other.

We still don't know who was calling *me*.

"Look," Nat says finally, putting her perfectly functional and unshattered phone back in her bag and breathing out slowly. "You know what? I'm sure it's nothing to worry about: probably a random sales call or something. It could have been anyone, right?"

I nod, trying to quell the queasiness in my stomach. After all, the chances of dying in a plane crash are one in eleven million, and yet eight million people get on an aeroplane every single day.

The chance of you being *you* – of your specific parents

meeting and combining your precise genetic material – are one in ten to the power of 2,685,000… and yet here you are.

And the odds of being obliterated by an asteroid are one in 1,600,000, unless it's a really *big* asteroid, in which case six miles of the Earth's crust will immediately peel away, hypersonic shock waves will destroy everything in their path, debris will blast into orbit, firestorms will obliterate all known life and dust will stop sunlight reaching the Earth and precipitate another ice age.

But we all just walk around every day, assuming that won't happen.

So if a lifetime of analysis and data has taught me anything, it's that we *have* to trust that statistics are on our side.

Because otherwise, all it takes is one.

15

That doesn't mean there aren't other things to worry about.

My brand-new phone is smashed to smithereens and I spent the money my parents gave me for insurance on an official Ravenclaw phone case, so everybody would know how smart I am.

Ironically, that broke too.

Something tells me I may not have been sorted into the right Hogwarts house after all.

"Come again?" Dad shouts when Nat and I have returned to the Magical Kookaburra Shanty and I've finally found the courage to call my parents, as directly specified in our Australian Travel Without Parents Agreement. "You spent the insurance money I could have spent on funky neon trainers on *what*?"

It turns out you can hook the outdoor cinema screen up to a web call and unwisely I chose this one to give it

a try. Which means my father is yelling at me at three times his natural size and in high definition.

Technological advances are not all they're cracked up to be.

"It doesn't matter," I mumble, trying to look somewhere other than up his enormous, foot-sized nostrils. "The important thing is I'm *safe*. Bodily, and in my mind and soul. Let's focus on the positives, shall we?"

"It was a lift door, Harriet," Annabel says calmly from where she's seated next to my dad, now approximately ten feet tall: a bit like Galadriel. "Not a weapon of mass destruction."

"Did you know 266 people have been injured in elevator incidents since 2002? I think you're massively underestimating the grand-scale danger I just escaped."

Then I open my arms out wide so they can appreciate how lucky they are that I'm unharmed.

Apparently they do not.

"Well, you're not having a new one," Annabel says, jogging Tabitha up and down on her knee. "They're really expensive, Harriet, and your dad has only just got his job back. We're not made of money."

Then my dad looms towards me. "We might, however, Harriet, trade *you* in for part-exchange and invest in another, less clumsy and more responsible teenage daughter."

"There's probably a buyback system," Annabel agrees. "Although we probably wouldn't use it."

"Onwards and upwards," Dad adds.

I scowl at my parents, then at Nat: grinning next to me.

"So what am I supposed to *do*?" I snap, folding my arms. "*Ninety-two per cent* of teenagers go online every day. I'm supposed to check my mobile *a hundred and fifty times daily* on average. How am I going to do that without a phone?"

"Share Nat's," Annabel says simply. "Or do without."

Oh my God. It's like they don't understand being sixteen at *all*.

"Just because when you guys were my age you bounced rolled-up parchments off the backs of dinosaurs to each other doesn't mean that's an option now."

"Sure it is," Dad laughs. "Just don't use a stegosaurus or they get stuck on the spikes."

"So annoying," Annabel smiles. Then she gets closer to the webcam. "Harriet, where's your grandmother? You're not being too much trouble, are you?"

And what exactly is that supposed to—

OK, I'm not even going to bother finishing that sentence.

"I'm here, darling-heart," Bunty replies, swaying in from the side with a tray full of home-made banana cake.

"And everything is perfection. We're living every moment to the max, aren't we, my darlings? Squeezing out every single drop."

Nat and I nod fervently, grabbing two slices each.

"Not to the *max*," Annabel frowns. "And, Mum, you need to leave some drops in. Do you remember what we talked about?"

"Yes, Bels," my grandmother smiles. "I may or may not have signed a very long and boring legal contract I didn't read."

Then she sits gently next to me and puts a small blue velvet bag on my lap with a wink.

Curiously, I open it.

Inside is the largest phone I've ever seen.

It looks and weighs like a black brick, there are prominent buttons with numbers on the bottom half, the screen appears to be in greyscale and there's a thick plastic *antenna* coming out of the top.

The average British child makes its first mobile-phone call at the age of eight, and I'm pretty sure this is the one my grandmother used for that very occasion.

"Cooool," Nat says, gazing at it in admiration. "That's so freaking *retro*. We should *definitely* use it in our future shoots."

Disturbed, I prod the screen. Nothing happens.

How do you even send messages on this thing? Are

they telling me I'm expected to press 7 *five times* just to get the letter S? I'm going to be forty-five by the time I've sent a basic goodnight text.

More importantly, *where is the camera?*

Then I glance up and see Bunty's triumphant face, and – glancing a little further – I spot the fierce expressions of my oversized parents.

Yup: they've seen it too.

"I *love* it," I say obediently, throwing my arms round my grandmother. "Thanks *so* much, Bunty. This is *so* helpful and *so* practical."

"You're very welcome," she beams. "There's a new loaded SIM card inside, darling, and if you put cash on it it'll work like a charm. Plus if you get bored you can play *Snake*!"

I look in alarm at the monstrosity in my hand.

Never mind play *Snake*; I might be able to fight and kill one with this beast. "*Brilliant.*"

Quickly, I say goodbye to my parents.

I blow Tabby a sympathetic kiss: after all, I've left her alone with them for the next two weeks, haven't I?

Then – with considerable effort – I spend twenty minutes carefully jabbing into the phone all my important numbers: Nat, Bunty, Rin, Toby, Jasper, Wilbur, home, the new agency and the nearest Australian bookshop.

We use thirty-four muscles to move our fingers. By the

time I've finished I think I've sprained at least fourteen of them.

Finally, I send Jasper the shortest, most complicated-to-construct text ever written:

SRY 4 CALL – RING U TMW AT 2. Hxx

Seventy-one button presses: no photos, no attachments, no links, no smiley faces or tiny unicorns, no internet access, no dictionary, no predictive text (not that I ever had that switched on).

Yup.

This is going to be a nightmare.

16

The rest of the night is spent working hard in my new position as Nat's Social Media Chief Controller President™ (SMCCP).

(I decided to combine all the titles and then – for luck – register the trademark.)

This obviously includes:

- Following the editor-in-chief of every major Australian fashion magazine.
- Writing *Check out this epic new fashion designer! She's super COOLIOKO* ☺ under every single post.
- Typing *Why aren't you following us back?* on all of Rin's social media accounts.
- Uploading the photo of me and Kenderall with #pic of @CirenK in #NatGrey #Paris Fashion Week #LOL #Throwback #Greendress #Purpleparty #Oops
- Waiting for Kenderall to repost to her 287K followers.
- Realising she's not going to.

By morning, we've managed to lose the colonic irrigation company and gain a company that sells wigs for hamsters, and I'm not entirely sure that's the *Haute couture* audience my best friend is looking for.

"How's it going?" Nat says over breakfast. "Is our venture taking off yet, Miss Internet Mogul?"

She's been buried in some new design ideas and I'm not entirely sure how to tell her that there are 2.3 billion active social media users in the world and so far we've only attracted three of them.

One of whom is her mum.

"Mmmmm," I say, staring hard at my toasted soldiers. "It's taking off like nobody's business."

Literally, like a business belonging to nobody.

In January 1986 the NASA Space Shuttle orbiter *Challenger* (OV-099) broke apart 73 seconds into its flight, disintegrating over the Atlantic Ocean off the coast of Cape Canaveral in Florida.

This venture is *taking off* very much like that one.

"Harriet," Nat says after a pause. "Look at me."

I stare at the ceiling above her head.

"Harriet."

Swallowing, I gaze at the front door.

"Harriet Manners," Nat sighs. "You've *got* to work on making eye contact when you're fibbing. Give me that laptop right now so I can see what you're doing."

Reluctantly, I hand it over and wait while my best friend studies each page intently. Then I wait a bit longer as she slumps on to the table and starts gently smacking her head against a coaster.

"*Dude*," she says in exasperation, finally lifting her head. "Did you just spam the editor-in-chief of Australian *Vogue* five times? Did you use *fifteen heart-eyed cat emojis?*"

"It's not *spam*," I say indignantly. "In 2013, emojis were officially named the fastest-growing language in the world: I am *communicating internationally*. What would you suggest?"

"I don't know," Nat admits. "This isn't really my area of expertise."

We stare at each other for a few seconds.

"I could post a picture of a kitten in a jumper?" I offer tentatively. "They seem to be quite popular."

Nat puts her head back on the table again.

"I give up," she mumbles into her arms. "I mean, who needs a creatively satisfying career? I'll just sit with you in the cafe after I finish college, drinking Jasper's coffee and watching Toby wear a chocolate moustache every day for the rest of my life."

"Oh, we won't be there," I say without thinking. "Toby's already got a place at Oxford, I'll be at Cambridge and Jasper's taking a gap year in Paris."

Nat groans loudly and begins head-butting the coaster again.

"I *mean*," I correct quickly, patting her shoulder and trying to lever her away from frontal lobe damage, "we will be *there for you in spirit,* and everything's going to be dandy, you *wait and see.*"

Also I don't want to karmically jinx my spot at Cambridge University.

I may have been working on my personal essay for the last six years, but you just never know what they're looking for: there's nothing to lose by trying to harness Bunty's helpful cosmic spirits to my plan as well.

"Maybe I'm crap," Nat whispers miserably from under her armpit. "Maybe my designs are awful. Maybe I've been kidding myself all along. Maybe I can't actually do this at all."

I can literally *feel* her natural confidence starting to evaporate, and the guilty stomach-spike starts again: slowly unscrewing my stomach from my abdomen.

I've never seen Nat doubt herself about *anything*.

This disaster is entirely because of *me*.

Which means it's up to me to fix it as well.

"Right," I say in a businesslike manner, standing up from the breakfast table abruptly. "We're putting social media on the back burner while we wait for people to respond the way they're supposed to. It's time for Plan B."

"Plan B? We have a Plan B?"

I stare at Nat in shocked silence. "Are you joking?"

"Of course I am," she laughs, pushing my arm. "Bet you've got the whole Plan Alphabet, and probably some Roman numerals too. Go on then, hit me with Plan B."

Relieved, I drag the Brick out of my satchel.

It's just past eight am, although I'm surprised there's enough technological know-how in this thing to tell the time: I'd half expect it to come with a sundial dangling on a string.

Luckily, it's capable of receiving SMS text messages.

Spangle-kitten! 11! B @TopModellz 4eva!
Sparklification ON! Your gravy boat. FG

One day I'm going to get a message from Wilbur that doesn't look like it's been written in abstract FBI code.

That day is clearly not fast approaching.

Also, I'm not sure how long the appointment at the new modelling agency is supposed to last but *forever* seems a little ambitious.

"We've got three hours," I say, dragging Nat over to the walk-in closet. "Which gives us just enough time to get ready."

With a flourish I open the door and gesture at the remaining clothes triumphantly.

"Ready?" Nat frowns. "Ready for what?"

I turn to her with a bright smile.

"If the fashion world won't come to us, Natalie Grey, then it's time for us to go to them."

17

How do I put this?

Right at this precise moment in history, there are twenty-six sovereigns around the world: kings, queens, sultans, emperors, grand dukes and emirs who reign over forty-three countries, including Cambodia, Monaco, Swaziland, Britain and Tonga.

There are, however, currently no empresses.

At least, there *weren't* until Nat and I walked into the biggest and most prestigious modelling agency in Australia wearing our very best and most fashionable outfits.

That's right.

What I'm trying to emphatically say is: we *rule*.

Literally *everyone* is staring.

The receptionist, paused with a sandwich halfway to her mouth; two models, seated on chrome chairs in the corner; a cleaner, coming out of a bathroom with a mop;

and an agent, passing by the internal window with a folder held close to his chest.

At Nat, in a beautiful calf-length black silk slip with red flowers embroidered round the neckline: nipped in at the waist, then floating around the knees. And at me, in a long, yellow satin gown with scalloped neckline and a shiny white ribbon round my waist, now wound firmly round the door handle.

It's fine: I'm pretty sure nobody has noticed I'm tied to the fittings yet.

They're all too busy staring at my gold trainers.

"Are you *sure* this was a good idea?" Nat whispers as she subtly disentangles my ribbon and we continue to swish our way regally towards the front desk. "It doesn't feel very... *chilled.*"

"Really?" I whisper back. "The air conditioning is on full. Personally, I'm very glad I bought the faux fur coat."

Then I whip out a cropped, bright orange, fluffy number, pull it snugly on and immediately start to perspire.

Nat opens her mouth, then shuts it again.

She protested quite hard when I explained Plan B, but I *knew* evening gowns would be perfect for our first official Australian engagement. Not just because they're gorgeous and Nat's proud of them, and not even because they won her design prizes at college.

Everybody knows that if you want to make a lasting

impact, you've got to stand out. And nothing says *look at me* like wearing floor-length satin and a faux fur jacket in forty degrees of mid-morning heat.

Plus our Australia badges, just for... you know.

Luck.

Lifting my chin, I approach the woman at the desk.

The sandwich is still stranded three centimetres from her lips: that's how much of an unexpectedly majestic vision we are.

"Good morning. I am Harriet Manners and I'm here for an eleven o'clock appointment. And yes, I *am* wearing an original Natalie Grey design. Please, do take a professional business card that I definitely did *not* print out of my computer at home."

Carefully, I do a spin on the spot, curtsy and place an *NGrey Designs* business card on the reception desk: shiny silver side up.

Then I turn to Nat, who's hiding behind a large stone pillar.

"Show her your dress again," I whisper encouragingly. "They work much better as a duo."

"*Harriet*," she whimpers, retreating further. "*Jeez*."

"You're the who what where now?" The receptionist blinks at the card, then takes a nonchalant bite out of her sandwich. "Wait, are you guys *British*? Yeah, that makes *loads* more sense."

OK: why do people keep saying that?

I'm about to ask when the door opens and three more models saunter in: tall, thin, tanned and possessing the kind of healthy, netball-playing beauty I could never hope to achieve in a trillion years.

I may know that the game was invented in England around 1890 and is a derivation of early basketball, but that's as far as my netball prowess goes.

"Strewth," the brunette in tiny white jean shorts blurts, stopping short in front of us. "Did we miss Cinderella's ball?"

"Nu-uh," a blonde in a miniskirt and halter-neck giggles. "It's the Annual Disney Princess convention, remember?"

"That yellow one is Belle, right? If *only* there was a beast around hahaha."

From the corner of my eye I can see Nat's face getting redder and my stomach churns guiltily again.

Do something, Harriet.

"Actually," I snap, spinning round. "I *think* you'll find that your most dangerous indigenous creature is the Tasmanian devil and it has been absent from the Australian mainland for 3,000 years."

Nope: that wasn't the scathing retort I was looking for.

"*And*," I keep going desperately, "you should know that the Tasmanian tiger was—"

"Calm down, chook," the third girl interrupts, looking up from her nails. "They're only mucking with you. They're just not very funny."

The other two models promptly stop laughing. "Harsh," one of them says in a hurt voice.

The girl who interrupted me narrows her eyes, dyed silver crop glistening in the sunshine. "These dresses are cute," she decides after a beat. "Totes inappropriate for mid-morning, but they've got kind of something."

Confused, I glance to the side and see Nat's face abruptly changing colour again.

"Yes!" I shout enthusiastically, quickly putting my SMCCP metaphorical hat back on. "Exactly! They're made by a brand-new designer from England and she's won awards and—"

"I made them," Nat says calmly, walking out from behind the pillar. "They're mine."

"Yeah? Because I've got a big show next week, front row, and I need to wear something fresh. Do you make to order?"

If you didn't know Nat, you'd think she was taking this 180-degree turn of events completely in her stride: coolly and professionally.

But I do, and she's not.

One of her earlobes has gone pink and her left nostril is twitching. She starts fumbling in her handbag and haphazardly pulls out a lipstick, an eyeshadow and our apartment keys, so I triumphantly slam four business cards into the girl's hand.

"Always at the Cutting Edge of fashion!" I yell. "That's our famous strapline!"

Also *ha*: Dad was clearly wrong: business cards are *not* "outdated and redundant".

("*You're* outdated and redundant," I told him.

"Touché," said Dad.)

"I could probably sort something out." Nat shrugs casually as her right nostril begins twitching too. "I mean, I could *try* to fit you in."

"Brill," the girl nods, slipping the cards straight in her pocket and heading past the receptionist's desk into the agency. "I'll call you this arvo, yeah?"

"How does she do it?" the blonde model says as she picks up a sheet of paper from the reception desk and turns towards a side door. "She *always* spots the up-and-coming designers."

"And this one's *British*," the other one adds. "That's *so cool*."

"Also explains a lot," the blonde concurs as they disappear too.

The second they've gone, Nat's nonchalance breaks.

"Oh my God," she squeaks under her breath, grabbing my arm. "OhmyGodohmyGodohmyGod—"

"Told you so." I grin smugly, wriggling out of the faux fur jacket. "Told. You. So. I am a veritable marketing *genius.*"

I'll make up the song and dance for this triumph later.

"Harriet Manners?" a voice calls from the back. "Eva's available now. Would you like to come through? We're ready for you."

4Eva.

Ah. Wilbur wasn't asking me to sit in a modelling agency for the rest of time after all.

Carefully, I assess my best friend: shining with hope and confidence and – I'll be honest – the gloss of slightly damp-under-the-armpit silk.

"So much to do," Nat murmurs, pulling her sketchpad out. "Material to research, patterns. A-line skirt, or circle bias cut. Silver, to match the hair, or maybe pink…"

Grinning, I watch my best friend submerge herself in the world she loves: motivated and content.

Plan B: *tick.*

Then – still grinning – I head towards my next great adventure.

The Australian modelling world is ready for me, is it?

Perfect.

I think I'm ready for it now too.

18

Just north of Melbourne is a mountain.

It's 800 metres high, and covered in plants and trees: mountain ashes, grey gums, red stringybarks, narrow-leaved peppermints and candlebark. In fact, it has so many trees that when British explorers Hume and Hovell climbed it in 1824 they realised the view was rubbish, decided it wasn't really worth the climb and named their discovery *Mount Disappointment.*

Which is officially the best mountain name of all time.

I kind of understand how they felt.

To get to this modelling agency, I've travelled 10,650 miles, used two planes, three taxis, one suitcase and precisely forty muscles just to move my legs. I've missed two study groups, one Saturday crossword and maybe even a potential first date with my nearly-boyfriend.

And I have to be completely honest: now I'm actually here, I don't totally understand *why*.

* * *

"Harriet…" Eva says for the fifth time, leaning back in her chair and flipping through my modelling portfolio with one tanned finger. "Harriet, Harriet, Harriet."

I've been in here six minutes, and that's basically all she's said. There are 14,221 people called Harriet registered as living or having once lived in Australia, and I'm becoming slowly convinced she's going to name all of us one by one.

"Yes," I confirm, smoothing out my gown. "Harriet."

"Harriet," she murmurs again, then more hopefully: "Harriet…?"

"Manners, from England."

"That's the one," she says, pausing on the photo of me in the Hatfield House maze. "Got it. Wilbur's protégée from London. Wonderful."

Then she closes the book and smiles at me.

We're tucked away in a tiny side-office with glass walls, which means I can see the hub of the agency very clearly. It's mainly open-plan with private rooms shooting off to the sides and five enormous round desks: each with eight agents and dozens of phones, computers, huge piles of paper and files.

On every wall are boards covered in glossy, glamorous images or headshots and there's a lot of activity: phones ringing and beeping, printers whirring, agents chatting, models and clients walking in and out of side rooms.

It's just that none of that action is in here.

Literally none of it.

Apart from a fly, hovering by the window, nothing is even moving. Eva continues smiling at me with the benevolent, disinterested expression of a lion who has already eaten in a David Attenborough documentary.

"So…" I prompt, clearing my throat.

"So," she agrees, nodding.

"So?"

"So."

So is the 41st most commonly used word in the English language: I think we're about to push it up a few places.

"So… what can I do for you, Harriet?" Eva leans back in her chair once more. "How can I help?"

I blink and straighten my dress out. What do modelling agents normally do for models in a modelling agency? Is this a trick question?

Maybe it's a test to check how intelligent I am.

"I thought maybe I could print out the casting itinerary?" I suggest, immediately rising to the challenge. "So I can study it properly and get it all scheduled in. Or you could put it on my USB-stick, if you like."

Proudly, I place a memory stick shaped like an ice lolly on the desk.

I thought it was very summery and Australian and also cute in an 8GB-of-storage kind of way.

"Perfect," Eva beams with a nod, lobbing the stick into a drawer. "If anything comes up, we'll let you know."

Then there's a silence.

Lobsters hear with their legs: maybe I should give mine a shot too, because I definitely caught that last sentence wrong.

"Sorry, if anything comes up?" I say blankly. "*If?*"

"*When*," Eva corrects easily. "It may take a little while – four weeks, maybe five. Sometimes six before anything starts coming through for our new girls."

I stare at her in confusion.

"But I don't have six weeks," I blurt. "I've only got eleven days left in Australia. Then I have to go back to England and do my exams."

"Excellent!" Eva says more brightly. "We like girls with lots of qualifications. Why don't you come back in the summer holidays, and then you'll have much more time!"

That is *not* what I meant at all.

Never mind Mount Disappointment: this has turned into the Volcano of Disillusionment and it feels like I'm about to fall straight in.

Plus it doesn't make any sense.

Wilbur heavily implied days ago that there was modelling work waiting for me in Australia. *A foreign agency has asked me to loan your prodigious sparkliness to them for a few weeks, possum. They've been watching your ascent for a while and we think this could be what tips you into Supermodel-land.*

I've even got an Ideas For Breezy Australian Modelling Facial Expressions list, printed out and folded in my wallet: I've been practising them secretly in the mirror every morning.

I've been walking on my tiptoes pretending I'm wearing heels at any given opportunity, just in case.

I'm dressed in a flaming yellow evening gown, for goodness' sake.

I am *ready* for this Supermodel-land adventure.

And I have to be honest: I don't feel very *tipped* anywhere right now. In fact, I'm about as vertical as a human being can get.

"We'll be in touch," Eva says, putting her bare feet on the desk and crossing them at the ankles. "Thanks for coming in, Harriet. It's an absolute *pleasure* to have you on our books."

I open and shut my mouth a few times like a goldfish.

Or maybe a cow: they only breathe through their mouths when there's something wrong with them too.

"Uh," I say, picking awkwardly at my skirt. "OK. I've... got a new phone number. Would you like it?"

"Why not?" Eva shrugs pleasantly.

Hastily, I scribble Bunty's Brick number on a piece of pink paper on the desk, and draw a few hearts and flowers round it to try to make it a bit more distinctive.

Then I push it across the desk as memorably as possible.

"Lovely!" Eva says, sliding it to the bottom of a huge pile of other girls' phone numbers. "Catch you around, Harriet!"

Around? Around *where*?

"Umm," I say as she opens the window and the fly zooms out. "Thanks for seeing me."

"It was a pleasure," Eva agrees, making it clear that this was very much a one-time occurrence. "Nice dress, by the way."

Swallowing, I grab my portfolio.

"Thanks," I say lamely.

Then I'm waved back out of the Australian fashion world just as sunnily as I was waved in.

19

A "moment" is defined as ninety seconds.

It's a medieval unit of time, introduced before the invention of the mechanical clock: the movement of a shadow on a sundial covered forty *momenta* in one solar hour, so each one changed in length depending on the length of the day and the season.

And for years Annabel has been encouraging me to "take one", before I react to any difficult or confusing situation.

So as Eva shuts the office door behind me, I obediently start counting slowly down from ninety.

Eighty-nine, eighty-eight, eighty-seven, eighty-six...

The agency is still buzzing.

Models are appearing with portfolios held tightly under their arms and disappearing into offices. Agents are making busy, efficient phone calls, probably booking exciting jobs, organising exotic travel, discussing availability for brand-new and life-changing experiences.

110

Eighty-five, eighty-four, eighty-three…

Arranging photo shoots and fashion shows in places I've never been to: possibly involving some species of animal I've never met, adopted, freed or annoyed before.

Eighty-two, eighty-one, eighty…

And I'm finding it quite difficult to believe that with all this fashion action going on, I'm not suitable for *any of it.*

Seventy-nine, seventy-eight…

I mean, I've travelled this far: they could give me a *chance*, couldn't they?

Seventy-seven, seventy-six, seventy-five…

Just *one* little casting?

Seventy-four, seventy-three…

The youngest person ever to fly in space – twenty-five-year-old Gherman Titov – performed seventeen loops round the Earth in twenty-five hours. I could go round the world seven hundred and forty times in the time Eva wants me to wait for a modelling job.

And set a new world record while I'm at it.

Seventy-two, seventy…

Oh my God, a moment is so long.

Seven…

So so long.

Sev—

You know what? There's a reason we have watches.

Quickly – before anyone spots me – I gather my yellow satin skirts and swish into a side room full of machines and paper and folders and pens: possibly because it feels a bit more homely to me.

Then I close the door, lump my portfolio down on the machine in front of me and get the Brick out.

I quickly scroll through to the number I need, then firmly press the button and lift the heavy handset to my face.

There are a few rings, then a *click*.

"Baby-baby Dingo! How's it hanging, my sparkly koala bear? Upside down, by the feet?"

"Wilbur," I whisper urgently. "I think I need your help."

20

OK, not *help.*

Guidance. Instruction: counselling and enlightenment. Suggestions, information, tips and pointers. Direction and recommendations.

Or... you know.

The answers to a few billion questions.

For some reason, Wilbur is already laughing.

"You need help?" he snorts down the line. "That's *very* unlike you, my little platypus-face. Is this definitely Harriet Manners I'm talking to? Because that is *totally* out of character, Sugar-wombat."

Sometimes I think the people in my life don't see me the way I see me at all.

"I've just had my appointment at the Australian agency," I say, "and I think there's been some kind of clerical error, because they don't have any jobs for me. None whatsoever."

"Baby-baby Kangaroo," Wilbur says gently. "It was

never guaranteed employment, more like a fab potential opportunity. I thought you understood."

Judging by the big gaps I left in this fortnight's schedule with GUARANTEED MODELLING DAYS!!! written on them, I definitely did *not*.

"They said I might have to wait more than a month."

"That's perfectly normal, bunny," my British agent confirms. "You've been super lucky so far. Modelling is like a game of Scrabble. Sometimes you've got the right letters, sometimes you don't. And sometimes, tiny blobfish, you've just got to sit your little tush down and wait until you do. Why don't you go see the sights with that twinkly grandmother of yours?"

Frowning, I leaf through my folder, then press a button on the machine in front of me.

Wilbur's making no sense, as per usual. Last time I played Scrabble I managed to get ninety-three points out of the word *SYZYGY* using a blank tile and a Z double letter score, and Jasper was so irritated he wouldn't talk to me for three hours.

It's an alignment of three celestial bodies like the sun, the moon and the Earth, just in case you're wondering.

There is *always* a word you can play.

"So I should be patient?" I clarify, absent-mindedly pressing another button. "You think something will come up?"

"*Mais oui*," Wilbur agrees. "Just relax, my little candy-cassowary. And what are those beeping noises, Muddle-mop?"

Umm.

The sound of me photocopying my entire portfolio in case I need extra copies of it in the future?

"I'm just… organising documents and… enjoying a bit of… Australian warmth."

This photocopier was made in Taiwan, but there you go.

"Perfiddlyection," Wilbur says as another copy of my snowflake headshot pops out. "It's raining dragons here but one of my new girls snagged a top Gucci campaign and I'm flying to Mauritius with her next week, whoop to the whoop!"

A tiny unintentional sigh escapes my lungs.

Mauritius is famous for once being the only home of the now-extinct dodo and being composed of eighty per cent sugar cane.

I'd *love* to start sketching that itinerary out.

"Tell you what, my little gingernut," Wilbur says as the machine stops whirring and I tuck the warm pages back into my portfolio. "I'll give Eva a bellio tomorrow, see if I can't squeezify you into some kind of casting. How does that sound?"

A wave of intense gratitude rushes through me.

I *knew* Wilbur would help.

Or – you know. Guide and inform. Ahem.

"Yes, *please*," I say with immense relief. "And I'm really not fussy, I'll do literally *anything*."

"No, you won't, sugarplum," my fairy godmother laughs. "You're my model and Peak Models has a reputation of epic-ality to maintain, honey. But I'll see what I can do."

OK, so: where was I?

Seventy. Sixty-nine, sixty-eight…

Carefully, I look both ways and scoot out of the stationery room before anyone catches me.

Sixty-seven, sixty-six…

Holding my warm portfolio to my chest, I start scurrying down the corridor towards the exit. I've just got to wait until tomorrow. That's not so long, right?

Sixty-five…

Maybe we can visit the Sydney Sealife Aquarium in the interim: they've got a gentoo penguin called Steven.

Sixty-four…

And a manatee called Pig.

Sixty-three…

A door to a room on my left opens and a woman walks out.

Sixty-t—

"Thanks for coming!" a voice calls out: "I think she was the last on the list. Is there anyone left?"

Sixt—

Six—

Wait a second.

Maybe it's time to be my own fairy godmother.

Grab My Moment...

"Hello," I hear myself say, taking a step forward and holding out my hand. "I'm Harriet Manners. Sorry I'm late."

21

Sometimes being a geek can be slightly problematic.

Like when you go up to the whiteboard at breaktime and correct a teacher's maths equation and they reduce your A* to an A grade.

Or when you spend ten minutes informing the person studying the menu in front of you in the cafe queue that a single cup of coffee contains eleven per cent of the recommended daily dose of riboflavin, six per cent of pantothenic acid, three per cent of manganese and potassium, and two per cent of niacin and magnesium and then they leave without buying anything.

Or when you correct your friend's grammatically incorrect texts with *you're or *their and they don't reply for three days.

Oh, who am I kidding?

More often than not, being a geek is a life-hazard and should come with some kind of preliminary warning attached: a flashing headlight, or at least a little red badge.

118

But, every now and then, it can be handy.

And as I step impulsively into an unknown casting with a head full of random knowledge, something tells me this might be one of those times.

This might be the fashion hub of Australia but any questions thrown at me, I reckon I can probably answer. A beauty contest held in Singapore in 1998 awarded sixty per cent of the marks for knowledge of the internet.

I am *already* prepared.

"I'm so sorry," the pretty blonde lady in front of me says. "I thought we were at the end of the list from the agency. Did we miss you off?"

"Oh," I laugh, tossing my head with as much nonchalance as I can muster. "I've just arrived from England. They didn't think I'd be able to make it in time, but here I am! Phew! Thank goodness there are 102,465 flights a day worldwide and I was on one of them!"

Excellent, Harriet. Life-grabbing and assertive.

Enthusiastically, I thrust my still-warm portfolio at them.

Then I grab eight or nine of the photocopied sheets and arrange them in a neat fan across the table, for good measure.

"Great!" an even blonder young man in jeans and a blue T-shirt says with a strong Australian twang. "I'm Jack and this is Emily. And it's a niche job so the more the merrier!"

Together, they bend over my book.

And – as they flip slowly through – I can feel the excitement in the room growing: the way a balloon expands if you put the neck over the mouth of a milk bottle and then heat the bottle up.

They nod vigorously at the *Baylee* headshot, and at the Elizabethan *Vogue* Polaroid. They murmur with fierce approval at the Mount Fuji shot for Yuka Ito and the glass Manga Girl box picture and the gold tutu.

By the time they get to Charlie the octopus, Jack and Emily are grinning widely.

And I can feel hope inflating inside me like hot air too.

I *knew* this would work. I just *knew* it.

This is My Moment and I have grabbed it all by myself: without help from *anybody.*

"An octopus!" Emily says, smiling brightly at me. "What an absolute treat!"

"Charlie was a *callistoctopus macropus*," I agree delightedly. "Also known as the Atlantic white-spotted octopus, found in the IndoPacific region and shipped to Japan especially for the shoot."

"I do hope he wasn't hurt," Jack frowns.

"He wasn't hurt at all," I promise. "In fact, did you know that common octopus collect crustacean shells and other objects to construct fortresses round their lairs?"

"It's lovely having an expert in our midst," Emily smiles, and I feel a surge of pride: I have spent my whole life hoping somebody would call me that.

"Well," I say as modestly as possible. "I prefer to call myself an *enthusiast*, really."

"These pictures are amazing, Harriet," Emily says, picking up the photocopy of the sumo photo in Tokyo. "It's like you're a proper fashion model as well."

I beam with delight. I've been called many things, but a *proper fashion model* has never been one of them. "Thank you so much!"

"And how did you make the transition?" Jack asks, jotting something down on a piece of paper. "Was it tricky, or did it come naturally?"

I think about that excellent question for a few seconds. "It was hard at first, but I think I've adjusted to it now."

I mean, there have obviously been a *few* mishaps in the process, but there's no need for them to know all the details of my personal fashion journey.

"You're so *young*. When did you start?"

"I was fifteen. In my country that's quite normal, I think."

"You must have trained incredibly hard. What's been your most challenging location so far?"

The rollercoaster at Luna Park, without a doubt: I was so scared I nearly climbed out at the top. "Coney Island,

New York," I say thoughtfully. "I think my heart stopped beating completely!"

"Hahahah!" they laugh. "Sometimes it must feel like that, right? But you know what they say: we are all born of the ocean, and each of us has a little ocean inside us."

I blink. *Roll with it, Harriet.* "Did you know that the blood has a ninety-eight per cent similar chemical composition to seawater, and almost exactly the same pH, so that saying is really almost *literal*?"

The clients glance at each other with unmitigated joy.

And I can feel myself physically expanding: my breadth of knowledge swelling inside me until the balloon of information is about to explode.

Being a geek *rocks*.

"But what can you tell us about breathing? Because," Emily smiles modestly, "I'm afraid we're coming at this mostly from the fashion angle. I'm sure you know *much* more."

Excitement tingles through every fibre in my body. Oh my God, what can I tell them about breathing?

Basically *everything*.

"Well," I say quickly, "we all have different lung capacities, but the *vital capacity* for the average woman is 3.1 litres, while the *inspiratory capacity* is about 2.4."

Their eyes open wide.

"*And*," I continue, "breathing actually has *very* little to do with oxygen. Air only has twenty-one per cent!"

They nod, enraptured.

"And the oxygen is used to break down glucose in the cells into carbon dioxide via ATP."

OK: I'm going to stop now.

Mainly because I'm so excited my own lung capacity feels like it's shrunk by at least half.

I am *nailing* this.

Emily and Jack glance at each other, then close my portfolio with a triumphant *snap*.

"Well," Jack says with a broad grin. "I think that's all we need to know. We've been looking for someone who could combine experience and detailed knowledge with fashion, and you're perfect."

I stare at them. "*Really?*"

"Absolutely," Emily says with a happy grin. "You're just what we've been waiting for, Harriet. The job's yours if you want it."

22

Dragonflies have the best vision in the animal kingdom.

While humans see colours as a combination of red, blue and green, Japanese researchers have discovered that the dragonfly has *thirty-three* different types of light-sensitive proteins, which means they can see colours we can't even imagine.

And I know exactly how they feel.

Because as I quickly scribble my phone number and email address on the back of my photocopied headshot and walk proudly out of the casting, the world suddenly looks so bright it's as if I have 30,000 facets in my eyes too.

As if everything consists of a billion beautiful colours.

Dragonflies are also the most deadly predator on the planet, with a ninety-five per cent hunting success rate: twice as successful as a great white shark, and four times as efficient as a tiger.

But, frankly, they can take a back seat because at one hundred per cent my current success rate is even *better.*

I secured my first Australian modelling job.
All by myself.

Beaming, I bounce back into the reception area, giving my *Lucky Country* badge a celebratory polish.

Nat's still hunched over her art pad, biting her thumbnail. When concentrating, Natalie Grey is approximately eighty per cent human, twenty per cent ingested nail varnish.

"I got it!" I squeak triumphantly, lobbing my portfolio on to the seat next to her and jumping around with my fingers wiggling in her face. "I got a job!"

"*No way!*" Nat exclaims, putting her art pad down. "Already! *How?* You were only gone like three minutes!"

Frowning, I glance at my watch.

It took forty-eight minutes for those last two scenes to take place, so either Nat can't tell the time or she has consumed waaay too much acetone.

"I *gatecrashed* a casting," I whisper as we swish out of the building. "The agent wouldn't put me forward for it, so I did it myself!"

Nat turns to me, super impressed.

"Was that a good idea, Harriet? I mean, isn't that the fashion agent's job? Don't they work tirelessly to do exactly that?"

OK, I definitely misread that facial expression.

"They'll be really happy I got work," I reassure her as we cross the road towards a gloriously sunlit park. "Anyway, I think Eva just forgot, because I was *perfect* for it. I could answer all the questions and everything."

"You can *always* answer all the questions and everything," Nat smiles. "Getting you to *not* answer the questions: that's the valuable skill."

I stick my tongue out at her happily.

After a wobbly start, everything's going exactly to plan. And maybe it's not the plan I originally had but that's OK.

It's a different, impromptu, *better* one.

"What was that girl's name anyway?" I say as we start walking back towards Bondi Beach, arms linked. "The one who wants the dress?"

"No idea, but I'm sure she'll tell me when she rings tonight. Thanks for doing those business cards, H. *So* much more professional than writing my number down with liquid eyeliner. Can I see them?"

"Sure," I say, grabbing one out of my satchel. "I already had the card left over from the Night of Stars party and there's a special setting on Dad's computer that he never uses."

Then I hand it over and drift into a reverie of how great my life is going to be now I'm fully in control of my own fate.

Maybe I should send Cambridge University an early application.

Or perhaps a preliminary letter.

I can tell them about the 89 Nobel Prizes they've won in all six disciplines – thirty-one more than Oxford (although Oxford has produced more Prime Ministers) – and they'll be so impressed by my initiative that they'll—

"Harriet," Nat says sharply, suddenly stopping on the pavement. "Tell me this isn't the only card."

I blink at her. "Of course not. Don't worry, I made hundreds."

Nat's face is changing colour yet again: from pink to a funny grey colour. "I meant, tell me this isn't the *only version* of the card. Tell me they're not the same."

I don't think she understands how printing works.

"They're *all* the same," I say patiently. "That's what computers do, Natalie. They make lots of identical things."

"Harriet, there's nothing on it."

"What?"

Nat holds the silver card up and turns it over. "There is *nothing on it.*"

I grab at the business card but she snatches it out of my reach.

"There is," I insist anxiously as Nat rips off her *Lucky Country* badge and hurls it to the ground. "There's your name and your email and your phone number and your social media accounts. I wouldn't make a blank business card. What kind of idiot do you think I am?"

Then we stare at each other in horror.

Mainly because – let's be honest – the answer to that question is almost always the same.

"Check," Nat says in a panicked voice. "Check the others."

Mouth dry, I turn my bag upside down and empty its contents on to the floor. Every single silvery card is blank.

The printer must have run out of ink.

And I think my brain did too.

"Nat," I say, searching fruitlessly through the cards on the floor to no avail. "I'm so, so sorry. I'm sure that girl can reach you somehow. I mean, she just has to…"

Guess your name and phone number.

"Say it," Nat says, narrowing her eyes. "Go on, tell me the statistical chance of her guessing who I am and how to reach me."

Flushing, I look at the floor.

"Twelve digits," I mumble under my breath. "Each digit can be zero to nine, so that means ten possibilities. Probability of getting one digit correct, one in ten. Probability of getting all twelve digits correct…"

I pause. This is not encouraging maths.

"*Say it*, Harriet."

"One in a trillion for your phone number," I say in a tiny voice. "A whole lot more for your name."

I like to think of myself as a life-affirming person: capable of looking at the bright side of any situation.

But those statistics are dreadful.

"*One in a trillion*," Nat groans loudly, throwing the last card on the floor. "I *know* you were trying to help, but *oh my God*."

"I'm sorry," I bleat, face starting to flame. "I'm really really— WAIT. Maybe she's still in the office? We need to—"

Before I can finish, Nat is away: strong legs pumping, hair and evening gown streaming in the wind. Me, tripping over paving slabs at an increasing distance behind her.

But by the time I catch up, I know it's too late.

Nat's face is like thunder.

Which is an analogy that makes no sense because thunder is *sound* so technically it doesn't *look* like anything, but I don't have time to find a better one because my best friend is about to kill me.

"She's *gone*," Nat snaps, slamming the agency door behind us. "Nobody knows who she was, she's not in the diary and there's no way of finding out."

I open my mouth and shut it again, trying to find a version of this story where it isn't entirely my fault.

"She could try searching Google?" I offer weakly.

"With what information?" Nat stomps back out on to the sunny streets, me running behind her. "You want her to scan through millions of photos until she finds mine buried on my college website?"

I blink. Why not? That's what I would do.

"We're not all you," Nat sighs, even though I'm pretty sure I didn't say that out loud. "I love you, Harriet, but that was my big break. Right now I'm too angry to talk to you, OK?"

I nod. That seems fair and reasonable, given the circumstances.

"Sorry," I mumble again as I scoop up her discarded lucky badge from the pavement.

"I know," Nat sighs.

And we make the rest of our way home in silence.

23

Nat sulks for the rest of the day.

She sulks while I make her apology flapjacks and arrange them into the shape of SORRY on a plate, and sulks as I download *The Devil Wears Prada* and project it on to the cinema screen.

She sulks when I write a heart-shaped note that says *Please forgive me?* with a quick sketch of a kangaroo wearing a cowboy hat, and stick it on the pillow in front of her, and then on the bedpost, and then on my own forehead.

She even sulks as I sit on the edge of her bed: staring at her with my saddest, sorriest expression.

"Are we OK now?" I say hopefully.

"No."

A few minutes later: "What about now?"

"Nope."

"Now?"

"Harriet," Nat sighs, pulling the duvet over her head. "I need a bit of space."

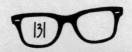

Which is fine and everything, but currently scientists have calculated space to be approximately 93 billion light years in diameter.

And I never know quite how much people are asking for.

"Darling," Bunty says when I finally give up and shuffle into the living room. "She'll be fine in two shakes of a fox's tail. Come sit with me and tell me about the shoot tomorrow."

She's been lying on the green velvet sofa, wrapped in a rainbow fluffy blanket while Moonstone sits primly in a nearby rocking chair, doing a crossword with a scratchy biro.

Obediently, I plonk myself down next to her.

"The flight leaves at eight am," I say, reading from the email Emily sent me twenty minutes ago. "The shoot should take all day, and then I'll fly back in the evening."

For the first time ever, my parents haven't insisted that I take Bunty or a guardian or some kind of babysitter with me for this trip. Maybe now they're ready to trade me in for a better version they're not as bothered what happens to the old one.

"Tell you what," Bunty smiles. "Why don't we make another cake for when you get home? You need *lots* of sustenance after an adventure."

I cheer up significantly. "How about a lamington? It's

a traditional Australian chocolate sponge coated in desiccated coconut and I haven't tried it yet."

"Absolutely," my grandmother laughs. "Darling, you must always try *everything*."

Suddenly feeling a bit homesick, I lie with my cheek on her lap.

"You know," Bunty says, stroking my hair gently. "Life is like a flower, sweetheart. The more you nurture it, the more light you give it, the more it opens up and the more beautiful it gets."

I nod, then glance over curiously at Moonstone.

She mutters under her breath, then crosses out the word she just filled in.

"You just have to be gentle with it," Bunty continues. "Love it, appreciate it for what it is, but never crush it and never try to hold on too tight."

I nod again. I mean, I'm not a trained gardener but even I know you're not supposed to mangle flowers with your hands.

"Life is transient, so let it change and enjoy each precious moment for what it is."

Frowning, I glance at the coffee table.

The Daisy-Chain Guide To Living Your Most Petal-Filled Life is lying there: battered, bright sky-blue, with a big white and yellow flower on the front and gold lettering.

It contains a lot of sparkly bookmarks.

Although if Bunty's direct-quoting now, it would probably be more efficient to just give me it so I can read and annotate it myself: that's kind of my speciality area, after all.

When I glance up, Moonstone is nodding at her crossword.

"OK," I agree, nestling closer, suddenly sleepy. "Did you know that the word *daisy* comes from the Old English expression *daes eag* and means *day's eye* because it opens at dawn?"

"Well, there you go, darling. Isn't it lovely to know that even flowers are watching over us?"

"Mmm," I murmur.

Then there's a comfortable silence while Moonstone makes aggressive noises with her pen. I'm starting to nod off when my satchel makes a strange sound and my head lurches upwards with a jolt.

BEEP BEEP.

As if it's actually *saying* the word aloud: that's how low-tech my phone is.

Dragging the Brick out, I stare at the green-lit screen.

Breaktime! Video call? Jasper x

I sit up straight: time to meet my schedule for once.

Laboriously, I type:

Ys!

Quickly, I give Bunty a kiss and jump off the sofa.

Leaning over Moonstone's shoulder, I murmur "Six down, four letters, sharp comment: *barb*, you're welcome."

Then I go outside and press a few buttons until the enormous cinema screen switches from a picture of a red shoe to the familiar scowl of Jasper King.

"*Finally*," he says as soon as he sees my face.

Which is kind of funny.

Because that's exactly what I want to say to him too.

24

Here are some facts about Aboriginal Art:

- It comes from the oldest continuous living culture in world history.
- Paintings are based on Dreamtime Stories, handed down through generations for 60,000 years.
- As there is no written language, these stories are communicated through colour made from ochre, iron and charcoal.
- An artist is not allowed to paint a story that does not belong to them through family lineage without permission.
- The most valuable Aboriginal painting was sold for $2,400,000.
- I learnt all this during my Year Seven Art Project.

Obviously, I don't tell Jasper that last bullet point.

I totally forgot I'd promised to visit the Art Gallery of New South Wales, and he asks about it almost immediately. By the time I've panicked and regurgitated every Australian art fact I know, I've nearly convinced myself I actually went there too.

Maybe I should have: it's fascinating.

"What did you think of the Yiribana gallery?" he continues in excitement, leaning forward. "Isn't that Emily Kam Ngwarray painting insanely beautiful?"

"Yiribana means 'this way' in the language of the Eora people," I remember diligently, looking slightly to the left of the screen. "And it acknowledges the location of the gallery on Gadigal land."

"And what about John Bulunbulun's bark painting? Did you see it? We studied his cross-hatching technique last term."

"Uh, yes," I say, swallowing, because I've now totally run out of relevant knowledge. "It was very..." *What?* "Tree-y."

"But did you take any photos? I'd really love to use some as inspiration."

My stomach is starting to twist guiltily.

Honestly, I'd kind of automatically assumed Jasper would have totally seen through my fact-spouting by now, and I'm not entirely sure what to do as he hasn't.

This is uncharted territory for me.

"Ah," I say, shaking my head. "I *did*, but I... smashed my phone. Soooo annoying."

At least *that* bit is true.

"Don't worry," Jasper reassures me. "It won't have ruined the memory card, so with Toby's help we can access the photos when you get back."

Bat poop. I did *not* think this one through.

"*Anyway*," I say, making a mental note to download other people's gallery photos before I return home. "What's been happening since I've been gone?"

So Jasper tells me.

About how Rin and Toby have officially dubbed themselves *Roby* and bought matching winged trainers; about the carved-leaf art project he's finally managed to finish because I'm not there to spill things on it.

About how yesterday Alexa Roberts abruptly walked into the cafe, glided round like a basking shark and then left without buying anything.

"Do you think she was looking for me?" I say, mildly curious.

"Obviously," Jasper nods. "That girl needs to get a life."

And I can't help feeling a bit chuffed.

Because it's becoming very clear that after years of feeling like I was the one with the problem it was actually the other way round. And now I've left my bully behind me completely, in more ways than one.

Finally, Jasper and I slow to a silence.

I'm not entirely sure what's supposed to come next.

We may have been good friends for six months, but Jasper and I have only kissed a total of seven times.

(Not that I've been counting, obviously: I mean seven times *roughly*.

Or – you know.

Precisely and accurately and ticked off in my diary.)

Whatever this is feels quite close to the beginning.

"Did…" I start.

"Have—" Jasper says at the same time.

We both stop, and I flush slightly.

"You go first," I insist, because I was about to randomly ask if he knew that the Ewok language is a combination of Tibetan and Nepalese and it's not really a pressing question.

"I was just going to ask if you've seen anyone you know while you've been out there?"

And my mouth suddenly goes dry.

One person produces roughly 20,000 litres of saliva in the average lifetime: enough to fill fifty-three bathtubs. Right now, I couldn't even fill a thimble.

"W-what's that supposed to mean? Who?"

"Rin was saying that Yuka Ito is in Sydney at the

moment," Jasper replies. "She's your old boss, right? We thought she might have made contact."

And – just like that – I can swallow again.

"Oh, *Yuka*," I say in relief. "Hahaha. Of *course*. Umm… no. We haven't seen each other for ages."

"Well, maybe you should contact her," Jasper says, turning away as his dad starts yelling from the cafe counter. "She was an important part of your life, right? And you're in the same country. You might not get the opportunity again."

Then he turns to look directly at me.

For just a second, I'm not sure if we're talking about Yuka any more. And it suddenly feels like there's a huge distance between us: much, much bigger than ten thousand miles or ten hours' time lag.

"Mmm," I say vaguely, swallowing with difficulty. "Maybe. It's just… we didn't leave things on good terms and Yuka is really insanely p—"

I abruptly stop.

Powerful.

Oh my God: *that's it.*

And – with a loud crunch – my next fate-changing idea slots straight into place.

"Jasper," I yelp, suddenly sitting upright. "Can I call you back tomorrow? We're on to speak at seven pm, right?"

"Yep." Jasper stands up and starts tying on his apron. "Sure. I've got to go now anyway. Good luck for the shoot tomorrow."

"Thanks," I say as he reaches for the button. "Goodb—"

But Jasper's already gone.

25

So, this could be kind of awkward.

Given that:

a) the last time I saw Yuka Ito, I was standing in an underground crypt in Paris, surrounded by bones, wearing feathers and trying desperately not to empty my bladder in front of her and

b) the time before that, I directly told her to leave me alone because I didn't need her help any more.

As I grab my laptop and scan through emails from the last year, I'm trying to convince myself that Yuka won't remember any of that.

The brain can store 2.5 petabytes of data, which is 2,500,000 gigabytes. But Yuka's one of the world's top fashion designers, and she's always extremely busy.

If I'm *very* lucky, she'll have somehow copied over anything pertaining to me.

With a burst of enthusiasm, I type:

Dear Yuka Ito,

I read online that you were given a Lifetime Achievement Award by the Council of Fashion Designers of America! Congratulations! Although I didn't know you were even eligible – it was very clever of you to register your business in the US like that.

Anyway, I am the Social Media Chief Controller President™ *of an up-and-coming designer called Natalie Grey and I was wondering if you would like to repost some of her images on your website?*

Just two or three should be plenty! ;)

You won't regret it!

Harriet Manners xx

Quickly, I press SEND.

Then I realise I didn't actually attach any photos or links, so I write another email.

Dear Yuka Ito,

Whoops! I forgot the photos.

Don't worry, I've attached thirty-two images to this email so you have PLENTY to choose from! ;) ;)

Harriet x

I press SEND again.

But the file's too big to send, so I carefully separate the photos out into four emails of eight photos each and ping them to Yuka.

Then I realise I forgot to say please and thank you.

So I compose a seventh email.

Dear Yuka Ito,
  Please and thank you very much!
  H x

Yup: that should do it.

I'm getting pretty good at Taking The Initiative, even if I do say so myself. Maybe I should run an after-school class in Seizing Your Carp when I get home.

A few seconds later, Nat emerges from the house: rubbing her eyes and wearing the enormous T-shirt I gave her with a photo of Team JRNTH printed on it and which she swore she'd rather "eat with ketchup than wear, Harriet".

I think this is her touching way of saying she's forgiven me.

Either that, or we're about to have a really weird dinner.

"Hey," my best friend says sheepishly, standing in the doorway. "Whatcha doing?"

"Nothing," I say, quickly closing the laptop. "Just

making sure I'm on top of my logarithms and integral changes of variables in time for the new term."

Nat doesn't need to know what the next stage of Plan B is yet: not until I know that it's going to work.

"Sometimes I worry about you deeply," she says and smiles, sitting down beside me and elbowing me affectionately. "So what's the next Sydney sightseeing plan, bestie? Hit me with our schedule."

And – as if by magic – I see that all my stupid blunders are forgiven and forgotten.

That's the thing about space.

Scientists have ascertained that the universe is already 13.8 billion years old and many billion light years across, and they predict that it will last for another five billion years. In other words: it's big, it's old and there's plenty to go around.

So maybe Bunty is right: maybe I don't always have to hold on so tightly.

Because the people I love always find their way back in the end.

26

I have been a model for nearly seventeen months.

Or – if you want me to be a little more specific – nearly twelve thousand hours, seven hundred thousand minutes or forty-four million seconds.

And it's fair to say they've been pretty insane.

In that relatively short amount of time, I have destroyed a hat stall in Birmingham; jumped around in the snow outside the Kremlin; floated in a light-up dress in *Lake Motosu-ko* in Japan and been hit by a bike on Shibuya crossing.

I've watched the 250,000 streetlights of New York flicker from Brooklyn Bridge; been draped in unhappy snakes in Jemaa el-Fnaa in Marrakesh and rolled around in the orange sands of the Sahara Desert; danced in clouds of Holi paint in India and been unceremoniously water-sprayed by an elephant.

I've been terrified by the Catacombs of Paris and have fallen into Le Piscine Molitor wearing a giant bunny head,

146

and crashed on to quite a few floors in the general London area.

What I'm trying to say is: thanks to modelling, I have probably done and seen more in the last 637 days of my life than I did in the 5,572 days before it.

Although possibly not quite as much homework.

But just as soon as I think I've *got this,* the fashion world somehow manages to throw a new challenge at me. And as I board the plane in sunny Sydney for a two-hour flight north, I realise that this is one of them: me, on a one-day shoot on the other side of the world from where I live, all by myself.

And I can't help wondering how the Harriet Manners of a year and a half ago would have reacted. You remember: the girl who hyperventilated into crisp packets and hid under tables.

She'd probably have put the sick bag over her head already.

Except, as the plane roars smoothly into a bright blue sky, I suddenly realise that girl doesn't exist any more. Bit by bit, I've left her in tiny pieces in all these different places over the last year and a half: scattered across the world like anxious confetti.

Because I don't feel nervous any more.

I don't feel overwhelmed or scared; I don't feel like I can't do this, or I shouldn't be here or I don't belong.

And yes, I am still Harriet Manners, geek girl to the core. But all I feel right now is freedom and excitement and adventure: the door opening to my place in the world.

A whole new chapter.

"Ladies and gentlemen," the air hostess chirps as the plane slowly glides north. "If you look to the left, you will be able to see the Tasman Sea, stretching all the way to Tasmania."

Obediently, I peer out of the window next to me.

"Those of you on the right-hand side of the plane should be able to see all the way to Tamworth and Dubby."

Leaning over, I stretch the other way.

Miles of gold and green are patchworked and scrambled and flecked with blue beneath us.

"And if you lean over to look below," the lady's voice continues as I eagerly follow her instructions, "it's a clear enough day to see the eastern coastline of Australia. We're now crossing over the Gold Coast, towards Brisbane, Yamba and Byron Bay."

I sit bolt upright.

Then, swallowing, I gingerly peer down at the landscape underneath us. I see squares of buildings, a few white strands of beaches scattered along jagged turquoise edges, roads etched out like delicate veins on the back of a hand.

I peer a bit harder, and for just a second I almost think I can see people: moving around below us like ants.

Living their lives, oblivious to us gliding above them.

Which is obviously impossible: we're far too high up for that kind of detail.

But I swear that for a fraction of a moment I see it.

I see a little brown house with a big backyard: a gnarled tree and a surfboard against a falling-down porch; an attic with a window that looks up to the stars.

For a moment, I think I see *him*.

"And now we're heading up past the Sunshine Coast," the air hostess continues as my neck twists painfully so I can watch the tiny town retreat behind us. "Where the plane will begin our descent into Proserpine."

Blinking, I try to focus.

The final email through from Emily and Jack last night completely confirmed *how* utterly suited I am for this job.

I am ready to tell them *everything*.

I can tell them that Queensland is the second-largest state in Australia: five times the size of Japan, and seven times the size of Great Britain. I can point out that it's home to more than four million people and two hundred national parks including the Riversleigh Fossil Fields and the Wet Tropics.

I might casually throw in the fact that it's known as the Sunshine State because it receives between eight and nine hours of sunlight every single day, and also that the sea surrounding it contains ten per cent of all the discovered fish species on the planet.

That there's a natural structure in Queensland so big you can see it from *outer space*.

I am ready to blow their *minds*.

Slowly, the plane begins to descend into a warm, golden light and every passenger is peering out of the windows.

Below us are a million shades of blue: from deep ultramarine to indigo, sapphire to cyan, azure to pale turquoise. Stretching to the horizon, mixed with swirls of bright white as if somebody has dropped an ice-cream cone from the troposphere and it's melting everywhere.

Cast into the shimmering water at random are splotches of dark green: forest-covered islands that curve in mounds as if giants are curled up and sleeping beneath them.

The edges of these countless islands are ragged and delicate, as if they've been ripped from the pages of a huge emerald book.

And dotted between them in the sea are tiny white boats.

Tourist boats and yachts that get bigger and brighter

as our plane gently lowers towards a bronzed, rust-coloured runway, lined with gently swaying palm trees.

If the human eye were a digital camera, it would have 576 megapixels: more than twice the power of the highest-quality camera you can buy. And as the excitement in my stomach starts building, I find myself trying to capture an epic film of this moment so I can keep it in my brain forever.

Because in spite of all the amazing things that have happened in the last seventeen months, I have never, ever been close to one of the Seven Natural Wonders of the World before.

This is officially number four.

Just below Mount Everest in Nepal, Victoria Falls in Zambia and the Grand Canyon in America. And just above the Northern Lights in Iceland, Paricutin Volcano in Mexico and the harbour of Rio de Janeiro, Brazil.

Out of the blue, I get to start checking off a whole new lucky list.

And it begins with:

1. The Great Barrier Reef.

27

Here are some facts about the Whitsundays:

- There are 74 islands, and only eight of them are inhabited.
- 2,900 different reefs spread across their Marine Park.
- They were named by Captain Cook who thought he'd first seen these islands on the Sunday Feast of Whitsun.
- He got the date wrong: they should actually have been called the Whitmondays.
- Whitehaven Beach is regarded as one of the top five most beautiful beaches on the planet.

I'm not exactly sure what the plans for the photo shoot are, but I'm sincerely grateful for the huge bottle of SPF50 Nat shoved into my satchel at the last minute. Something tells me that today is going to involve bikinis, frolicking in turquoise shallows and developing the kind of sunburn

only redheads on reflective white sand can really hope to achieve.

"Harriet! Sweetie, you're here!"

Emily bounces across the Proserpine arrivals lounge in tiny jean shorts and a black crochet crop top, then kisses my cheeks enthusiastically.

"We're *so* glad you could make it," she beams as Jack appears, grinning behind her.

"We are indeed," Jack agrees, pumping my hand up and down vigorously. "The agency told us not to expect much on our budget, but here we are! We landed ourselves the perfect model!"

"We're *so* lucky."

Never mind just dragonflies: I'm so happy there are probably a few possums and cats that can see me shimmering in a billion colours now too.

I've been called many things in my life, but *the perfect model* has never been one of them.

I wish Eva were here to hear it.

And maybe a few people from school.

And Stephanie from Infinity Models, Aidan the photographer, Peter Trout, India, Poppy, Shola, Rose...

Actually, it would be nice to have quite a lot more witnesses.

"You're *so* welcome," I beam as I'm led into the blinding yellow sunshine, towards a slightly dusty grey car. "This is a dream come true for me too. I've never been to the Whitsundays before!"

Jack and Emily's eyes widen into circles. "Whaaaat?"

"*No!* That's crazy! We'd have thought it would be the *first* place you'd have come!"

"Apart from Crystal Bay in Bali or Elephant Head Rock in the Similan Islands."

"Or Barracuda Point in Sipadan."

"Maaya Thila in the Maldives."

"The Great Blue Hole in Belize."

"The Komodo Islands."

"Oh, who are we kidding? There are *so* many amazing locations, how do you even pick?"

I grin at them widely.

I have no idea what they're talking about, but I'm pretty sure that at the head of my *How to Be A Top Model* list it says *Agree With Whatever The Paying Client Says*.

So I nod as fervently as I can.

"I guess you just pull it out of a hat!" I laugh brightly. "That way the decision is made for you, like in *Harry Potter*!"

They start chuckling heartily.

"This is *so* much fun, isn't it?" Emily says, cheeks shining.

"We're new at this," Jack nods, putting an affectionate

hand on Emily's shoulder. "Probably should have explained this at the casting but it was a bit of a whirlwind. Em is the creative and I do the photography. It's our first proper shoot, so this is kind of exciting for us."

"Not kind of, Jack," Emily frowns for a split second, then beams again. "It's *super* exciting."

This is incredible. I've never seen two clients so happily enthusiastic and utterly uninterested in playing it cool.

I think I've finally found *my* kind of fashion people.

"Do I need to prepare anything?" I say as the car starts driving towards the coast and I gaze out of the window at rows of lush spiky flowers I am yet to know the accurate Latin name for. "What kind of *look* are we going for?"

So far my modelling CV includes: scared, blank, delighted, confused, ecstatic, distracted, amused, embarrassed, heartbroken, loved-up and humiliated.

I am a veritable *smorgasbord* of human emotion.

"Oh, you'll see when we get there," Emily laughs. "And don't worry, Harriet. No doubt you'll be the one telling us what to do!"

Aww, she knows me so well already.

"Right," Jack says as the car pulls up next to a small pier. "If it's OK, we'll get you ready on the boat. That gives us more time for the fun stuff."

Then he leaps out and opens the car door for me.

The golden sunshine hits me with full force, like

opening an oven door half an hour into baking a cake. (Which I've been told ruins the process but how else are you supposed to know how it's going?)

"After you," Jack says, gesturing towards a compact white speedboat. "I'll grab the equipment out of the boot."

In the meantime, Emily is heaving an enormous, plastic-covered bag out of the boot, followed by a big black box. "I'm probably not the most experienced stylist you've ever worked with," she laughs as a hairbrush falls out of the box.

"*Ems*," Jack says, shaking his head. "We can do this, remember?"

"Sure," Emily says, flushing. "Right?"

"*Right.*"

Their nervous excitement is suddenly almost tangible: as if you could reach out two fingers, pull the end of it and unravel it like a spool of cotton.

With a minor stomach lurch, I turn to look back at the speedboat. There's the driver and two assistants on board already, so at least it won't just be the three of us, out there on the ocean.

Because for the first time since I impulsively gatecrashed the casting, it's beginning to occur to me how little I know about what we're actually doing here.

And the tiniest seed of anxiety is planted.

I've been so focused on telling these clients what *I* know and what *I* can do that I forgot to ask any questions about them at all.

Which may not have been my cleverest move.

"Great!" Jack says jubilantly, dragging out of the boot what appears to be a thick blue full-length Victorian leotard. "This is going to be *such* fun."

Another mini-wave of consternation.

"Is that for me?" I say dubiously. "Am I modelling… wetsuits?"

"Oh golly, no," Emily laughs, unzipping the bag. "That's for Jack. Your look is quite the opposite, I'd say."

With a proud flourish, she pulls out a dress.

It's long and white: tight on the bodice and covered in tiny sequins and lace to a beaded silver waist, where it abruptly puffs into the biggest ruffled skirt I've ever seen.

It's also – there's no nice way to put this – falling apart.

Even from metres away I can see the stitching starting to unravel, the beads coming loose and the bottom half slowly separating from the top.

"I made it myself!" Emily adds as she leads me into a cabin on deck and helps me carefully into it. "By hand!"

Several hundred sequins promptly fall on to the floor.

"Whoops," she says chirpily. "Luckily I've brought some glue."

"Uh," I say as it begins to seep through the lace. "Brilliant."

It's also surprisingly heavy: within minutes I have to sit down on a bench because my leg muscles are quivering.

With a firm hand, Emily proceeds to give me blue eyeshadow up to the eyebrows, bright pink blusher and hot pink lips that are completely ignoring my natural lip shape.

Then I'm led back outside, scattering beads and sequins as I go.

"Let's not forget the veil!" Emily squeaks, pinning a long piece of fraying chiffon to the back of my head. "And the tiara!"

She attaches a crystal-covered plastic crown on top of it.

Then with a practised air of feigned modesty, she opens the big bag again and slowly pulls out eight more dresses. Each one is long and white and elaborate: covered in flowers and sparkle and lace and ruffles and embroidery and feathers.

And each – in its own matrimonial way – is disintegrating rapidly.

By the time they're all out of the bag, the floor is covered in tiny bits of random white fluff: like the aftermath of one of Victor's particularly vicious pigeon attacks in the garden.

The boat engine starts to hum and I twist round in growing panic, looking for my phone.

Maybe I can call Wilbur.

Maybe I can call the Australian agency.

Maybe I can speak to Eva, explain that I took this job without telling her and I'm not entirely sure that—

But it's too late: the boat has started motoring away from the land, and we are surrounded by sparkling, turquoise, infinite, expansive sea.

Umm.

What the *sugar cookies* have I got myself into this time?

28

The Nightingale of Kuala Lumpur.

That's the name of the most expensive gown on the planet: designed by Faiyzali Abdullak, made of pure silk and covered in 751 Swarovski crystals.

It's worth an estimated thirty million dollars.

On the upside, at least I don't have to worry about destroying something quite that valuable today. On the downside, when Wilbur finds out exactly what part of the fashion industry I'm modelling for, he may never speak to me again.

I don't think his *standards* include plastic crowns and Hobbycraft glue, drying on my neckline.

"Umm," I say as the boat starts purring into the open ocean and I glance at my satchel: thank heavens the Brick is in it.

Buy some time, Harriet.

"Forty-two per cent of all marriages end in divorce. Is this really a growing business market, do you think?"

"But just think of the fifty-eight per cent that *don't*," Emily says chirpily, stapling together a tiny rip in my skirt. "Isn't that wonderful? Isn't it *romantic*?"

OK. Try again.

"I'm sixteen," I say desperately. "I don't think you're legally allowed to get married in Australia until you're eighteen."

"Ha!" Jack laughs, emerging from the cabin wearing the wetsuit. "Unless we're planning on marrying you to a whale, then I think we'll be all right!"

"A woman once married the Eiffel Tower," I tell him, staring worriedly at what appears to be a camera entirely encased in thick plastic. "Search Google for long enough and you'll find anything is possible."

Then I frown at the ocean.

Marry me to a whale? What is *that* supposed to mean?

The boat is slowing down to a puttering stop, and the bright blue sea around us is dotted with other small boats, packed full of shouting and laughing tourists.

All of whom are wearing snorkels.

Lots of them also wear wetsuits, flippers and goggles and have air tanks attached to their backs, and are lowering themselves gently into the water or plunging off backwards with big squeaking splashes.

Click, click, click.

The realisation dawns slowly, like watching an enormous

unstoppable steam train appear on the horizon and puff laboriously towards me. Huge, heavy and making a lot of noise.

And I've tied myself to the tracks so diligently I've no time left to escape.

Just enough to patiently wait for it to get here.

"We're not going to moor on an island?" I ask hesitantly, watching as the anchor gets thrown overboard and winds its way towards the bottom of the ocean. "This wedding shoot isn't on a tropical golden beach?"

Emily and Jack glance at each other, then erupt into gales of good-natured laughter. "On a *beach*? What a waste of your unique talents that would be!"

I blink. "Sorry?"

"That's why we told the agency we needed someone special," Emily says, adding yet more pink lipstick to my already neon face and leading me towards the edge of the boat. "Someone like *you.*"

"Indeed!" Jack says, strapping a big aqualung to his back and pulling goggles on. "Can't wait to see what you can do down there, Harriet!"

I blink at them again: then at the water.

Then at the people splashing into the deep blue sparkling ocean with full diving gear on.

"Down there?" I say blankly as the train finally reaches

me: steaming and screeching with no sign of slowing down. "As in... perpendicularly?"

"Absolutely!" Emily chirps as Jack waves, puts his breathing tube into his mouth and plunges into the water. "Why else would we have picked a model who's *also* a trained freediver?"

And there it is.

Sixty-five tonnes of solid steel: smashing into my consciousness. Because the casting at the modelling agency is starting to run through my head again, except now I'm actually listening instead of focusing on getting all the answers right.

And it sounds kind of different.

How did you make the transition? You're so young. You must have trained incredibly hard. What's been your biggest challenge so far?

What can you tell us about breathing?

It's like you're a proper fashion model as well.

I'm an A* student in English, I have a gold medal in grammar and a certificate that proves I am in the top one per cent of the UK's teenage linguists.

Yet I never once thought to ask: as well as *what*?

"A trained... s-sorry?" I stutter as I'm gently helped up to the edge of the boat: puffy white dress unravelling around me; veil fraying in the breeze.

"Freediver," Emily grins, adding yet more blusher. "We

can't believe our luck. Honestly, we thought we'd end up getting an expert who had no idea how to model!"

Oh my God. *They think I'm a professional mermaid.*

"I-I…" I stutter, throat starting to close in sheer panic. "I don't… I'm not sure I… How do I…"

"Don't worry," Emily reassures me. "The dress has weights in the belt to hold you down and Jack's learnt *all* the sign language. You'll be able to communicate with each other perfectly!"

I sincerely doubt that, given that:

a) I don't know diving sign language and
b) I'm not even able to communicate coherently now.

"Umm," I say, staring at the deep water.

I'm searching as hard as I can, but I can't think of a single honourable way out of this mess. I didn't wait for Wilbur's help; I went over Eva's head; I pretended the agency sent me and I took a job I knew nothing about, without asking any questions.

I wasn't even patient enough to count to ninety beforehand.

Now two lovely people with a brand-new business have spent their entire budget on flying me to Queensland because I convinced them I'm a professional. And if I fail, their first ever photo shoot fails too.

This situation is all my fault.

As per bat pooping usual.

"How…" I say anxiously, tottering on the edge of the boat on my tiptoes, "uh, *long* will I be under there, exactly?"

"Up to you! Four or five minutes should be plenty!"

Four or five minutes would definitely be more than plenty.

Swallowing, I stare at the bright blue ocean as my internal well of biological trivia begins to whirr.

You can do this, Harriet.

Humans can hold their breath for twice as long underwater as they can on land because the body automatically decreases the pulse rate in order to minimise oxygen requirements.

The average person can manage thirty seconds.

So all I've got to do is get each shot done in one minute or less.

"Good luck!" Emily grins, patting me on the back.

Nodding, I hyperventilate as many times as possible to lower the general carbon dioxide levels in my body: the way professional diving champions do.

At least I've been practising *that bit* my whole life.

Then I take a deep breath, wrap my disintegrating skirt round my legs with one hand and pinch my nose between my fingers with the other.

And I jump in.

29

Now, I know a lot about water.

I know that the average human body is made up of fifty to sixty-five per cent water, while the brain consists of over seventy-five per cent fluid.

I know the original metric system was created by the weight of water, which means one litre of water weighs one kilo and one cubic metre of water is exactly one tonne.

I know that there's the same amount of water on Earth now as there was when our planet was formed, so we're drinking the exact same water as the dinosaurs, Cleopatra and Shakespeare did; I know there's a water reservoir floating in space equivalent to 140 trillion times all the water in every ocean on Earth.

I even know the precise chemical structure of water and could draw you an accurate diagram.

But as I plunge into the Coral Sea and start sinking slowly, I also know that not one of those facts is going to help me now.

Because all that matters is that this water is dense and wet and I can't breathe in it. (Mainly thanks to not being able to absorb oxygen molecules through gills in the side of my neck, like a fish.)

Stay calm, Harriet. Channel your inner Little Mermaid.

Blinking, I focus on the retreating surface above me.

The sea is transparent; shimmering rays of light flicker through it, and waving gently beside me and below me are hills of beautiful corals in pinks, blues, greens.

Tiny clownfish in orange and white flit round me in skittish circles; a large silver and pink bass glides slowly past; spotted yellow fish with pouty lips hover towards me and then flick away. A bright blue starfish sits to my left, and a tiny green seahorse bobs up and down between the rocks.

A stingray soars calmly over my head like an aeroplane.

And I keep sinking.

Down to where the light rays are thinner and the water is bluer; the fish are larger and the coral darker. Finally – just when I think I'm going to keep going until I hit the bottom – I see Jack: peering through the underwater camera, one hand up with his fingers in a circle.

With immense effort, I push upwards to stay suspended.

And as Jack flattens his palm and gives a nod, I compose my face, throw my arms widely above my head and point my toes together.

Click.

Then I quickly shift: lifting one knee, curving my elbows and touching the backs of my fingers together. *Click.* Opening my eyes wide, I extend my back and reach to my right with my fingertips. *Click.*

My chest feels as if it's about to burst.

Go, Harriet. Go.

As fast as I can, I kick my toes outwards as gracefully as possible while touching my palms above my head in a delicate prayer-shape.

Click.

Yup: I've modelled internationally and shot for some of the biggest fashion designers in the world.

And I'm now underwater, doing the "YMCA".

My father would be so proud.

Finally, just as it feels like my head's going to explode, Jack holds a thumb up and – with a flush of relief – I kick as fast as I can towards the surface.

Go go go go go go go –

I burst into the sunlight gasping for air with my wet red hair slapped across my face and poking up my nose.

Looking nothing like Ariel whatsoever.

"Perfect!" Emily chirps, helping me – dripping, bright red and panting – up the ladder on to the boat. "And again!"

So in I go.

This time in a dress covered with minuscule loose pearls.

Slowly, I sink.

Frantically, I attempt "The Robot": arms held out rigidly at right angles and feet squared, face frozen.

Click click click.

Quickly, I swim back to the surface, clamber out, get into another dress, jump in and try "Picking Apples": fingers stretched out, up on tiptoes.

Click click.

Out, dress, splash. "Knee Shuffle".

Click click click.

"Saturday Night Fever".

Click.

"Big Box Little Box".

Click.

Until I'm hot and cold and I've run out of disco moves and everything is a whirl of water and sunlight and coral and fish and satin and floating and falling and I don't know which way up I am or what I'm doing any more.

Just that I want it to stop.

I will do *anything* for this to stop.

Finally, Emily gives me a radiant smile.

"Just one more!" she says happily, helping me into the last wedding dress. "You're such a star, Harriet! Well done you!"

I blink at her, chest heaving.

Trembling and trying to swallow, I'm led to the edge of the boat.

I stare at the sea for the seventh time.

And then I start falling.

This time I don't stop.

As the sunlight flickers and sparkles around me, I'm suddenly calm, peaceful, serene. Spinning upwards and falling downwards: weightless and drifting, like a dandelion seed.

Or a bird, hovering in the air.

Maybe a pretty kestrel or a tiny blue merlin or a red-tailed hobby or a peregrine falcon or an iridescent hummingbird with a pink throat and those little green wings that go buzz buzz buzz I don't think I've ever seen a hummingbird maybe I should go to Mexico or Costa Rica or Ecuador or—

Everything gets darker.

Slowly, the lights flicker and dim.

And I'm just closing my eyes when a hand reaches out and grabs mine.

Dragging me back to the surface again.

30

31

"Harriet?"

32

"Harriet? Open your eyes."

33

"Come on, Manners. Look at me."

34

Slowly, I become aware of voices.

Then the rocking motion of waves slapping against the boat, the warm sun on my face, a light breeze on my legs; a hard wooden deck against my back.

A hand, still holding mine.

I know this hand.

I recognise the shape of the fingers, the shortness of the nails, the roughness of the palm, the way my thumb is being pressed on the outside.

This is a hand I've held before.

Slowly, I open my eyes.

There's a face directly above me: tanned but angular, the mouth wide and full, tilting up in the corners with two little dents in the bottom lip. The nose slopes up gently: there's a mole on the left cheek and a tiny line etched into the forehead.

Above it is a mass of dripping black curls.

And staring at me are two dark, familiar eyes: slanted

like a lion's and studying me intensely, as if they're slowly trying to piece me together from little bits too.

"Hello," I say calmly, then choke up a bucketful of seawater as the meteor hits and the Earth explodes, ripping everything away from the surface in one fell swoop: trees, people, buildings, pavements, mountains, rivers, seas.

Me.

"Oh, thank hell," Nick says, touching his forehead to mine.

And everything goes black.

35

7, 451, 533, 451

7, 451, 533, 493

7, 451, 533, 511

"What's she saying?"

"Is it a telephone number? Do we need to ring it?"

"We can't, it keeps changing."

"*Do* something!"

"Guys, it's OK. Just give her a few seconds."

Cautiously, I open my eyes again.

Nick's still there.

My non-imaginary, statistically improbable, fully three-dimensional ex-boyfriend.

"7,451,533,631," I croak blankly, staring at him. "Approximately that many people are in the world right now. It goes up really quickly."

"It goes down pretty quickly too," Nick sighs. "Manners, what the *hell* do you think you were playing at?"

Blinking, I try to sit and cough up another lungful of seawater.

Behind him, Emily and Jack are peering at me anxiously: hovering with glasses of water and cups of tea and plates of snacks.

"Here," Emily says, wrapping me in a large piece of silver tinfoil like a turkey at Christmas. "Eat some cake, Harriet. Or a biscuit. We've got sandwiches too. Jack! Sandwiches!"

"I'm getting them," he calls out frantically, diving into the cabin. "Harriet, what do you like? Cheese? Ham? Tuna? There's some kind of beef with—"

"*Just any sandwiches*," Emily shouts. "For God's sake, Jack!"

Blinking, I look back at Nick.

He's wearing a plain black wetsuit and flippers, goggles are wrapped over the top of his head, his cheeks are flushed and his eyes are bright, and I suddenly feel like I'm weightlessly floating and sinking, falling and flying again.

7,451,639,128…

"I…" I start weakly.

"Drink the tea," Nick says firmly, grabbing a cup and handing it to me.

"I don't want any—"

"You've swallowed a lot of seawater and you're going to dehydrate if you don't. Drink it, Harriet."

Obediently, I take a few sugary sips.

"Jesus, what were you *thinking*?" he snaps over the top of my cup, standing up and starting to pace around the deck. "Harriet, do you have any idea what you... Did it even cross your mind what could have..."

For a second I imagine I can see his long lion's tail twitching angrily and an unexpected giggle nearly pops out of my mouth.

"I'm *fine*," I insist hoarsely, putting the cup back down and gratefully tucking into a piece of cake. "Just got dizzy for a second, that's all."

"What were you *doing* down there?" Emily yells at Jack, whacking him on the arm. "Why didn't you *notice* there was a problem?"

"The manual said arms over your head means you're OK!" he responds, sounding mortified. "Harriet, I'm so sorry."

"Honestly, I'm *fine*," I insist through a mouthful of cake, then swivel back to Nick again as if my eyes are compasses and he's the North Pole.

"How?" I blurt. "*How* are you here?"

"I'm a diving instructor on that boat," Nick says simply, pointing at a green motorboat packed with squealing

179

tourists, fifty metres away. "It's my last day on the job. So... luck, I guess."

Just like that.

As if it's not the least likely thing that has ever happened to anyone, in the history of the planet.

As if I didn't already calculate the chances and they were nigh on zero. As if there aren't twenty-three million people in Australia, five million people in Queensland, seventy-four islands and 344,400 km^2 of Great Barrier Reef.

"You didn't know I was here?" I ask, searching his dark eyes. "You didn't... follow me, just in case I got into trouble?"

"Nope," he smiles despite himself, anger finally relenting. "And let's be honest, Manners: that would be a full-time job. You're always getting into trouble."

"I am *not*," I say, flushing bright red. "Just *sometimes*."

"Almost all of the time."

"No more than anyone else."

"Literally so much more than anyone else."

Jack and Emily awkwardly clear their throats: I'd completely forgotten they were still there. "Umm, why don't you take a few minutes to adjust while we get packed up," Jack says. "You're sure you're OK?"

Eyes still glued to Nick, I nod.

"Drink more tea," Emily insists again, holding a fresh

cup out. Then – whispering – they sidestep away like two anxious crabs.

Nick and I continue to stare at each other.

7,451,276,176...

6,836,392,019...

3,283,109,482...

1,917,201,928...

99,716,039...

7,819...

997...

82...

There are billions of people in the world, but it suddenly feels like they're disappearing.

Until all that's left in front of me is...

One.

36

Mathematics, I love you.

But this time you have let me down badly.

Because I didn't see this coming, I'm not prepared in the slightest and frankly I may never trust a calculator again.

Coughing, I wobble to my feet.

The only words in my head are *it's you it's you it's you you you you you it's you it's you I can't believe it's you* – and I don't think I should start with that.

After all, I'm standing in front of my ex-boyfriend, wearing a tinfoil cape and a sodden *wedding dress*.

My outfit's making me look keen enough already.

"So," Nick says finally. Behind us, somebody on the green motorboat whistles and beckons but Nick holds a Just A Second finger up high in the air, then turns back to me. "This is… unlikely."

I nod blankly.

One in three million, eight hundred and twenty-nine

thousand, nine hundred and thirty, if we're going on the
likelihood of us standing in the same two metres squared,
and that doesn't include the ocean.

'Unlikely' doesn't even begin to cover it.

"How... umm... are you?"

It's not enough – I know it isn't – but it has to be one
of the most common sentences in the English language
for a *reason*.

"I'm good," Nick says, nodding and glancing at the
green boat again.

"And how's the..."

I stop.

How's the Everything. How is everything in your life
and all that's happened in the six months since I knew
every tiny thing that happened in each day and night
and all the thoughts in between.

"Great," Nick says, scratching his ear. "All of it,
yeah, great." The man on the boat whistles again and
Nick mutters, "For the love of...", then cups two hands
round his mouth and yells: "*All right, I've got it, one*
minute."

And I can suddenly feel my old friend panic starting
to rise.

I have one minute.

Just one minute to say everything there is to possibly
say after six months of saying literally nothing. Mankind

has existed for six million years: 2,184,000,000 days or one and a half billion minutes.

I could have started as a tiny legless amoeba and I'm *still* not sure it would be enough time to say what I need to.

"And you?" Nick says, clearing his throat. "How are you?"

"I'm coolioko," I nod, coughing once more. *Not coolioko again, Harriet.* "I mean, I'm... fantastico." *No.* "Supastic." *No.* "I mean... I'm OK and stuff."

"Excellent. Toby and Nat?"

"They're great. Rin's in England now. She's going out with Toby."

"Really? Great."

Apparently, if you spread the brain out without wrinkles it would be the size of a pillowcase. Someone needs to take a look at mine urgently, because it feels like it's unfolding into a flat, shiny pulp.

It never used to be like this.

Things between Nick and I were always... easy. Whether I was having a panic attack on the kerb, or being pushed into Red Square in a wheelchair, or live on camera in a television studio, we always knew how to communicate with each other.

As if we were two yoghurt pots with some kind of magic invisible string between us.

But now his face seems sad and distant, and I don't know how to read it any more.

"Plus Jasper," I blurt desperately. "He's my new boyfriend."

I don't know why I say it: it's not even true.

"Oh?" Nick says, smiling rigidly. "That's great!"

My brain flattens out until it's duvet-sized.

"Yep," I continue quickly. "He's a really talented artist and has *heterochromia iridium*, which means having two different-coloured eyes. It's a genetic defect that affects six in a thousand people."

Shut up, Harriet.

"Great news," Nick nods, taking a step towards the edge. "About Jasper, not the eye thing. I'm glad you're happy."

The horn on his diving boat sounds.

"*OK!*" he yells. "I'm coming! Jeeeez."

Then he picks up his oxygen tank and my stomach flops over and my brain starts to whirl harder and all I can think is – *don't go.*

Don't go don't go don't go don't—

"Nick," I say suddenly, taking a step forward. "Did you try and call me a few days ago? Because I promise I wasn't ignoring you, I dropped my phone, it smashed, I couldn't see who it was and I couldn't hear all of it and then Nat threw it on the—"

"I didn't try and call you," he says flatly, sitting on the

edge of the boat and swinging his flippers round. "Honestly, I didn't know you were even in Australia until a few minutes ago."

"Oh."

With an abrupt vibration, our boat engine purrs to life and Jack yells, "All aboard for cast off!"

No no no no—

Not yet not yet not yet not yet—

"Anyway," Nick says, strapping his goggles over his eyes. "I should get going. It's been nice seeing you again, Harriet."

It's been nice seeing me again, Harriet.

As if I'm somebody he once accidentally shared a short car-journey with and never thought about again.

"Y-you too," I say numbly.

"Bye, Manners," he says with a tiny sad smile, putting in his mouthpiece.

I stare at him in silence.

The English language has what are called *ghost words*. Due to printing errors, translation and interpretation mistakes, words like *dord, kime* and *abacot* are officially in dictionaries all over the world even though they don't actually exist.

They're just the shapes of words: without meaning, without purpose, without intention.

Outlines with nowhere to go.

"Bye," I finally manage. "Nick?"

And as he splashes into the ocean and disappears, the words I was really looking for go with him.

I missed you: drifting like phantoms across the ocean. Evaporating into the air.

37

I have no idea what happens after that.

The next thing I know, I'm back on dry land and in my own clothes. Then I'm at the airport, I'm saying goodbye to Jack and Emily; I'm flying back to Sydney with the window blinds tightly closed.

I'm getting out of a taxi outside the apartment.

I'm walking towards the front door.

But I'm not entirely sure how, because something inside me feels like it's unravelling and I don't know where it's trying to go.

Or what it was made of in the first place.

"Hi," I manage faintly, opening the Kookaburra door. "Is anyone—"

"Harriet!" Nat squeaks, lobbing her arms round me so hard I have to steady myself against the doorframe. "Oh my God, you're back and you'll never *believe* what happened today!"

She's right: so far, I don't.

"What?" I say weakly as I untangle her arms. "What's happened?"

"The *girl*!" Nat yells, grabbing my shoulders. "The girl at the agency! She's not a model, she's a fashion blogger and SHE FOUND ME! She did a Harriet on the internet and somehow *found* me."

OK, that's not called *Doing A Harriet.*

That's displaying unbelievably good research skills.

"Amazing!" I mumble. "So you're... uh..." *Focus, Harriet.* "Making her a..." *What's it called?* "Dress?"

"Yes!" Nat grins, clapping her hands. "I went material shopping this afternoon! It's going to be pink, with a red lining and a—" She stops. "Harriet – what's happened? Oh my God, are you OK?"

"Hmm?" I drop my satchel on the floor. "I'm fine."

Nat puts a concerned hand on my cheek. "You're not fine, Harriet. You're burning up."

"I'm fine."

"You're not fine."

"I'm *fine,*" I insist, turning with a wobble towards the kitchen. "I think I just caught a bit of sun." But I can still feel Nat frowning behind me, so I add: "Did you know that ten trillionths of a suntan comes from the stars in galaxies beyond the Milky Way?"

She immediately relaxes again.

Ha. Apparently Distraction Facts *do* work on Natalie Grey after all.

"So – the girl – what happened?" I say, turning on the kettle.

I've already decided that this is Nat's Big Moment and there's no way I'm ruining it.

Especially when I did so spectacularly last time.

"Well," Nat says in excitement, following close behind me. "It turns out her name's Silva, with an *a* not an *er*. She remembered what you said about 'At The Cutting Edge' and Googled it! Harriet, she has a huge blog and a YouTube channel and she's already talked about me! Apparently she reckons I'll be the Next Big Thing! Look!"

Practically skipping on the spot with joy, she grabs her phone and holds it out.

I blink at it.

"You've got seven and a half *thousand* followers?" I scroll through her social media accounts. "Since this *morning*?"

"Yeah!" Nat says happily. "Pretty good, right?"

Little hearts and stars and bubbles are popping up frantically, and the follower count is rising by the second: 7,549… 7,553… 7,576…

"Nat," I gasp. "That is *amazing*."

"Right?!" she agrees brightly, then frowns. "But you might have to take over again, Harriet, because I've got to make the best dress ever and I don't have time to reply to everyone. Is that OK?"

She's right: comments are appearing in their hundreds.

Amazeballs! Silva's so on it! OMG I LOVE that jacket! Omg THIS. Where can I get it? GURRRRL YOU RULE! <3 <3

As yet nobody has asked for more information about the wiring in Sydney Tower.

Sometimes I worry about people on the internet.

"Sure," I say quietly as Nat runs over to a coffee table strewn with fabric, sits down contentedly and starts happily sifting through it. "Don't worry. I've got this."

Except I'm not sure I have.

My cheeks are starting to feel like they're on fire, my stomach hurts, a dull ache is slowly spreading through my arms and legs and I'm starting to feel hot and cold and shaky all over: as if I've just been dipped in liquid nitrogen.

I blink at the wall.

No: that analogy doesn't work. Liquid nitrogen is −321 degrees Fahrenheit: all of the skin would be ripped from my body in seconds. Hmm… something similar but more scientifically accurate.

I can't think exactly what right now.

"And how did it go?" Nat suddenly remembers, concentrating on her needle as she makes tiny stitches in a piece of lace. "Was it a great shoot? What did you wear?"

"Hmmm?" God, I'm so *hot*. "Oh, the usual. Dress. Beach. Pose. So on."

"Amazing," she sighs, needle flashing in and out of the lace. "We're so *lucky*."

"Mmmm," I agree weakly, fanning myself. Good old stupid, statistically unlikely *luck*. "I'm just going to..." *Where am I going?* "Go do some... social media strategy work in the..." *Where?* "Bedroom."

And maybe I'll have a little nap first.

A welcome few minutes of darkness and silence while my brain stops whirring.

Nat finally looks up. "You sure you're OK?"

I dredge up a smile. "Fine!"

Shivering, I grab my satchel, shuffle to my bedroom and shut the door.

I'm just crawling into bed when the Brick starts ringing loudly. It takes me six seconds to reach it, seven to decide whether to answer it or not and two to actually press the button.

That's how exhausted I feel and how little I want to have this conversation.

"Hello?" I say finally, closing my eyes tightly.

"My little bumblebee!" Wilbur trills. "Light of my life, flower of my heart, what the *billy-boo* have you done this time?"

I had kind of hoped today's epic screw-up would stay between me, the sky and the sea.

Guess I was wrong.

Again.

38

According to my fact books, the average Briton apologises at least eight times every day.

Watch this, because I'm about to use mine up in one go.

"I'm sorry," I whisper, curling up into a tight ball.

"Baby-bonsai-tree," Wilbur continues chirpily. "I would have *sworn* on my shiny green Louboutins that we spoke yesterday about patience and whatnot. But I've just had a call from Eva and I must have been imaginifying it, because apparently that did not sink in at *all*."

Shivering, I pull the duvet over my head. "I'm so sorry."

"What happened, Bunnycakes?"

"I..." *Didn't listen to experts, assumed I knew better, refused to wait, made my own plans, forced myself into a situation I didn't belong in and created total havoc. Again.* "I Did a Harriet."

"You did," Wilbur agrees gently. "You went Full Harriet.

194

And now I'm being asked why this fandango occurred. Any ideas, my little crinkle-cut-crisp?"

It's a very, very good question.

Just not one I have an answer for right now.

"I'm really sorry."

"I *did* try to remind you of normal agency rules when I called on your first day in Oz, Puddle-bum," Wilbur sighs. "But I *knew* it had gone right over your little head. Whoosh, like a sparkly rocket."

I blink at the wall numbly.

Oh my God: that broken phone call was from *Wilbur*?

Intense heat is moving from my cheeks, into my chest and wrapping itself round my throat so I can't breathe.

"Sorry."

"It's OK, Muffin-chops. But you know that long, long list of models that you weren't at the top of? You're further down it. A lot further down it. Lots and lots and lots further."

There's a pause.

"Let's put it this way," Wilbur continues thoughtfully. "Now it's less like Scrabble and more like Snakes and Ladders. And you've just hit the big green one that goes back to the beginning and there aren't really that many ladders."

"I'm really sorry."

Wilbur hushes me. "I'm not cross, my little ginger snap.

They'll get over it. In the greater scheme of things, this little *disasteroo* doesn't matter in the slightest."

Except that it does.

I'm slowly beginning to realise how ironic it is that I'm so good at learning lessons inside school, and so terrible at learning any outside it.

And I'm tired of saying sorry.

On the upside, clearly nobody told Eva or Wilbur the whole story, or I suspect this phone call would be from my parents and possibly Annabel's legal firm.

"Wilbur," I say dully, curling up even tighter and wrapping my arms round my stomach. "I *promise* nothing like this will ever happen again."

My fairy godmother laughs with a tinkle.

"Oh, Bunny," he says fondly. "I think if there's one thing we know about Harriet Manners, it's that something like this will *always* happen again."

I've got three sorries left to spend.

Saying goodbye to my agent, I get my laptop out and blearily type out an email, apologising profusely to Emily and Jack.

Then another, apologising to Eva.

Finally, I scroll slowly through my texts for the one I got approximately three hours ago and didn't answer.

Time for another appointment! Want to talk? J

I type:

Sry, not feelng so gd. Spk tmw Hx

Then I turn my phone off.
  And close my eyes.

39

I spend the next three days in bed.

By the end of the first evening, it's become abundantly clear that I'm suffering from some kind of exotic waterborne sickness: probably picked up from an errant stingray or ailing jellyfish.

Maybe Chikungunya or Chagas disease.

Possibly West Nile virus.

None of which are commonly found in Australia and all of which are usually spread by mosquitos and not sea creatures, but facts mean nothing to me any more.

All I know is I hurt all over.

I can't sleep or eat or talk or read or study.

And I have no interest in getting out of bed again.

Ever.

On the second day, Nat forces Bunty to call a doctor.

"It's not normal," I hear my best friend whisper at the door. "She turned down chocolate and banana pancakes

with whipped cream *and* an offer to watch a documentary about locusts."

I must be really, really ill.

Unfortunately, the doctor doesn't appear to know what he's talking about.

"You don't have guinea worm disease," he says firmly, pulling the thermometer out of my mouth and staring at it. "Or African trypanosomiasis. And you absolutely certainly don't have Crimean-Congo fever."

I gave him a few options, just to speed up the diagnosis.

"Are you sure?" Nat says worriedly from the doorway where she's been lurking all morning. "How do you know?"

"Because we're not in the Congo," the doctor replies. "And her temperature is 37.1 degrees. If she had any of the above, I think it would probably be a bit higher."

I'm extremely alarmed at how cold I am for a second, and then remember Australia uses Celsius and not Fahrenheit. Although that's still 0.1 over the average: he's being very offhand about my wellbeing.

"Have you checked for Naegleria fowleri?" I say weakly. "It's a brain-eating amoeba that comes from warm lakes, springs and pools. I definitely *feel* really confused and disorientated."

The Australian doctor laughs heartily.

"We'll keep an eye on you but it looks like basic

exhaustion to me. Have you been physically exerting yourself more than normal recently?"

I glance at Bunty, standing behind Nat with her arm wrapped round Nat's shoulder.

There's no way I can risk her overhearing about the shoot, in case she tells my parents, so I shake my head vigorously.

"Of course not," I say indignantly.

"Well," the doctor says with a smile. "Get some sleep, eat some food and you'll be right as rain in a day or two."

"Actually," I say, lying back on my pillow. "That saying doesn't really mean much. In 1400 it was originally *right as an adamant*, which is a magnet, and it was slowly corrupted to *right as a gun* in 1622, then *right as my leg*. *Right as rain* stuck just because it's alliterative."

"Hmm," Nat says drily from the doorway. "She's definitely getting better now."

I stick my tongue out at her.

"We'll take care of Harriet," my grandmother smiles warmly. "Thank you, doctor."

Then she gives a little nod and Moonstone walks in with a tray packed with sandwiches, croissants, cakes and biscuits that for some bizarre reason don't look appealing at all.

I nestle under my duvet again.

"You stay there as long as you want to, darling," Bunty says gently. "We're here when you're ready."

By six am of the fourth morning, my mysterious illness has passed.

On waking up, I suddenly feel an urge to pick at a biscuit and sip a glass of strawberry milkshake. Then – bored of being horizontal – I swing my legs out and start to wobble around the apartment, looking for a book to read.

And also – frankly – for an excuse to get out of my room.

After three days of refusing to open the curtains and using the en suite bathroom, it's starting to smell like the cage of an incredibly lazy hamster.

With the lights still off, I give a big yawn and tiptoe to the kitchen for a glass of water. I've just finished draining it when I hear chatter coming from the cupboard on my left.

Frowning, I shuffle over and hold my empty glass up to the wooden door. This action focuses the audio waves into a smaller area, thus making it easier to hear and also making you look a bit like a spy.

Because either the cupboard is actually talking to me or I'm having a flu-addled hallucination.

Regardless, I should probably listen.

"No, darling," it says in a whisper. "Not yet." Pause. "The doctor's been and she's just a little under the weather. I promise I'm taking care of her, sweetheart, don't worry. But this definitely isn't the right time."

I blink sleepily. Is that Bunty?

And, for your information, "under the weather" is *another* inaccurately used idiom. It comes from sailors who had seasickness and were sent below deck so that the rocking of the boat would be less pronounced.

Although after Queensland maybe it's not that far off.

"Don't worry about *that*," my grandmother continues warmly. "I'm as strong as an ox, darling. You know me. But I still think we should wait a little while longer."

There's another silence, and I suddenly realise Bunty must be talking on the phone. My brain is so muddled, for a second I thought my grandmother was conversing with the furniture.

"But I keep thinking about Yuka, sweetheart. It's so *sad* that we haven't spoken properly for a decade. We were so close once upon a time." Bunty's voice gets lower. "The argument we had was so ridiculous. Burning a hole in a ceiling is *not* that big a deal."

She must be speaking to Annabel. There's an intimacy in her voice, the kind you reserve for a daughter.

The kind Annabel always reserves for me.

"*OK*, yes, the roof fell down," Bunty sighs reluctantly.

"*OK,* maybe the whole house went up in flames with it and the cat disappeared. But I *did* offer her a *lovely* bed in my caravan and it had fairy lights and whatnot."

Knowing Yuka, that would not have gone down well.

"Also," Bunty continues, "it's not good karma to leave things on bad terms, darling. The universe doesn't like it."

I blink. Huh?

Leave things? Is Yuka going somewhere?

"We'll tell Harriet soon," Bunty says more gently. "But I'd like to see my old friend first. We're in the same city, and it feels like fate is trying to bring us together at the... Well, *the end* is a bit melodramatic, isn't it? At a temporary parting of ways."

I take a huge step back, eyes wide.

There are approximately five and a half litres of blood in the human body, and it suddenly feels like the majority of mine have just evaporated.

The end? Parting of ways?

Is Yuka Ito... *sick*?

And I'm hit by a wave of memories.

Of Yuka: sitting on the chair in the dark of the Infinity agency, ordering me to turn round in my pinstripe suit. Yuka: standing in the snow in Moscow, glaring at me struggling to control a kitten.

Dictating to me through the earpiece during that

television show; sitting in the back of the taxi in Tokyo; walking away from the shoot by the lake; firing me on the train platform when I got back.

Standing in front of me in the Paris Catacombs.

Always, always, the same: in a long black dress, a tiny black net hat, long black hair, snow-white skin, brightly coloured lips, a freezing expression.

And always, always immortal.

As if there has always been a Yuka Ito and there will always *be* a Yuka Ito: as if the world needed a Yuka Ito, so here she was.

But she's not immortal at all.

And I can feel pain and sadness and shame starting to ripple through my chest in a three-coloured swirl: like some kind of emotional Neapolitan ice cream. Yuka is sick, and I've been *demanding things* from her.

Oh God, I emailed her *seven times in a row*.

Never mind that she's already changed my life and I never actually said a proper thank-you. Never mind that I didn't even think to ask how she was.

Hello, this is Harriet Manners and I want more.

Flushing hot, I put the glass back in its original spot as quietly as I can, and tiptoe silently into my bedroom. Then I crawl back into bed, shut my eyes and try to regulate my breathing.

By the time Bunty pokes her head in and whispers:

"Harriet, sweetheart, did I hear the door? Are you feeling better?" I'm pretending to be unconscious, complete with tiny snores.

Gently, my grandmother walks up to the bed and brushes a few strands of hair off my face. "Little girl," she murmurs softly. "What happened in Queensland?"

Then she leans down and kisses my forehead.

But as she creeps back out again – flowery flip-flops clacking against the wood floor – the final drop of blood in my head evaporates.

It's replaced with a realisation so sharp and vivid I suddenly sit bolt upright in bed.

Nick.

Yuka is his *aunt*.

That must be why he was so sad and distracted. Why I couldn't read him. *This* is what broke the string between us.

And my heart aches: for Yuka, for Nick, for everything they must now be going through. For finding out too late.

I sit up a bit straighter, staring blankly at the wall.

Except... *it's not too late, is it*?

From the moment we met, Nick has been there for me.

When I cowered under a table in Birmingham; when I hyperventilated on the pavement outside my first agency meeting; when I panicked on my first-ever photo shoot and didn't know what to say on breakfast TV.

He was there, skating with me on my first-ever date.

Kissing me under the Christmas tree; standing on my doorstep in Tokyo; helping me through the sumo shoot; guiding me into the lake by Mount Fuji; sitting with me by the crossing in Shibuya.

He turned up at my house when I had a cold.

Winked at me from the catwalk in London.

Came to New York with sixteen purple balloons and sixteen cupcakes on my birthday; turned up at the Gotham Ball with a gift for me; let go when I asked him to on Brooklyn Bridge.

Watched me model in Paris, hidden and smiling in a crowd.

Nick has always been there: whether I knew I needed him or not.

Another wave of intense shame sweeps over me.

But what did I do for *him*?

I sat around: waiting to be saved. Hoping my prince would come and find me, over and over again. That he would climb the tower, fight the dragon, slay the witch, break open the glass box and get me out.

So isn't it *his* turn now?

I should help. Not as his girlfriend – not even as his ex – but as his *friend*.

Jumping out of bed, I rummage through the secret pocket in my satchel, get my planets necklace out and put it on for the biggest dose of good luck I've ever wished for.

Then I grab my laptop, a notepad and a pen and start making a brand-new, life-grabbing plan. Because after all the kindness Nick has shown me over the last year and a half, I think it's time for me to pay a little back.

For *me* to be the hero who swoops in when they're needed, without being asked to.

It's finally time for me to save Nick.

40

Now there's just the small problem of logistics.

So I spend the next two hours making bullet points, checking and double-checking timetables, booking tickets and scanning maps.

I know exactly what it is I have to do.

I'm going to have to go *Full Harriet.*

"Good morning, Nat!" I call at nine am, pulling the curtains abruptly open. "Good morning!" I shout to Bunty, who's standing in the kitchen in a fluffy pink robe with her hands wrapped round a floral cup of coffee. "Good, uh... never mind," I say to Moonstone as she glares at me silently from the corner armchair.

Then I gesture at the table, laid perfectly outside.

"If you could make your way to the poolside," I say politely, "there is a lovely breakfast awaiting you, complete with green smoothies, avocados and bowls of buckwheat. To say thank you for looking after me when I was sick."

After all the planning was completed I only had seven minutes left and it turns out the cupboards in this apartment are *packed* with disgusting-looking health food.

Nat must have eaten all the chocolate croissants.

"Oh, *delicious*," Bunty beams, taking a comfortable seat on a sunlounger. "I love a wonder grain. Are you feeling better now, darling? You certainly *look* much perkier."

Nat emerges from the bedroom, rubbing her eyes.

"What's happening?" she says, blinking in the sunlight. "Ew, what colour is that milkshake?"

"It's *very* good for you," I say, pushing a sludge-coloured one towards her. There was some kind of mix in a packet so I just added water. "Drink up and behold!"

Then I turn to the laptop and hit a button.

Immediately, the enormous cinema screen lights up. I know I haven't done one of these in quite some time, but I clearly haven't lost my touch: this PowerPoint presentation might be my best yet.

There are interactive spinning images and *everything*.

"I'm confused," Nat says, blinking at it. "Yesterday you were shuffling off this mortal coil or whatever you called it. When on earth did you prepare a school lesson?"

"It was just a transient sickness," I announce, pushing her firmly into a bean bag. "I'm better now, so if you're settled I shall begin."

Then I gesture at the screen with one hand while clutching the remote control with the other. "Did you know that the coastline of Australia is 22,293 miles long?"

I flick to a page filled with photos of beautiful white sand.

"Oh God," Nat groans. "It's not even nine am yet."

"There are precisely 10,685 beaches in Australia," I continue, pointing at the images. "That means you could go to a different beach every day for *twenty-nine years* and you still wouldn't see them all."

Smiling broadly, I hit the *next* button.

It pans out to a big map of the country, complete with tiny photos of koalas I pasted on for cuteness purposes.

"More than *eighty per cent* of Australia's population lives within a hundred kilometres of the coast, making it one of the world's biggest urbanised coastal dwelling populations."

With a hand-wave, I click the button again.

"Oh, this is *delightful*," Bunty sighs happily, leaning back in her lounger and eating a spoonful of buckwheat soup. "What an unexpected treat."

Nat takes a sip of her sludge smoothie, then spits it on to the floor.

"H," she sighs. "Get to the point already."

OK: that was harsh.

Where else does she think this is heading?

"*So*," I conclude, skipping to the final slide, "the point I'm making is that the Australian coastline is *big*. Eighty-five per cent of the population live within fifty kilometres of the *sea*. I think that *we should be some of them*!"

Then I flick to a page with photos of Nat, Bunty and me, stuck on top of an Australian flag.

"We *are* some of them, darling," Bunty points out fondly. "We're sitting in front of the sea right now."

Sugar cookies. I did not factor our current location in.

"*More* of it," I say hastily. "We should see *more* of it. Why stay in one place when there's a whole *world* to explore?"

Then I hold out my hands and spin in a circle.

Bunty breaks into applause. "I couldn't have said it better myself! That was *fabulous*! Shall we go today? I'll get my bag."

I can feel satisfaction pulsing all over me.

Ha. That was *so* much easier than trying to convince my parents of anything: they were an excellent if somewhat critical training ground. Now I just have to grab my suitcase, get us to the bus station and—

"Wait a minute," Nat says, leaning back in her bean bag with her eyes narrowed: looking at me carefully. "You want us to leave Sydney, right now, to go and see *all the beaches in Australia*?"

"Yup," I say, looking at the floor. "Basically."

"No beach in particular?"

"N-ooo." I shift my gaze to an interesting tree behind her. "Just… any of them. As they come. As we go up the coast."

"Sure." Nat's eyes have narrowed to slits. "And none of these random beaches would begin with a B, would they? Followed by another B?"

Bat poop. She was paying *way* more attention to what I've been saying over the last year and a half than I thought she was.

"Well, of course," I say, quickly turning the presentation off before she sees the little red star I drew on the coastline. "There's Bells Beach in Victoria. Burleigh Heads Beach on the Gold Coast…"

"Byron Bay, fourteen hours' bus-drive north."

We stare at each other as only lifelong best friends can: with all the words on the planet even though we're not saying any of them.

"Oh my *God,*" Nat finally shouts, jumping up and flinging her napkin on the table. "You spoke to Nick, didn't you?! What happened? Did he ring again? Harriet, you didn't ring *him*, did you?"

She knows.

I don't know how, but somehow Nat saw straight through my PowerPoint presentation to the truth. There may be 10,685 beaches in Australia, but I'm only planning on heading to one of them.

Byron Bay: Nick's childhood home.

"Umm," I say, chewing my bottom lip. "Actually, I saw him."

There's a long silence.

Nat's eyes are so round she looks like a cartoon character: as if they're about to fall out of her head with a *boing* sound. "*You saw him?* WHEN, EXACTLY?"

"He turned up on my shoot. And…" I glance at Bunty. Obviously I can't expose what I know about Yuka, because then she'll know I eavesdropped on her private conversation. "I need to see him again. As soon as possible."

Nat closes her eyes for a second.

The muscle between her eyebrows twitches briefly and her bottom lip tenses.

Then she opens them again and looks straight at me.

"No," she says coldly. "Absolutely not."

41

Ninety-five per cent of the universe is unaccounted for.

Astrophysicists have looked at all the stars, black holes and galaxies they can find in the sky, and they only make up five per cent of known mass: leaving a huge amount of "dark matter" which they dedicate their entire lives to hunting for but are still unable to find.

What I'm trying to say is: we might *think* we know everything, but there are frequently mysteries right under our noses.

The unknowable is always lurking.

I've been best friends with Nat for over a decade, but I never, ever saw this dark matter coming.

"No?" I say, sitting down abruptly on a sunlounger. "What do you mean *no*?"

"I mean no," Nat says, a familiar pink flush climbing up her throat. "No, you are not seeing Nick again. No, you don't *need* to see him. And *hell no*, I'm not coming

214

with you or backing this idea in any way, shape or form."

My mouth falls open.

Nat has never failed to support me wholeheartedly: not even when my ideas are stupid, trouble or poorly thought through.

In fact, she's normally the first to join the front line.

Like a kind of sacrificial soldier for bad ideas.

"I don't think you understand," I start tentatively as Nat rips a red flower from a nearby bush and starts yanking the petals off, one by one. "This isn't about *me...*"

"*No*," she hisses, throwing another petal on the floor. "Nu-uh. Not going to happen. Never. Over my dead body."

She throws the stalk on to the floor and steps on it.

"Nat," I say slowly, standing up and holding my hands out the way cowboys do when trying to calm a wild horse. "I understand if you don't want to come or if you're too busy but—"

"That is *not* what I'm saying," she snaps. "Oh my *God*, Harriet. How many times are you going to do this? *What is wrong with you?*"

In fairness, people have been asking me *What is wrong with you?* my entire life.

I kind of assumed my best friend already knew.

"What are you talking about?" I say, feeling hot and cold again. "Do *what*?"

"Hurt yourself again!" She takes a step forward until she's definitely too close to yell but is doing so anyway. "Dammit, it's like watching a puppy run at the same wall time and time again, and at some point *somebody has got to stand in the way.*"

I stare at Nat in amazement. I'm not a *puppy.*

And if she would just calm down, I could take her aside and gently explain the situation: about Yuka's illness, about the overheard phone call, about Nick's imminent loss.

But she's too busy pacing round the table like a strident tiger and I'm a bit scared of touching her arm in case she bites me.

"Nat," I say again, "I have a *reason* to—"

"Of course you do," she snaps fiercely, throwing her hands in the air. "You'll have found some kind of *reason,* even if it requires a huge leap in logic based on no kind of reality whatsoever. Even if you've had to construct an entire narrative round it."

My eyes get wider. "My logic isn't *leaping.*"

"Yes, it is, because it always does. It's what you *do.* Your brain makes its own weird random pathways, and you'll have somehow convinced yourself that Nick *needs you* and that you're going to be there for him, whatever it takes, *as a friend.*"

I open my mouth and shut it again.

"When it's *not* just as a friend," Nat continues furiously. "You're still in love with that boy and you're going to destroy yourself on him all over again. For the third time. Even the *Titanic* only sank once, Harriet!"

And a coldness inside me suddenly hits with full iciness.

Like an unexpected iceberg, appropriately.

"I am *not* still in love," I say frostily. "I'm not going to *destroy myself*. And you have no idea how serious this situation is or why I need to be there."

"Oh my *God*," Nat fumes. "Why do you think you were in bed for three whole days after seeing him? Your *body was literally closing down.*"

I blink. "I had an unidentified sea *flu*."

"Sea flu, my butt. You had *heartbreak*. And now you're just going to go get some more voluntarily?"

I stare at her in amazement. "You don't always know everything, Nat. You think you do, but you don't. This is important. I *need* to do this."

"You *don't*," she snaps, red rash rising. "You need to get *on with your own life*. You're not a couple. And Nick *doesn't want you to be there for him or he would have asked.*"

Blankly, I stare back at her.

She obviously doesn't know Nick at all. He would *never*

ask for help. He would shut the world out and go through it all on his own.

I'm starting to wonder if she knows me either.

"I'm not asking for your permission, Natalie," I say, lifting my chin with as much strength as I can find. "I'm going and there's nothing you can do to stop me."

"Fine," she says, standing up and hurling her smoothie into the bush. "Go, then."

"I will," I say with my arms folded.

"Good," Nat says, turning to storm back into the house. "But this time it'll be without me."

42

I've always been proud of my door-slamming skills.

But Nat's trump mine. As she disappears into the house every single piece of glass looks like it's about to smash into the garden, along with a bit of rooftop.

Reeling, I turn to Bunty.

It feels like the air is still vibrating with Nat's rage, but my grandmother is lying quietly on her sunlounger.

I prepare myself for another fight.

Honestly, I don't *want* to fight my grandmother: especially when she's so sweet and her hair is all fluffy and soft, like a pink *kawaii* bear, but if I have to in order to get on that bus then that's what I'm going to—

"I'll come with you," she says, standing up slowly. "My bag's already packed."

I blink at her, astounded. "Really?"

"My bag's always packed, darling. It's good to be prepared for any adventure."

"I mean, you're really coming with me?"

"Of course. If your heart is telling you that this is what you have to do, then you need to do it. Our hearts have voices and we should *always* listen to them."

Another wave of frustration washes over me.

"It's not my *heart* speaking," I say tersely. "It's my…" Which bit of my body is this decision coming from? My lungs? My liver? My kidneys? "It's my *brain*. The motor cortex, which controls my *voluntary* actions."

"Then you should *definitely* listen to that." Bunty smiles, leaning briefly on the table. "I mean, if we didn't have brains what would we be?"

"Corals. Or jellyfish. Starfish, sea urchins, sand dollars…"

"Exactly!" Bunty laughs. "And who wants to be a jellyfish?"

"Quite a few people, probably," I admit, starting to calm down again. "A lot of them have bioluminescent organs that glow in the dark and that would be pretty cool."

Grinning, my grandmother takes a few steps forward.

Then she turns to Moonstone. I hadn't even realised her friend was still here: that's how dark the tree shadow she's been sitting in is.

And how like a shadow she is too.

"Moonie," my grandmother says firmly. "My granddaughter and I are going to take a little trip up the coast. If we leave on the night bus, we can arrive in the morning and catch the bus back tomorrow evening. I'll need you to stay here and look after Natalie for me."

Moonstone frowns. "What is Annabel going to say?"

"Annabel doesn't need to know," Bunty says with a sly wink at me. "I mean, if a grandmother can't run away with her granddaughter now and then, what is the point of *any* of this?"

She waves a hand around and there's silence.

"Exactly," Bunty continues in triumph. "So let me go grab my *Daisy* book and we'll be back before you know it."

Moonstone looks me up and down a few times.

Something tells me she does not like what she sees, although in fairness I haven't had a shower or washed my face or brushed my teeth in nearly four days so it's kind of understandable.

"Fine," she says, relenting visibly. "But if you need anything, I can get a flight up there in two hours flat."

"We won't need anything," my grandmother assures her confidently. "Just a little bit of luck."

By that evening, I'm clean and packed and at the Sydney bus station with my brightly twinkling grandmother by my side.

I didn't say goodbye to Nat because I didn't need to.

Her hot-headed temper tantrums are just one of her little ear-bone tics, and I accept them even if I don't always agree with them: I need to give her space to calm down again, that's all.

Then everything will be fine between us.

"Well," Bunty says as an enormous red coach with a blue greyhound painted on its side turns on its engine and we queue up alongside it. "This is *exciting*. You're never too old for an adventure, darling-heart."

"You're never too old for *anything*," I say as we approach the front and hold out our tickets. "Did you know that Sophocles wrote *Oedipus at Colonus* when he was eighty-nine, and Justice Oliver Wendell Holmes started studying Greek at the age of eighty?"

We take a few steps up on to the bus.

There's a long, narrow line of thirty small, vivid blue seats covered with little red and yellow geometric shapes, and – somewhere at the back – a tiny toilet cubicle that already smells of urine.

OK: maybe there *are* some things you can be too old for.

These look like seats built for four-year-olds, and between us my grandmother and I have the combined age of an octogenarian.

Slightly perturbed, I turn to Bunty.

"*Such* fun," she says without a flicker of concern,

putting her battered patchwork bag in the overhead hold and settling into one of the seats with a warm blanket. "This reminds me of my teenage years. Nothing like seeing a country from the road, darling!"

I look dubiously at the tiny, rather sticky seats we're now crammed into. Because – as my grandmother closes her eyes and settles uncomfortably in for the night – it's starting to hit me that it's going to be a very, very long road indeed.

Thirteen hours and fifty-three minutes long, in fact.

And I have no idea what's waiting for us at the other end.

43

Here is the official list of the five biggest cities in the world:

1. Tokyo, population 37,833,000
2. Delhi, population 24,953,000
3. Shanghai, population 22,991,000
4. Mexico City, population 20,843,000
5. São Paulo, population 20,831,000

Suffice to say, Byron Bay is not on it.

It's a seaside town in Eastern Australia with a population of only 4,959 people and a three-kilometre radius, which means my chances of finding Nick are pretty promising: even in the limited eight hours we have here.

And as the bus drives down a pretty avenue lined with green trees and parks and cotton-coloured houses, I can feel my optimism rising.

I mean, he somehow found me in *Tokyo*: the most populated city on the planet.

Twice.

This can't be *that* difficult, can it?

"Okeydokey, darling," Bunty says as we clamber off the bus. She's been asleep for the last fourteen hours: napping against the vibrating window on her folded headscarf. "I've got a couple of friends living *just* down that road. Why don't we have a calming cup of camomile together first?"

I look twitchily around in a circle, fiddling with my planets necklace.

Because it's just starting to hit me that any minute now I might see Nick again, and I haven't decided yet exactly what I'm going to say.

Or how I'm even going to track him d—

Oooh.

"Actually," I say as a tall, tanned, dark-haired boy skateboards down the road and my stomach flips over. "Can I meet you later, if that's OK? I've just had an idea."

Bunty smiles. "Darling, you are *full* of those, aren't you?"

She can say that again. Right now I'm so full of them it feels like my head is going to explode.

"Mmm," I twitch.

"Text if you need me, darling," my grandmother says, kissing my cheek. "And remember to follow your heart."

"It's *my brain* I'm following," I clarify quickly. "My *brain*."

"Of course," Bunty laughs. "Although I'd suggest you take them both with you anyway, just for good measure."

As soon as my grandmother has gone, I get the Brick out of my satchel. This is going to cost an absolute fortune, but where there's a will there's a way.

And there's *definitely* a will.

I can feel it pounding in the centre of my chest, making me feel queasy and light-headed. An octopus has three hearts, and from the way mine has started hammering I think mine may have tripled too.

Swallowing, I switch the phone on.

Then I quickly scan through the flurry of text messages suddenly popping up after four whole days of being switched off.

Hey! Did you get my last message? Jx

You OK? Jx

Is something going on? Jx

Harriet, your grandmother says you're sick. Do you need to come home? Can change flights. Annabel

I'M not worried. I bet you've eaten too many jam doughnuts. LIKE FATHER LIKE DAUGHTER AMIRITE? LOL Dad. xxx

Grimacing, I close the messages. I'll deal with them later.

Then I scroll impatiently through my contacts.

I'm about to thrust myself into the life of somebody who isn't expecting me. I'm about to try to find someone who hasn't made their whereabouts known: to be there for somebody, despite not being asked to. And there's one person in my life who knows how to do that, better than anyone else.

Consistently, with five years of practice.

The phone rings and then there's a click.

With a sudden rush I'm crouched inside the bush outside my house again: freezing cold and lit by a green, wise light.

"Greetings, earthling. This is Toby Pilgrim."

"Toby, it's Harriet. I need you to teach me how to stalk."

44

OK, *stalk* is the wrong word.

I'm merely... geographically locating somebody without their knowledge. After all, I only need to *find* Nick and explain why I'm there and then I'm no longer a stalker: I'm a concerned old friend who is worried about his wellbeing.

Which is *much* less socially inappropriate and/or illegal.

"Hold on just a tickety," Toby says cheerfully. "I'll put you on speakerphone." Then there's the long, loud sound of somebody blowing their nose into a Batman hankie.

And before you ask, I know it's a Batman hankie because Toby showed it to me before I left.

Even though I absolutely begged him not to.

"Right," he continues, sniffling a bit and (probably) sticking it back up his jumper sleeve. "Rin and I are *all* ears."

"Hello, Harry-chan!" she calls sweetly. "Are we all

ears? I have two, Toby-kun. You have just two. Where are others?"

"It's an expression from the English idioms book I got you," he says affectionately. "Remember?"

"Ah, like stealing the Mickey Mouse. Or itching your feet. Popping one's clogs together."

"Close enough."

"I'm in Byron Bay," I say quickly, because I'd love to chat but this call is costing me approximately seven hundred pounds a minute and I've only got one day to find him. "And I just need a few... uh." How do I put this tactfully? "Tracking pointers."

Tracking pointers. That sounds a *lot* less creepy.

"Ah," Toby says wisely, like the keynote speaker at some kind of Stalking Conference. "Harriet Manners, you are going on a Polar Bear Hunt."

"You are going to capture a very big one!" Rin giggles. "Like the nursery rhyme!"

"Exactly," Toby agrees. "Although in a thoroughly humane, metaphorical sense only."

OK: this conversation is proving to be a *lot* less constructive than I initially thought.

Not to mention a lot more expensive.

"What?" I sigh flatly.

"We've talked about this before, Harriet," Toby explains patiently. "You need to embrace your inner polar bear. So the first thing you've got to do is blend seamlessly into your environment. As you're in a beach town, do you own anything yellow that might conceivably look like sand?"

I look down at my red shorts and crossword T-shirt. "No."

"That's a shame. Do you – perchance – have any *glue*? Because then you could just roll around on the ground for a few minutes and that should do the trick."

I am beginning to regret making this call.

"Let's say I stay in my own clothes and leave the ground alone like a non-insane person. What else?"

"A polar bear's sense of smell is so powerful they can track prey from seventeen kilometres away," Toby states knowingly. "Does your target have a recognisable scent?"

Lime-green shower gel and wet grass.

"I'm not sniffing my way round town, Toby. Next?"

"Polar bears are invisible to infrared cameras so you're going to need night-vision goggles. I'd send you mine but they're quite heavy so they may take some time to get there."

I glance up at the glorious Australian sunshine beaming down on me. "It's daytime, Toby," I say through gritted teeth. "So I probably don't need them either."

"Got it," he says, completely unfazed. "In that case, cover your nose with your paw. It'll help deflect attention and also conserve warmth."

I am never asking Toby for advice on anything ever again.

"Toby, I don't *want* to deflect attention. I actually want to be *seen* or there's no point in this at all."

"Got it," he says breezily. "But remember that a hunting polar bear can swim up to seven hundred kilometres, non-stop, for nine whole days. Stalking can sometimes get quite boring so you might need to take a book."

"Manga," Rin agrees sweetly. "I shall send some observations."

I'm starting to feel more than slightly impatient.

I love my friends dearly, but my return bus to Sydney leaves at eight pm tonight: I only have the rest of today to source, save and comfort Nick.

I *really* need some actual help.

"Toby," I interrupt. "All I need to know is how to *find* someone. Like, where would they be? What would they be doing? How do I guess?"

Toby has always seemed to know exactly where I am: what I'm doing, and when I'm likely to be there at any given time.

And I've never understood *how*.

"Oh," he says in surprise. "Well, that's easy. You just need to think about the person in question and then you'll know."

I blink. "What?"

"Imagine you're them, Harriet. Think about what they like and how they feel and what makes them happy. Then go there too. It's really not that complicated."

And suddenly my head is full of the conversation Nick and I had, seven months ago on Brooklyn Bridge.

I haven't been home for more than ten days in three years.

I miss being shouted at by Mum.

I miss my friends.

I miss surfing and sunshine and playing the piano and waking up, knowing where I am and who I am.

I miss being in one place.

If I was Nicholas Hidaka right now, where would I be?

"That's incredibly helpful," I say with real relief, jumping off the wall. "Thanks so much, guys."

"You're welcome." Then there's a short pause while Rin whispers: *Ask her, Toby-kun.* "Harriet? We won't tell Jasper where you are or what you're doing, right?"

An unexpected wave of shame washes over me.

It's so intense I can feel it pulsing through my fingertips, through my shoulders, up my neck, into my cheeks. Because – just like Nat – Toby and Rin know exactly who I'm trying to find without being told.

And obviously they don't think I should be doing this either.

"Umm," I say, biting my bottom lip. "If you could keep it between us, that would be great."

It's not that I'm *not* going to tell Jasper.

I'm just not going to tell him right *now*. Some topics are delicate and need a little longer to explain: like the fact that I'm currently on the other side of the world, tracking down my ex-boyfriend.

"All memory of this conversation has been wiped from our brains," Toby says loyally. "It never happened, Harriet Manners."

And a sudden fond lump jumps into my throat.

The polar bear is the strongest mammal on the planet.

They're loyal and tenacious and brave.

In fact, the Inuits believe that polar bears are so magical and wise that the very word *Arctic* comes from the Greek *Arktikos* which literally means "the constellation of the bear".

Polar bears are so amazing, they named a *continent* after them.

And I feel incredibly lucky that this one tracked me down and never let go.

"Thank you, Toby Pilgrim," I say gratefully. "You're a true genius."

"I know, Harriet," Tobes says, blowing his nose again loudly. "I went and did the test."

* * *

Feeling much calmer now, I put the Brick down.

Then I get a carefully folded-up piece of paper out of my bag. I found it this morning, attached to an email from last year. In the foreground, Nick is grinning: hair a mess of curls, nose crumpled, hand held up against the sun.

And in the background is a little brown house.

Whenever I'm sad or lost, the first place I go is to my local launderette. But *after* that, I go home: to Annabel, to Dad, to Tabby, to my dog and my bedroom. Something tells me Nick might do that too.

Here goes Stalker Plan Number One.

45

There are 2,481 houses in Byron Bay.

That means – without an address, and with the limited time I have left – I would have to visit over a hundred houses an hour, or 1.7 a minute, for the chance of finding the one Nick grew up in.

Conformance to a linear sense of time tells me this would be almost impossible.

Luckily, one short remembered conversation has increased my chances significantly.

"You live on *Ivanhoe* Street?" I'd laughed when he told me last summer, my feet propped on his lap. "But your house is in *Byron* Bay: did they have to pick a Sir Walter Scott poem?"

"Yeah," Nick grinned, tugging on the toe of my sock. "Sadly 'She Walks In Beauty Like the Night Street' was already taken."

I chuckled. "Still has a better ring than 'Prometheus Avenue'."

"Or 'Childe Haroldе's Pilgrimage Place'."

And – as I walk quickly down the road with the photo clutched in my hand – I can still hear us laughing.

Finally, after examining eleven houses on Ivanhoe Street, I see it.

And I feel like I'd have recognised it as his immediately, even if I didn't have a picture held out in front of me.

It's two storeys, and small by Australian standards.

There's a pointed roof and a cute balcony with sun-faded towels hung over it; under which are sunloungers, a dining table and a hammock. The house is brown and slatted; the windows are large and open.

It sits in the middle of a lush green garden full of ferns and palm trees, surrounded by trees so thin and tall and stretched-out it looks like a giant has tried to pull them from their roots.

There are three beaten-up surfboards covered in old, scratched-up stickers that say PRAY FOR WAVES and *Good Vibes Only* and SHUT UP AND SURF leaning against a wall, and a blue barbecue pulled out next to them with a burnt sausage lying on the grill.

A brown dog sits on the lawn, panting.

Scattered at random – here and there, like confetti – are unmistakable hints of Nick.

In the piano I can see through the living-room window;

in the pile of laundry, just visible in the hallway; in the winding stairs to the porch that he sometimes used to jump down while we were on epic four-hour phone calls together.

To the left is the big, hollowed-out tree he fell from when he was eleven, breaking his arm and leaving behind two metal pins that always make the security gates at airports beep. To the right are the little holes he made in the wall to climb on to the roof.

Starting to flush, I hold the photo up and I can almost see him standing there again: squinting in the sun.

Because somewhere in that house right now is possibly...

I take my deepest breath.

You can do this, Harriet.

Bending down, I give the brown dog a quick pat. He must be a new addition to the family.

Then I touch my necklace again, approach the front door and ring the bell. It chimes around the house – bouncing off the walls – and through the mosquito net I can hear voices: yelling.

"Get that?"

"I'm busy!"

"*You* get it."

"Oh my God, am I the doorman or what?"

"*Fine.*"

I wait with my breath held as I listen to the sound of steps coming through from the back of the house, getting closer and closer.

Finally, the shadowy shape of a woman emerges.

Slight and small, with long, straight black hair tied in a ponytail that has a hint of grey at the temples. Her face is round and her eyes almond: her skin is very pale.

And I have to blink a few times: that's how familiar she is.

It's as if somebody has copied and pasted Yuka Ito into a different document and then edited her, like a human game of Spot the Difference. There are smile lines round her mouth and eyes where Yuka has none; and this face is warm and open, whereas Yuka's never is.

Plus this woman is wearing a long, loose pale blue dress with a denim pocket on the front, and I think Yuka Ito would scoop her own eyes out with spoons before she let that happen.

The brain of a spider is so large it actually spills out into its legs, and that's what mine suddenly feels like it's doing: emptying into my feet and toes and leaving my head completely.

Keep it together, Harriet.

And try not to breathe so hard: you look like you ran here.

Brow creasing, Nick's mum pulls open the screen door

238

and holds a hand up against the sunshine, exactly the way Nick does in the photograph I'm holding. There are infinite possible sentences in the English language: uncountable ways to make your thoughts known.

Suddenly I don't have any of them at my disposal.

"H-hello," I finally manage as she looks me up and down curiously. "I'm—"

"Harriet Manners," she finishes for me. "I know."

46

We're always only twenty-five per cent aware.

Even when we're wide awake we only know what a quarter of our bodily functions are doing. Our heartbeat, lungs, eyes, fingers, lips: they all keep going without our intervention.

But as Keiko Hidaka – Nick's mum and Yuka's little sister – stares at me quietly and patiently, I swear I can feel every tremor, every movement, every muscle in my being.

And it's taking every bit of focus I have to keep it all functioning as normal: otherwise it feels like it might just shut down.

She *knows* me? How does Nick's mum *know* me?

Also I have to say it: she doesn't *look* like the kind of mum who would yell at her son for not picking up socks. She doesn't look like the kind of mum who would yell about anything, actually.

But maybe not many mums do.

"Hello." Keiko smiles gently as I open and shut my mouth repeatedly. "What can I do for you, Harriet?"

Her English has a faint echo of the same delicate intonation and lilt that Rin's has: the carefulness of a second language.

"I..." I clear my throat.

You're here for Nick, Harriet. Focus on being here for Nick.

"I was just in the, uh, area." Awkwardly, I gesture around the porch, as if I've found myself at this precise spot by total accident and I'm as surprised by it as she is. "And I thought I would... see if Nick was... about."

About.

Like a seven-year-old with a bike, looking for a playmate. Not a sixteen-year-old ex-girlfriend from the other side of the world who had to take two aeroplanes and sleep on a bus overnight to get here.

"Ah," she says with a curt nod.

"Who is it?" a loud Australian voice yells from the back. "Jeez, Keiko, you're going to let all the flies—"

A tall, thin, tanned man with very curly, greying hair lopes towards the door and stops. He looks exactly like Nick will in thirty years, and my brain now feels like it's spilling out of my shoes on to the floor.

"Is that...?" Nick's dad says, squinting at me.

"Yes," Keiko agrees. "I believe it is."

"Is she...?"

"Yes."

"Do we..."

"I don't know just yet."

It would take thirty-eight minutes to fall through to the centre of the Earth and emerge on the other side, if it was physically possible without burning to ash within seconds of breaking through the Earth's mantle.

I'm so embarrassed I might just go ahead and give it a try anyway.

I'd be combusting but at least I'd be on my way home.

"Who is it?" another voice yells as my ears start to flame. "What is everyone— Wwwhooaa."

A small face has appeared from round the corner.

It has familiar dark skin and slanted eyes, but the hair is a buzz-cut, he's short and there's a speckling of acne on his cheeks.

"Is that who I think it is?" says Nick's little brother Josh.

"Umm," I say, shifting on to my other foot. They're all staring at me with round eyes as if I'm a woodlouse and I've just started juggling. Nick's not here, or they're not going to go and get him for me. Either way this is definitely the most awkward situation I've ever put myself in.

And – given how well you know me now – that's really saying something.

Be brave, Harriet.

"I was wondering if you could... perhaps... tell me where I might be able to find him? I'm only in town for the day and it would be really nice to... uh."

Make a declaration of support and kindness.

See his face again.

OK, where did *that* thought come from?

"Say hello," I finish weakly.

Nick's mum and dad glance at each other, then at the dog still sitting on the grass.

"Oh my God," his dad sighs. "When is that thing going to get off our lawn? Why won't it go home where it belongs?"

I flinch, trying not to read the obvious in that statement.

"I'm afraid we don't know where Nick is today," Keiko says, flashing her husband a stern stare that suddenly makes her look exactly like her sister. "But I'm sure he'll be sorry to have missed you."

There's something in her voice that suggests that might well not be true, and all at once it feels like I've been popped with a pin.

"Sure," I say as gamely as I can. "I'm sure I'll be in the... area again." You know: the next time I happen to pass through Eastern Australia on my travels to exactly nowhere. "It was... nice meeting you."

"It was lovely meeting you too, Harriet," Keiko smiles kindly. "Finally."

With a gentle yet firm hand, she closes the screen door.

But just as I'm walking away I hear Nick's dad whisper: "Do we tell him she came?"

"No," Keiko whispers back. "I don't think we should."

47

Right, that scene didn't go exactly as planned.

I mean, it went as it was *likely* to go – all things considered – but that's not the same thing, is it? On the upside, at least it gives me extra time to work on my opening speech.

Also, over 800,000 Britons are profoundly deaf.

If I try hard enough, I can probably completely block out what I just heard.

Pulling my shoulders up, I straighten my back and walk with feigned purpose down the driveway, trying not to notice the curtains twitching curiously behind me.

Then I re-evaluate my next step.

Reaching up, I fiddle anxiously with the chain of planets round my neck. About 264 BC in ancient Rome, gladiators known as *bestiarii* were made to fight bears, leopards, tigers, lions, bulls or any other predator that could give the audience the dramatic spectacle they were looking for.

The gladiator was usually ripped to shreds.

Breathing deeply, I get my map out and start walking towards the centre of Byron Bay. Because I know what's next on my Stalker List, and frankly I'd rather take on a hundred terrifying animals simultaneously.

Let's hope I get out of this particular arena alive.

Here are some things I would ideally like to never do:

1. Skydive
2. Bungee-jump
3. White-water-raft and/or rock climb
4. Go into a test or exam I'm not totally prepared for.

As I push through the door into the buzzy, packed, noisy *Oh-ganic Cafe*, I decide this is now at number five.

I've never seen anywhere so *cool*.

Literally everyone in here is tanned and beautiful. Everyone is nonchalant and relaxed and glowing with rude health; clad in bandana tops and leggings, board shorts and tees, crochet and tie-dye halternecks. They have dreadlocks with rainbow threads woven through them or tumbling glossy curls; piercings through eyebrows, tattoos of snakes and dragons; bodies conditioned by hours of complicated yoga moves and an outdoor lifestyle.

They're lounging on big cushions and bean bags strewn at random all over the cafe floor; leaning on low tables, chatting easily, eating bowlfuls of salads and cheesecakes that – according to the menu above the counter – have no cheese in them.

It's hip. Snazzy. Groovy. Nifty.

Happening and *now*.

And all the other words that Nat has told me never, ever to use in public again because they're just not cool. Ironically.

I've never felt more out of place in my life.

Although at least I'm not wearing a *pinstripe suit* this time, because I don't think they'd even let me through the door.

Clearing my throat, I straighten out my orange crossword T-shirt and look around the cafe more carefully. In the past, on the rare occasions Nick was in Australia, he'd ring me from this cafe and – over two or three phone calls – I met his best friends.

Jake: a blond, dreadlocked boy with a spike through his bottom lip and sleepy eyes. Tod: tall and black-skinned, with a quiet smile and a big afro of curls that "could beat Nick's any day, mate". Noah and Liam: identical twins who were surprisingly different-looking.

All of whom were lovely and welcoming whenever we spoke – even if they did mock Nick mercilessly for having a *posh English girlfriend* – but were also thoroughly intimidating in their collective confidence.

Even when Nick was there, gently guiding me through it.

Except this time… he's not going to be.

And I can tell within three and a half seconds of entering the room that he's not here, because whatever it is that sets off the Nick alarm in my head is totally silent.

Swallowing, I look around again.

Then I see them: sitting in the corner, laughing, drinking milkshakes, bent over Tod's mobile phone, looking at something super trendy and beyond my understanding.

"Hahahaha," Jake's snorting as I cautiously approach from behind him. "Look at that panda's face when the baby sneezes."

"Play it again," Noah chuckles. "Wait, put the sound up higher."

"It's up as high as it'll go. Hahahaha – there it goes again."

"Find that one with the foxes," Jake chips in. "It's *hilarious*."

"Wait, do foxes sneeze? Bro, that's ridiculous."

Surprised, I blink at the backs of their bent-over heads.

Are they seriously watching animal videos on YouTube?

Team JRNTH does that. Huh. Maybe Nick and his friends aren't *quite* as unlike us as I initially thought.

With a deep breath, I clear my throat.

"Foxes can sneeze," I say bravely. "Also, they're the only members of the dog family who retract their claws like cats."

Jake blinks and pauses the video.

Then slowly, one by one, they all turn round to face me.

There's a silence.

"Foxes also have whiskers on both their faces and legs to help them navigate," I add nervously after ten seconds or so.

Another silence.

"And a group of foxes is called a *skulk* or a *leash*," I blurt desperately.

"No way," Tod says finally, eyebrows lifting. "No *way*."

"*Way*," Liam grins. "*So* way."

I guess they recognise me too.

"Hi," I say, raising my hand as confidently as I possibly can. "I'm Harriet Manners."

48

There have been many awkward moments in my life.

The time my skirt fell down in the middle of my Year Three school dance recital and I stood there in my vest and knickers for thirty minutes, waving a wand: pretty humiliating.

When I leant against a grandfather clock in John Lewis and brought the entire set of them crashing down like dominos: that was kind of tense too.

Every netball match I've ever been a part of.

But all of them now pale into insignificance.

Because – standing in front of a group of boys, in a cafe on the other side of the world from home – I suddenly feel... *crazy.*

Demented. Insane. Mentally unsound.

Like the clichéd *bonkers ex-girlfriend*: the one every girl is warned to never, ever be, at any cost, ever.

And with a flash, I wonder if I should have listened to Nat: she *does* generally tend to have a firmer grasp on

social dynamics than I do. Because I might not *be* a stalker, but I certainly *look* very much like one at this moment.

"Hahahaha," Jake snorts, throwing back his head and laughing loudly. "What are you doing here, Harriet Manners? You're in *Australia*? Unreal."

My cheeks are getting redder and redder.

Until they've gone past red and started entering the puce and violet section of the colour spectrum.

"I was just… uh… passing," I start, then stop. That's not going to cut it this time – I don't think it did last time either. "I came here to see Nick," I admit. "I don't suppose you know where he is, do you?"

His friends all look at each other, and I can feel something unspoken passing between them.

"Nope," Noah says, more kindly than I was expecting. "'Fraid not. We haven't seen or heard from him since his last diving trip. Maybe he's at home?"

"I…" I swallow in humiliation. "I've already tried there."

There's another gale of good-natured laughter. "She's already been to his house," Tod chuckles. "Course she has."

"Oh, I'd *love* to have seen Keiko's face."

"And Ralph's. *A-mazing*."

Homo floresiensis, nicknamed the Hobbit, was a type

of early human, recently discovered to have once inhabited the Indonesian island of Flores. It stood at just over three feet tall and scientists believe it probably shrank over time to adapt to its environment.

Maybe I shouldn't stand here too long: I'm getting permanently tinier by the second.

"Have you come to win Nicholas back, crazy girl?" Jake grins. "Are you going to, like, go on one knee and propose?"

"Do we need to get our violins out?"

"I need a *hat*, man. British people wear *hats* at weddings, right?"

Seriously: just throw me to a panther now.

"I'm not trying to get him *back*," I explain, grateful I'm not in a long white dress for this particular exchange. "I'm just… trying to be a good friend, that's all."

They start laughing again.

And it's slowly starting to hit me how ridiculous I sound. *I'm trying to be a friend.*

When he's got four, literally sitting in front of me, and a whole family who clearly adore him at home.

When he already has a full life, without me in it.

Oh my God, what the *sugar cookies* have I been thinking?

"That's sweet of you," Tod says, standing up and stretching. "But I think he'll be OK."

"Yeah," Jake nods with his eyebrows raised. "We've got our boy's back."

"*Always*."

"We have *always* got Nick's back."

Then they look at me pointedly.

"Umm…" I say, taking a few jittery steps backwards. "That's great. So…"

One more try, Harriet.

"I don't suppose you have any ideas where he could have gone?"

"Nope," Liam says with a small, flat shrug. "None."

I take another step back, because he's clearly lying. "OK."

"Back to the diving, maybe?" Noah suggests, looking at me narrowly. "He's been *really* happy there."

"Yeah. *Happier* than he's been in *ages*."

"Back to being himself again. It's great to see."

The heat feels like it's slipping from my cheeks into my chest until there's a little roaring furnace in there. Because I know exactly what it is they're trying to tell me and I don't want to hear it.

Correction: I *cannot bear* to hear it.

"Cool," I whisper, taking another few desperate lunges backwards and scrabbling for the exit.

Go, Harriet. Go go go –

"Thanks."

Except it's a *push* door, not a *pull* door, and I'm tugging at an escape route that will never ever open.

Get out get out get out get out –

"To be honest, Harriet," Jake adds just as I launch myself desperately out into the street. "Even if we *did* know where Nick was, we definitely wouldn't tell *you*."

49

I manage to get out of sight before I start crying.

I stagger down the street at a run, turn the corner, turn another corner, find a random park and curl up under a tree microseconds before the tears come.

Which they do: in uncontrollable streams.

A few years ago a photographer called Rose-Lynn Fisher conducted an experiment called *The Topography of Tears.*

Each time, after crying for different reasons, she collected her tears, dried them on small glass slides and then photographed them under a microscope. She found that they all looked very different: that the chemicals and salt levels present in tears of joy, of anger, of heartbreak, of sadness, of shame, of frustration and happiness gave each tear a unique landscape.

Some looked shattered like broken glass.

Others were like snowflakes or plants; some were wiry and empty, others were wide and splodged like lakes.

But each of them was beautiful, each of them was hers, and each of them was totally unrepeatable.

Because if no two snowflakes are ever exactly the same, it stands to reason that no two tears ever really are either. They all come from different places: composed from different memories, different thoughts, different emotions.

They all make different shapes.

And they all have different parts of you inside them.

As I sit, sobbing quietly with my forehead on my knees until my legs are wet and shiny, I can't work out what these specific tears are made out of.

I just know they're hot, and they hurt, and they won't stop.

I'm suddenly certain that of all the things I should be doing and all the places in the world I should be right now, crying in a park outside my ex-boyfriend's childhood home is definitely not among them.

Yesterday, this plan made so much sense.

Yesterday, I was a hero, sweeping in to save the world.

I was a prince; a knight in shining armour.

Now I just feel like a delusional, emotional teenage girl – a crazy ex-girlfriend, verging on stalker – sobbing on the ground next to an empty crisp packet, a bottle of murky water and a steadily melting gummy sweet.

Nick's friends and family have made it very clear I'm not wanted.

He's *happier* now I'm not around.

And to make this ridiculous futile gesture, I fought with my best friend, dragged my ancient grandmother on a fourteen-hour bus ride and encouraged my friends to lie for me.

Because I'm not telling Jasper the truth, am I?

And somehow this whole mission doesn't feel brave or strong or smart: I don't *feel* like a hero or a polar bear.

I just feel... sad.

In every single possible definition of that word.

I cry until there's nothing left to cry with. That's the only good thing about sobbing intensely in a public place: there's only so much available liquid in the body, and once it's gone there's no other option.

Plus it's really hot, and I haven't had a drink for hours so I don't think my body has that much fluid to spare.

Sniffling, I wait a few extra minutes for the hiccups to go away.

Then I stand up and wipe my eyes.

I should go back to Sydney.

I should say sorry to Nat; apologise to Bunty for dragging her here; send Toby and Rin an expensively regretful text message. I should outline the situation to

257

my parents and somehow – *somehow* – try to tell Jasper what I've just done.

Basically, I should dust off my usual apologies and get ready to offer them all up on a big old silver platter.

As per freaking usual.

Except – as I pick the rubbish up and take it over to the bin before a gallah tries to eat it – a memory suddenly sweeps over me.

Of another time I cried on the ground of a foreign country.

And it's so strong, so intense, so *real*, it almost feels like I've been hit by a bike on a zebra crossing again. As if I'm curled up under my jumper in Shibuya.

Heartbroken and sobbing my heart out in Tokyo.

I don't know how long I cry for.

In fairness, people don't normally time themselves. All I know is that I cry long enough for my face to get all swollen and weird-shaped, and not quite long enough to forget what it is I'm crying about.

Not one person stops to ask if I'm OK. Not a single stranger asks if they can help. Not a human soul interrupts to offer poignant words of wisdom and kindness and—

"Are you OK?"

I sniffle and wipe my nose on my jumper. All right. Maybe I should have been a bit more patient before I attacked the entire human race. I nod.

"Are you sure?"

The voice is muffled and indistinct. "Yes. Thank you."

"Because," it continues, "for somebody who thinks they're OK, you spend a hell of a lot of time rolling around on pavements."

Slowly I remove the jumper and wipe my eyes.

"Hey," Lion Boy says with a small smile. "There's my girl."

And I know I'm not going home.

Because – as I post the bottle into the bin, rub my eyes with my wrist and straighten my shoulders – it suddenly hits me that maybe being the hero isn't always easy.

It's not always fun or cute or romantic.

Maybe saving someone doesn't always feel comfortable, or triumphant, or even very pretty. Maybe princes and knights get tired too, and feel embarrassed or humiliated. Maybe, sometimes, saving someone hurts and it's scary and risky and all you want to do is give up and go home.

Especially when everyone is telling you to do exactly that.

But Lion Boy has lifted me off the ground too many times for me to just leave him lying there. Somehow, I have to find the strength to lift him back.

And now I know where Nick has gone.

50

June, last year

"I don't really get sad," Nick said, staring at the ceiling. "I'm just one of those cool, aloof guys who stays chilled at all times. You know the type. We're everywhere in fiction."

We'd been dating for six months and were lying on my bed, talking, with the door open.

Or trying to, anyway.

Every three minutes my dad would poke his head through the door and ask if I had any laundry to do or whether I wanted a cup of tea, or tell us how the next-door neighbours were mowing their lawn *again*, and it was getting quite difficult to focus on our dialogue.

I'd never seen my father so keen to discuss housework repeatedly.

Smiling, I nestled into Nick's shoulder.

260

"Oh, right," I said with a wry grin. "You know, scientists have discovered that there are eight primary innate emotions that everyone experiences. Are there any others you're missing too?"

"At least six," Nick said thoughtfully, staring at the ceiling. "Maybe seven. But what are they again? Go ahead and remind me, Manners."

"Sadness," I repeated obediently, holding one finger up and then another. "Disgust."

"I really hate it when people pick their noses and then wipe them on public transport as if sitting on somebody else's bogey is some kind of travel bonus," Nick admitted.

"Tick," I smiled. "Fear?"

"Seagulls," he said immediately. "They're the bird versions of the head witch in *Witches*. Who I also am not a fan of." He laughed. "Please don't make me watch it again."

"That's two down. Surprise?"

"This girl crawled beneath a table I was under once, totally unexpectedly. That was rather discombobulating."

I laughed. "*Discombobulating?* Where did *that* word come from?"

"I might have stolen it from you."

"You can have it *on loan*."

"Thanks. I'll check it back in when I don't need it any more." Nick leant down and kissed my forehead. "What else? Maybe I'm more emotionally dynamic than I initially thought."

I held my fingers back up. "Anger."

"I generally only yell when I'm scared. Oh, and at my brother, Josh. He goes into my room while I'm away and *takes* things and *breaks* them and *puts them back* and when I ask him if he did it he says *no* and I want to physically *smash something*—"

Nick took a deep breath. "Yeah, OK. Anger. Tick. Next?"

"Anticipation?"

He rolled over so he wasn't looking at the ceiling any more and I could see all of his face. It was weird: the longer I knew Lion Boy, the less overtly *handsome* he seemed to me. The model-perfect cheekbones, the pretty ski-slope nose, the long eyelashes, the black, almond eyes: they were all there but I stopped really seeing them.

All I saw when I looked at Nick now was... *him*.

As if his face was made of glass and I could see straight through to the core of him.

"It's very confusing," he said, studying me back with the quirk of a smile. "When I'm about to see you, I get this... jumping. Here." He put my hand on his stomach and my hand suddenly didn't feel like a hand any more.

"As if there are lots of tiny insects inside there, but nice ones?"

262

"That's it. And I get a... tingle here."

Nick moved his hand to my shoulder, then along my arm, until he was holding my hand and his fingers were laced between mine tightly.

"As if you're full of fire?"

He leant back, closed his eyes and gave that abrupt laugh: the one that sounded like a shout. "That sounds really dangerous," he said. "Blimey, Harriet. Do we need to start carrying an extinguisher around for you?"

And I knew, with absolute certainty, that I loved him. For the first time, I just... *knew*.

"Shut up," I grinned, squeezing his fingers. "That means there's only two left. Are you ready?"

"Hit me with it, Harriet Manners."

"Joy."

There was a silence as Nick looked at my face. I could feel him taking it all in: every freckle, every crease, every pore. The grease on the end of my nose and the line between my eyebrows from too much frowning.

"Yes," he said finally. "Joy."

We each have one and a half gallons of blood in our bodies, but for that moment I swear mine became something else: something shiny and bright and golden.

As if I was full of light and heat instead.

Or – I'm just going to say it – fire.

"So the final one," I said when I could bring myself

to speak again. "Is acceptance. Taking somebody for all they are and all they want to be and everything they've ever been. The strong bits, the amazing bits, and the broken bits too."

Nick grinned and brought his face close to mine.

"Acceptance," he said quietly. "Tick."

And as he leant forward to kiss me – as I heard my father start vacuuming loudly in the hallway – I realised that I didn't just love Nick because he was beautiful. I didn't just love him because he was kind and calm, thoughtful and funny. I didn't even just love him because he made me so happy, wherever he was.

I loved all of this boy: the good bits and the bad.

And I knew that, when it came, I would love his sadness too.

51

Nick's sitting on his surfboard.

As I turn a corner and a breathtakingly beautiful beach stretches out in front of me – bright white sand, turquoise water, palm trees, exactly like a computer screensaver – I see him immediately.

His dark head is bent low, he's perched with his back to me on the end of a yellow board some distance away, and he's repeatedly jamming a piece of driftwood into the sand as if it's a sword and he's trying to fight four billion years of geological evolution singlehandedly.

Nick Hidaka is nearly eighteen years old. He's an ex-international supermodel, he's travelled the world: he's been to more parties, more fashion shows, more high-profile photo shoots, more countries, more airports, than anyone I've ever met.

But suddenly all I can see is a little kid.

An angry eight-year-old boy who's throwing rocks at other rocks, kicking trees, jumping on his tiny bicycle and yelling "I hate you" at seagulls before riding off precariously down the street.

I mean, isn't that what we all are deep down?

Although my inner eight-year-old never rode bikes: she was more into reading books, then accidentally spoiling the plot points for other people.

Quietly, I watch the rest of the scene buzz around him. The sunshine is at full pelt and the beach is packed: people are playing volleyball, laughing, swimming, shouting, running into the sea. But he seems oblivious to them all, seated on his plastic island with his big curls matted and sticking out.

It's just Nick, his surfboard and his stick.

And I'm certain I'm doing the right thing, because I've never seen anyone look sadder in my entire life.

Straightening my shoulders, I take my purple rubber flip-flops off. Carefully I hook them in one hand and start awkwardly shuffling across the soft, white sand.

I'm trying to work out exactly how to approach him without alerting him beforehand – maybe in short, jerky movements, like Victor trying to catch a sparrow – when the Brick starts ringing.

Quickly, I grab it before Nick looks up.

Although frankly this phone is so incredibly loud and analogue I'd be surprised if there were aliens in outer space who didn't react to its deafening *ring ring*.

"Hello?" I whisper, still looking at the back of Nick's head from some way off.

"It's me," Nat says briskly.

"Hello y—" I start, but she cuts me off.

"Just let me speak, Harriet. I may not agree with what you're doing but I should have got on that bus and come with you. I'm your best friend, I had one job and I didn't do it."

I blink in surprise. Unlike mine, Nat's apologies are few and far between. In fact, when we were younger I used to keep an Excel spreadsheet to prove how sparsely distributed they were.

She didn't like it very much so I stopped (and said sorry).

"Thank y—"

"I'm not finished," she continues. "You might be a puppy, Harriet, and you might keep running at that wall. But I shouldn't stand in the way, and I shouldn't get out of the way either. I should be your crash helmet. So when you do it, it doesn't hurt so much."

I turn round and laugh. "Nat, have you *ever* seen a puppy wearing a crash helmet?"

"Well... no. But I'm sure they *do* them. They do everything these days."

"Like a teensy pink one?"

"I'd quite like to be a blue helmet with stars on it,

267

please," Nat laughs. "And maybe with a little glow-in-the dark light on the back."

"Oh my God, a puppy would love that."

"It would be adorable," Nat declares. "We should set up a company called Puppy Protection Ltd."

"For All Your Wall-Hitting Needs."

We both start sniggering. Space never feels quite so big when there's somebody floating right next to you: even if she does spend a fair amount of her time shouting.

"So where are you?" Nat says when we've finally stopped giggling and making *woof* sounds. "Am I too late to help? Have you found him yet?"

I look over to where Nick is. He hasn't moved, although he appears to have found an even bigger piece of driftwood from somewhere.

At this rate, he's going to be back in England before I am.

"I'm looking at him right now," I admit. "I've just tracked him down."

"Did Toby guide you to your ex-boyfriend like some kind of nerdy Blue Fairy?"

"Yup."

"Thought so. That boy has crazy stalker skills. So what's the plan?"

"I'm going to talk to Nick," I say decisively. "I'm going

268

to tell him I'm sorry that Yuka is so sick. And then I'm going to come back to Sydney tonight."

"Wait," Nat says, breathing in sharply. "Yuka is... *what*?"

"She's really sick," I say quietly. "I heard Bunty talking about it to Annabel. I couldn't tell you yesterday because I didn't want them to know I'd... been eavesdropping. Again."

Hamlet's nosey father-in-law, Polonius, is clearly my kindred spirit.

With maybe a little bit of Ophelia thrown in for good measure.

"Oh my God," Nat exhales. "I'm so sorry, Harriet. Everything makes *so* much more sense now."

"Nick and Yuka might not seem it but they are really close," I explain, taking another step towards him, "and I just thought that maybe he needed someone to..." I blink. "Hang on, what do you mean *everything*?"

There's a pause.

"I didn't know whether to say anything," Nat says, "given how busy stalking you are and everything."

"I'm *not*—" Oh, I give up. "What's happened?"

"You know the dress Silva wanted? Turns out it's for a VIP fashion show she's attending. She's asked me to go with her as a plus one! Front freaking row, Harriet."

My entire face breaks into a huge grin: *Nat's Ultimate*

Fashion Target achieved. "Oh my *God*, Nat. *Front row?* That's ama—"

"Harriet, it's Yuka's show."

I blink. "Yuka is having a fashion show? In Sydney?"

"Yeah. It's called *The Show To End All Shows* and apparently it's some kind of enormous celebration to pay tribute to Yuka's designs from the last three decades. There was an article about it in the *Sydney Post* this morning."

And I can feel my stomach starting to hurt.

The Show To End All Shows.

Yuka's putting on one gigantic sartorial goodbye, and nobody in the fashion world has worked out why.

"*Sugar cookies,*" I whisper, looking back at Nick. "Nat, this is *awful.* Poor, poor Yuka. When is it happening? Where?"

"She must be really unwell, Harriet," Nat says gently. "Because it's just been moved forward five days."

And emotions are starting to hit me like a series of earthquakes: small at first, but getting bigger and bigger by the second.

I know I promised I'd never gatecrash anything again, but I might have to make an exception.

"It's soon, isn't it," I say numbly.

"Yes," Nat confirms. "It's tomorrow night."

52

There's no time to lose.

As I say goodbye to Nat, shove the Brick back into my satchel and start running haphazardly across the soft sand, I realise procrastinating is a luxury I no longer have.

Go go go, Harriet.

"Heeey!" somebody yells as I trip over their beach bag.

"Ugh," somebody else grunts as they get a mouthful of sand.

"Oooooy!" a small child shouts as I accidentally wipe out half their sandcastle.

"I'm sorry!" I call, turning and jogging backwards. "I'll come back and help you set it up ag—"

At which point I slam straight into a volleyball net.

Unfazed, I stand up and brush myself off.

Then I just keep running: over feet, round parasols and picnics, through groups of friends.

Until finally – huffing and puffing through my mouth like a dragon – I reach Nick. He's been watching me

271

approach, and I'd like to say that it's because he obviously has a Harriet radar built into his head like I do for him.

But I don't think he needs one.

I've seen videos of bulls on the loose in Spain creating less commotion.

"Nick," I pant, skidding to an abrupt halt. "I'm here."

There were so many more poignant ways to start this conversation, but I don't have time for any of them, or for embarrassment either.

Some things are more important.

"Hi," Nick says flatly. "That was quite an entrance, Manners. Even for you."

Something tells me he knew I was coming.

Probably thanks to one of the seven people I alerted by doorstepping them on the way here, like some kind of rampant telephone salesman.

"Nick," I say quickly, plopping myself down next to him. "I know I'm the last person you want to see. I know we broke up ages ago and this isn't my place any more. But I'm here, I understand, I can listen if you need me to and I want to say how sorry I am about everything."

Lion Boy looks at me carefully.

His expression is guarded and closed: I can't see past his beautiful features any more.

"OK," he says, nodding.

"I didn't... realise," I continue delicately, randomly

tapping a finger on his surfboard. "I didn't *know* about...
I didn't guess how much of an impact this would all have
on you."

Nick frowns. "I'm fine, Harriet. But thanks."

"So if you need anything..." I continue. "Or just want
to talk. Or maybe if you want to come with me to see
Yuka tomorrow..."

With a swift motion, Nick bounces up and shakes the
sand off his legs. "*Now* what are you talking about?"

I stare up at him from the ground.

He's much browner than I remember: the colour of a
roasted chestnut. He must have spent a lot of time on
beaches over the last six months, because there's a thin,
pale stripe just above his blue board shorts that I'm trying
really, really hard not to look at.

I'm also going to ignore his use of the word *now*.

"To see Yuka," I repeat in confusion. "She's in Sydney
and—"

"I haven't spoken to my aunt since last summer," Nick
interrupts shortly. "We fell out badly when I broke my
contract with her. None of my family has spoken to her
for nearly a year."

"But—" The pathologist who did Einstein's autopsy
stole his brain and kept it in a jar for twenty years. It
suddenly feels like somebody's just done the same to me.
"I thought that—"

273

Wait.

If Nick hasn't spoken to Yuka for a year, if he doesn't know what I'm talking about, if he doesn't understand why I'm here…

Does this mean he doesn't *know*?

As I stare at him in blank amazement it suddenly occurs to me that this is *exactly* the kind of news Yuka Ito would keep to herself.

"Look," Nick says, scratching his head and looking blankly past me at the sea. "Harriet, I appreciate you coming hundreds of kilometres to see me…"

"Seven hundred and seventy-seven," I say before I can stop myself, "point three."

There's a pause and I swear, for just a second, I see a tiny tug at the corner of his mouth.

"Yes," he says as it disappears again. "Point three. But you're right. We broke up and I've moved on. I think you need to now as well."

Stunned into silence, I stare as he picks up his long board.

"I'm going for a surf," Nick states, tucking it comfortably under his arm. "As planned. Then I'm going home."

He looks at me with an expression that I don't know how to read.

"Maybe, Harriet, you should too."

53

Now, I know quite a lot about surfing.

I know that Captain James Cook coined the term in 1778, and that it's one of the oldest sports on Earth: dating back to prehistoric stone carvings that are 5,000 years old.

I know that the "Father of Modern Surfing" was Duke Kahanamoku who started a surf club in Waikiki Beach, Hawaii, and that traditionally it was considered an elite and sacred activity.

I know that the first major surf competition took place in 1928 in Corona del Mar, California, and that studies have shown that sixty-six per cent of all surfers think about sharks while riding a wave.

I even know that it's a ten-billion-dollar global industry with more than twenty million participants worldwide.

All of which are facts I learnt while I was dating Nick.

But, suffice to say, *I don't know how to surf.*

Frankly, having researched it so diligently online I'm

pretty sure it requires muscles, strength and coordination that my body doesn't possess.

None of which is going to stop me now.

"Excuse me," I say quickly, jumping up as my ex-boyfriend literally runs away from me into the ocean. "Are you using that at this precise moment?"

About twenty metres away, a pretty blonde lady is sitting next to the blue surfboard I'm pointing at, eating a sandwich.

"Uh," she says in confusion. "Not right n—"

"Can I borrow it, please?" I say, bending down and velcroing the plastic rope round my ankle. "I'll bring it back really soon. There's just something I have to do."

She blinks at me, mouth still full.

And I can actually see the mental process swirling over her face: *If she was stealing my surfboard, would she ask first? Seems unlikely. Also it's very big and heavy: she won't get far.*

"Sure," she says, shrugging. "Knock yourself out. You're British, right?"

OK: do Brits have an international reputation for something I'm totally unaware of and yet am repeatedly representing perfectly?

Also, *knock yourself out* probably isn't the safest analogy for a water sport.

276

"Yes," I admit, struggling to pick up the long board that's surprisingly heavy and doesn't tuck comfortably anywhere on me. "I'll be back very shortly. Umm – which way round does it go?"

The lady blinks again. "You don't know which way round a surfboard goes?"

"Oh, I'm sure I'll figure it out," I say, starting to waddle with it held out in front of me like a penguin carrying an even bigger, flatter penguin. "I mean, there's only two options, right? Thanks again!"

The surfboard owner stares at me in disbelief.

Then – with a deep breath – I head towards a large body of water.

As if I've learnt nothing, ever, in my entire life.

54

There are many different types of waves.

Capillary waves, wind waves, seiche waves, seismic waves, breaking waves, inshore waves, kelvin waves, refracted waves. And that's not even including the type you get in A-level physics: transverse, longitudinal, P waves and S waves.

I have no idea which one I'm heading into now.

All I know is that they're bigger than they look from the beach and as I lurch awkwardly into the warm sea I'm not sure identifying them is really going to help very much.

So I'm just going to copy what everyone else is doing instead.

Glancing to the side, I wade confidently until I'm waist-deep in clear, turquoise water, throw the surfboard on to the surface and then try to lob myself staunchly on top of it.

It immediately rolls over and throws me into the ocean.

Then I try again except a little more carefully: shuffling on to the board on my belly, inch by inch, like a sporty and athletic sea snake.

Or – you know: that wretched alpaca Bunty told us about.

"Nick!" I call loudly, kicking furiously with my feet and using my arms like desperate oars on either side. "Wait!"

In the distance, I can see him gliding away.

Poised and graceful and strong: ducking his head and disappearing under a wave, then emerging smoothly again like an otter. I've never actually seen him in the ocean before, and I hadn't realised quite how *at home* he is: as if water is Nick's natural territory and land is something he tolerates in the gaps between.

A wave is coming for me, so I try to do the same.

Holding my breath, I grasp the front of the surfboard, press down and try to swim through the rising shelf of water.

It's nowhere near as easy as it looks.

"Nick!" I call again, spluttering as I burst out the other side with my hair plastered across my eyes and a streaming nose full of seawater. "Hang on a moment!"

He turns just in time to see another wave crest and smash me straight in the face. There's a short pause, then he rotates his board and starts paddling swiftly back towards me.

"Harriet?" he calls across the turquoise water. "What the *hell* are you doing this time?"

I mean, I'd have thought that was obvious: *stalking*, except now by water. Just like a polar bear.

Toby would be so proud.

"I'm *surfing*," I say as another huge wave comes and my board lifts up dramatically to a forty-five-degree angle, pivots for a brief moment and then plunges me seawards, face down. I come up, spluttering again. "Or... trying to."

This time it's unmistakable: I'm close enough to see his cheek twitch slightly. "Sure," he says, rapidly paddling closer. "My mistake. You're Kelly Slater."

"Winner of the Banzai Pipeline in 1992, 1994, 1995, 1996 and 1999," I tell him, rolling with the tide. "By 2011 he'd broken every pro-surfing record on the planet."

"Yeah, Slater's going to need to watch his back."

"You never know. I might have a hidden sporting talent nobody saw coming."

"Although you *can* ice-skate," he says, smiling a tiny bit.

"Exactly. It's basically the same recreational activity, except this water has melted."

Nick's board has reached mine now, and as they bump together for a second his hand accidentally touches mine and a bolt of electricity runs straight through it.

We both pull away at the same time.

"What's going on, Harriet?" he says more gently. "I thought I'd made how I'm feeling pretty clear."

We're somehow in a quieter spot: the waves are calmer, and with one smooth movement Nick sits up and swings his legs either side of his board.

With far less elegance, I scramble to sit on top of my board too.

And immediately roll over into the ocean again.

You know what? Maybe I'll just hang on to it with both arms and thank science and industry for warm water, air bubbles in plastic and proven displacement theory.

"You did make it clear," I admit, holding on as tightly as I can while trying to wipe away a dribble of snot without Nick noticing it. "But... there's something else I have to say."

"How unlike you," Nick sighs, rubbing water droplets off his face. "Also, do you have some kind of death wish, Manners? Because if so, there are easier ways to go than drowning."

"Ninety per cent of all drownings happen in fresh water," I say, ignoring the sarcasm. "It's more similar in chemical composition to blood, so it passes through the lungs into the veins by osmosis. That causes organ failure within two or three minutes."

I bob up and down silently for a few seconds.

"Ocean water has more salt," I continue, "which draws blood out of the bloodstream and into the lungs and takes longer. Between eight to ten minutes. That means there's more time to get saved."

And there it is again: the cheek twitch.

"As we both know," Nick says, lifting an eyebrow. "Given that I've already done that for you in the last few days. Are you out here so I can save you again?"

Even soaking wet, I feel myself flush hot. I am *not* looking to be saved. In fact, it's supposed to be the other way round.

And if something happens to Yuka before Nick makes up with her, I'm going to always feel like I could have done something to help.

However, this is *not* the kind of news you break to someone while bobbing around in the middle of the Pacific Ocean.

So I'm going to have to go Full Harriet *again*.

"Here's the thing," I say, taking Nat's advice and looking at him as steadfastly as possible. "I bumped into Yuka yesterday."

Nick blinks and shuffles on his board. "Yeah?"

"Mmm. She was..." *What would Yuka have been doing?* "Yelling at a model for eating a slice of her own birthday cake." *Good, Harriet. Believable*. "But she... mentioned you."

He frowns, studying my face. "Did she?"

"Yes. And Yuka's truly sorry, Nick. For the fight. She says she wants you to come to her fashion show in Sydney tomorrow. To make things up." *OK, this no longer sounds like Yuka at all.* "And also please can you make sure you don't wear those horrible blue socks because this is *fashion, Nicholas,* and they're an embarrassment."

That's better, Harriet. Much more realistic.

Nick throws back his head, and there it is: the laugh.

That loud, glorious shout I wasn't sure I was ever going to hear again.

"Those socks *are* an embarrassment," he agrees, visibly relaxing. "Although I'm pretty sure I left them at your house, so she doesn't need to worry."

I flush again. As you and I know, one of them is still in a box under my bed.

And I will die before I ever tell Nick that.

"So... will you?" I say tentatively. "Will you... come to Sydney and make things up with Yuka?"

There's a silence as we bob up and down together.

Every few seconds Nick's surfboard bangs into mine, and I feel a jolt of something.

For once, I'm not going to analyse what it is.

"Fine," he says, smiling broadly for the first time. "You know, Manners, this was an incredibly extreme way to pass on a message. You could have just rung. Or sent a postcard."

And I suddenly remember our race to the postbox last summer: happy and giggling and dizzy from the roundabout and the sunshine and the kissing.

"I could have," I smile back. "I guess this time I just wanted to get here first."

55

A British person makes an average of 396 friends in a lifetime.

So far I've made seven and lost three of them.

But as Nick grabs a bag from his house, says something I can't hear to his parents and starts walking with me down the road, I realise that I may have just gained another one.

Just like love, you don't always see friendship coming.

"And then I *fell* into the casting," I chuckle as we walk, eating mint ice creams we picked up on the way. "Straight on to the floor. I think I actually *said* 'oomph'."

"Ha!" Nick grins. "A bit like me on our first date, then."

I laugh, remembering him: sprawled on the floor of the ice rink outside the Natural History Museum, like the world's most ungainly starfish.

"I still can't believe you managed to answer Toby's quiz

questions accurately," I smile. "I've failed that about fourteen times now."

"Indiana Jones is a legend. Did you know that in *Raiders of the Lost Ark* the sound of the boulder chasing Indy was actually made by rolling a car down a gravel road? I was so disappointed I wasn't tested on that."

"At least Tobes didn't ask you how they achieve Wolverine's claw sound. He's added that on recently."

"They tore a turkey apart," Nick says promptly. "What a missed opportunity."

I laugh again: Jasper got that one wrong and was furious about it.

Jasper. I should really call him.

Swallowing, I take the Brick out of my satchel and press a few huge buttons, but the bizarrely long-lasting battery appears to have finally died.

I have to call him as *soon* as I get back to Sydney.

"And what was it like being a dive instructor?" I say, popping the Brick back in my satchel and trying to ignore an intense flicker of relief in my stomach. "How much of the ocean did you get to see?"

"Not all of it, sadly." Nick laughs and licks his ice cream. "There was a humpback whale and her baby and we could hear them singing to each other underwater. And there were quite a few dugongs, bustling around like the nannies of the sea world."

"Did you know that sailors thought they were mermaids? Apparently Christopher Columbus said they 'weren't quite as beautiful as they were said to be'?"

"What an idiot," Nick laughs. "I mean, if it's not bad enough that Columbus so-called 'discovered' countries that were inhabited already, he then goes around negging on sea cows?"

"Exactly! *Discovered.*" I point at a ginger cat, crossing the sunny street. "I discovered a cat! It's mine now."

"That house?" Nick points at a large one. "Discovered. *Mine.*"

"The sun? I've just come across it. Bagsy."

"Stars? All mine."

"Just wait a minute," I frown. "You can't have *all* the stars, Nick. That's just being greedy. Can I at least have the northern hemisphere?"

"OK," he agrees. "I suppose we can split the sky."

We both smile, and for a moment the three stars we decided to share when we were together – the three stars you can see from both the northern and southern hemispheres – hang silently and unseen in the air above us.

Then I look up the road.

Bunty is sitting outside the bus station: propped against a wall like a fluffy pink budgie, reading the *Daisy* book. Parts of her spangly outfit keep catching the sunlight and throwing rainbows on to surfaces around her.

She looks tired, and I feel a wave of guilt.

Should I ever decide to stalk somebody again, I'll do it on my own.

"Darlings!" she says, looking up with a sudden bright smile as we approach. "Harriet, sweetheart, you're dripping wet! Don't worry, I've got dry clothes in my bag." Then she beams at Nick. "Hello again."

"Hey, Bunty," he says, grinning warmly back. "How are you?"

"Full of camomile tea and oatcakes," she smiles, then turns to me. "Poppet, I've booked plane tickets back to Sydney for us in a few hours. Are you *terribly* disappointed that we're not going to hit the road again?"

The huge Greyhound bus is pulling in behind us.

Missing another cramped fourteen hours spent doing Sudoku puzzles and trying not to get static shocks from my fuzzy seat on the Australian highway? There may be eight primary emotions, but *disappointment* is not one of mine right now.

"I'll get over it eventually," I grin. "Thank you. Except…"

I look worriedly at Nick: I'd assumed we could just pick him up a bus ticket when he was here.

"It's cool," he says, shrugging and slinging his bag over his shoulder. "I'll just hop on the bus and see you at the show tomorrow. I've got friends I can stay with in Sydney."

"Nicholas," Bunty says warmly as a taxi pulls up next to us and the doors swing open. "I bought you a plane ticket too. Something told me we might need three."

Both Nick and I stare at my grandmother in amazement.

How?

How does she always know? Maybe whatever magical omniscience Annabel has is obviously passed on genetically from mother to daughter. It is *such* a shame I'm not related by blood to them.

Thanks very much, non-magic Dad.

"I booked it while you two were up the road chatting," she laughs, waving her smartphone. "Sadly my crystal ball is *far* too heavy to go in my overnight bag."

Oh. Right: that's probably how Annabel does it too.

Observation and the internet.

Nick and I climb into the back of the car, and I try not to notice that as he reaches over for his seat belt his hand briefly touches mine.

Or the spark that runs through my arm straight after.

"Darlings, did we get everything done?" Bunty says, stretching round to look at us carefully. "Is the universe aligned with everything in its rightful place?"

Nick glances to the side and smiles.

There's still a little distance but the plan is working and

I'm certain I've been the best friend I possibly can be.

Even if I had to break a billion rules of social etiquette to do it.

"Yes," I nod happily. "Everything's in the right place."

"Perfect," Bunty sighs, looking out of the taxi window with a tiny smile. "Then so are we."

56

As we know, I have many fact books.

And in one of them — intended by its publisher to be read on the toilet but actually propped on a Fact Shelf next to my bed — it says that human lungs are so elastic they are easier to blow up than a balloon.

Which is kind of funny.

Because as Bunty and I open the door to the Kookaburra Shanty, it appears that someone has done exactly that to Nat, and now she's being released slowly at the neck.

She's rocketing around the flat so fast she's practically making an *eeeeeeee* sound and smashing into walls.

"You're back early!" she cries, rushing over to the door. "How did it go?" She whizzes across to the coffee table that's piled a metre high with fabric. "Bunty, do we have any other scissors anywhere? These are blunt." She gets up again and runs to the cupboard. "Should I dismantle this dress, do you think? I can't find lace as pretty anywhere but it seems *such* a shame."

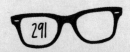

She starts breathlessly ripping up a pink gown, wavy hair in a chaotic, curly halo round her head.

Then she glances up. "Harriet, what *are* you wearing?"

Because Natalie Grey will never be too busy to not notice my outfit.

For the record, I'm wearing a knee-length patchwork dress with a flower belt and purple glitter smeared over my cheeks. I also have an amber dream-catcher necklace round my neck and seven bangles round my wrist.

"I went Full Bunty," I say with a little smile at my grandmother.

Then, putting my satchel on the floor, I glance guiltily at the phone charger in the corner of the room.

Maybe I'll just have a quick cup of tea first.

"Scissors," Bunty says efficiently, pulling a tiny pair out of her bag like Mary Poppins. How she got them past airport security will forever be a mystery. "Your wish is my command, darling."

"Ace, thanks!" Nat pauses in her enthusiastic ripping and glances behind us. "So where's You Know Who?"

As if Nick is Voldemort, or maybe Lord Sauron.

"He went straight to his friend's house," I say as Bunty wanders off to "source" Moonstone. "We'll see him at the show tomorrow."

Then my eyes flick towards the charger again.

"Cool," Nat nods, with slightly forced breeziness.

"There's so *much* to do, Harriet." She bossily pats the floor beside her. "Silva needs a dress and now *I* need a dress. *Front row*, Harriet. *Front freaking row.*"

I grin and perch next to the mountains of fabric.

Although, honestly, I'm not sure exactly what kind of service Nat thinks I can provide: during Year Seven textiles I managed to accidentally sew my trousers to Jessica's.

And we were actually both wearing them at the time.

"*Ooh*," Nat breathes, jumping up again and running to the sideboard. "I can't believe I didn't give this to you straight away. You've got a *very important* invitation, Harriet."

Then she runs back and hands a piece of card to me with an I've-Clearly-Already-Read-It wink.

It's small and cream.

Across the front, in formal gold script, it says *Harriet Manners* in writing so curly it's almost illegible.

And on the back it says:

To whom it may concern,

You will be taking part in my show.
  Arrive at Millers Point at 6:30pm ON THE DOT with a clean face, washed hair and nude underwear.
  As a previously employed model, you have already been compensated.

  Yuka Ito

I blink at it in surprise.

On the upside, at least now I won't have to gatecrash yet another fashion event I'm not actually invited to. Plus – after being blacklisted by every modelling agency in Sydney – I get to do what I actually came to Australia for in the first place.

But... this may be the last time I ever model for Yuka.

I'm suddenly filled with a wave of sadness.

And also gratitude: with this invitation, she's somehow managed to help me yet *again.*

"Soooo..." Nat grins cheekily as I read the card and try to work out whether *nude underwear* is an oxymoron. "Does this mean I *finally* get to see you on a catwalk for myself?"

I put it carefully in my pocket. "You could at least *try* to pretend you haven't been reading my mail before I have, Natalie."

"Sorry. Ahem. What's that fashion show invitation postcard from Yuka all about, Harriet? And does this mean I *finally* get to see you fall off a catwalk, sit down on one or crawl under it for myself?"

I stick my tongue out at her. "Haha."

"Oh," Nat adds as she sticks a bit of black thread through a needle and snaps it off with her teeth. "And Jasper's been texting me."

Apparently a heartbeat changes to mimic the tempo

of the music you're listening to, which is weird because mine has just sped up even though there's now total silence.

"Mmm?" I say, licking my lips and glancing at the phone charger again. "How... err... is he?"

Nat looks at me while I study a bit of lace so intently I've basically engraved delicate swirls and flowers on my brain.

"Harriet," she says finally. "I know you're confused, but you can't keep shutting Jasper out. He was your friend before he was anything else. Don't be such a ninny."

I open my mouth indignantly. "I'm *not* a..."

OK, the word *ninny* was first recorded in the 1590s and meant "fool"; possibly as a result of a mis-division of *an innocent* or from the Italian word *ninno*, which means "baby or child".

Yeah, Nat's got a valid point.

"Is he angry with me?" I say, picking at the lace nervously. "I *did* mean to call him, but the Brick ran out of battery and..."

Nat takes the lace off me. "I actually need that. Stop destroying it. Jasper's not angry, Harriet. But you need to talk to him."

"I will," I nod, stroking a red ribbon.

"Soon."

"I will." I wrap it carefully round my finger.

"Like, *now*."

I look up and Nat lowers her chin and stares at me from under her eyebrows, like our headmistress when I told her that I didn't think our GCSE syllabus was "expansive enough".

"OK, but first I just have to charge my—"

"*Now*," she says again, giving me her mobile phone.

Sighing, I take it and stand up.

She's right: I'm sixteen and a half years old, a legal adult in many countries (if not my own) and I don't have the excuse of being a child any more.

Fool, however, sounds pretty spot on.

"I'm not sure what to say to him," I admit quietly, twisting the red ribbon round my hand like an anxious cat's cradle. "I've never... been in this kind of situation before."

Honestly, I don't even know what situation it *is*: that's how completely inexperienced I am at anything even approaching a triangle.

I'm really much more of a straight lines girl.

"There's always the truth, Harriet," Nat says, glancing back at her fabric with a small smile. "Maybe you could start with that."

57

Here are some statistics about lying:

1. Ninety per cent of us have lied by the age of four.
2. Sixty per cent of people can't go ten minutes without stretching the truth.
3. Ten per cent of adults admit to lying "often".
4. Eighty per cent of women admit to telling "harmless half-truths sometimes".
5. One in every seven lies is discovered eventually.

That last one doesn't sound quite right to me.

Frankly, I'm not sure I've ever told a falsehood that hasn't been found out, so either that statistic is inaccurate or I'm a terrible liar.

What I *do* know, however, is that telling fibs is one of my least favourite things about myself.

In Greek tragedy, *hamartia* is the name for the fatal flaw in the hero or heroine that eventually leads to their

downfall. So in *Hamlet,* for instance, it's his indecisiveness; Victor in *Frankenstein* succumbs to his own pride; Romeo and Juliet both believe in love conquering all, including themselves.

And when it comes to lying, if I'm confronted, or pushed into a corner, or anxious, or want people to like me, or I don't want to let someone down, or I'm stressed or desperate or confused or need to get out of an awkward situation, I don't seem to be able to stop.

Especially when I don't want to hurt the person I'm lying to.

Or when that person is myself.

"Hi," I say as the phone finally connects.

I'm in my bedroom with the door locked, lying flat on my back on the bed: staring in vague surprise at a large cut-glass crystal strung from the ceiling directly above my head.

Where the sugar cookies did *that* come from?

"Hi," Jasper replies. "So I guess you're still alive, then. That's good to know."

I decided not to video-call so I can focus on the words I'm saying, rather than what I'm doing with my face while I say them. Nat assured me that Jasper wasn't angry, but he definitely *sounds* it.

And, honestly, I can't blame him.

It's now been six days since I spoke to him or texted him or acknowledged him in any way.

"I'm sorry I haven't been in touch," I say, closing my eyes tightly. *Just tell the truth, Harriet.* "This isn't an excuse, but my head's been... Who was that abstract artist you showed me at the Tate?"

"Picasso."

"No." Although actually he made quite a few pictures of women with two faces so that's a pretty accurate guess. "The one who laid canvases on the floor and then walked around, flinging paint at them randomly?"

"Jackson Pollock."

"Yes. That's what the inside of my head has looked like for the last week: like a big mass of messy swirling paint. Except it's not worth a hundred and forty million dollars."

"And nobody would want it on their wall."

"Exactly." I smile sadly. "I... didn't know how to hang my splodges on your wall, Jasper. So I disappeared on you. I'm so sorry."

There's a long silence: the kind of silence that feels like it stretches 21,300 miles all the way round to the other side of the world and back again.

"What happened?" Jasper says finally.

"I put my own life in danger," I say in a low voice, because it's starting to hit me that that's exactly what I did. "And someone I care about is very ill, and I..." I swallow. "I saw Nick."

The silence just keeps stretching: round and round, as if it's never going to end.

Keep going, Harriet. Say it all.

"And then I... lost control for a little while."

Because the truth is: I've spent my whole life arranging everything, managing everything, organising everything; keeping it all locked in boxes, in filing cabinets, in folders.

Putting everything in order, in lists, in bullet points, in charts.

And I think that for a few days, I couldn't keep it straight any more and everything fell apart.

"Did you kiss Nick?" Jasper says after a lengthy pause. "Is that what you're trying to tell me, Harriet?"

OK, I may not be a voice-reading expert but there's no doubt: Jasper is definitely *angry*.

"No," I say in surprise. "I wouldn't do that to you."

"Wouldn't you?" he snaps. "Because it sounds like that's what you're trying to tell me."

"That's *not* what I'm trying to tell you."

"Then..." Another pause. "I don't understand."

Frowning, I blink at the crystal hanging over my head.

When light hits sheer crystal, the rays pass straight through to the other side so it's transparent. But when light hits cut crystal, the rays refract from the cut edges and shatter into rainbows around the room. So, while it might *look* transparent, if you hold a cut crystal up to the light it's hard to see anything on the other side.

And I suddenly remember the day Jasper and I first met.

Me: trying so desperately to win that stupid toilet-roll competition after moving back from New York so that my brand-new sixth-form class might like me.

Him: thinking I was a conceited idiot.

How incapable he was of understanding what I was doing, or why, or how I felt, or who I was, or what I meant, even when I tried so hard to show him.

How difficult I have always found it to understand him too.

Because some people just can't see into you. Or you, them.

Even if there are beautiful colours and rainbows everywhere and you really, really want to.

Say it, Harriet.

"I want to go back to being friends," I say quietly. "I'm sorry, Jasper, but this isn't going to work. And if we try, we're going to lose our friendship too. I don't want that to happen."

And with a *whoosh* it suddenly feels like I've pulled out a splinter that's been worrying me since that first kiss outside the cafe: lodged in my finger but too tiny to even see without a magnifying glass.

Because I think I've known all along that if I felt the way I should about Jasper, I wouldn't need schedules and lists and itineraries to remind me of him.

He'd just be... *there*.

"Are you getting back together with Nick?" he asks after a beat. "Tell me the truth, Harriet."

I stare at the crystal for a few seconds.

"I don't think so," I say honestly. "I'm pretty sure that's over. But I just don't want this to get messy, Jasper. And I think it will."

There's another circular silence.

Then: "Yeah, you're right."

OK: *whoa*.

That's literally the first time Jasper has ever said that to me or – who are we kidding – possibly anyone. "I am?"

"I like you, Harriet. You're smart and funny and cute and a bit bonkers. But you're also *incredibly* hard work. Like, *seriously* high maintenance."

And a bubble of laughter abruptly pops out of my mouth.

I really am.

"What are you talking about?" I say as indignantly as possible, grinning at the ceiling. "Don't the girls you normally date give you timetables to romance them to?"

"There's generally a lack of schedules of any kind."

302

"Don't they merge your calendars the day after a first kiss so there's no availability misunderstandings?"

"Almost never."

"And they don't draft up a contract for you to sign in preparation for falling in love?"

"Absolutely not."

"I mean, what kind of crazy, laid-back, go-with-the-flow, organic, just-let-it-happen people *are* they?"

We're both laughing, and I can feel it: our friendship, slotting back into place like a jigsaw puzzle. As if it's a really important piece of a lovely picture that was never supposed to be pulled out of where it belonged in the first place.

"So I'll see you when I get back next week?" I say when we've both stopped chuckling. "In the cafe? Usual seat? Harrietuccinos all round?"

"They're actually called hot chocolates," Jasper says drily. "Weirdo."

"Grouch. Will you save me a burnt biscuit too?"

"Of course, although my parents are going to start working out why I burn them every time you're there." There's a tiny pause. "Harriet, Team JRNTH isn't the same without you."

"I know," I grin at the ceiling. "Because otherwise it's just Team JRNT and *nobody* would put that on a T-shirt."

Jasper laughs. "See you at home, freakoid."

And as I say goodbye, put the phone down and stare at the crystal hanging over my head – throwing reds and greens and blues and yellows around the room in bright rainbows – I realise with a flush of happiness that it's never too late to rectify the mistakes you might have made.

It's never too late to alter the direction of your own story.

After all, it starts with you.

58

The next twenty-four hours are chaos.

Which is ironic because the origin of that word is Latin, and meant *a gaping, wide, empty abyss* and only changed to *orderless confusion* in the 1600s.

We're definitely going with the latter version now.

Every spare moment and millimetre of floor space is filled with activity.

Whether it's sewing or cutting or ironing or trying to find skin-coloured underwear or washing my hair and face or just being bossed around furiously by my best friend because she's in hyper-perfection mode, we barely have time to sit down.

Although normally it's me doing the bossing so I'm giving Nat a free pass.

"Stick this to this," she says, handing me two bits of fabric and adhesive spray. "Hang that up in the bathroom to steam? Upload that photo. Wait, I'll dictate what I need you to say underneath."

All of which I do, gladly and without additional facts this time.

In 1896 there was a book called the *International Cloud Atlas* which defined the ninth cloud – the *cumulonimbus* – as rising to ten kilometres and therefore the highest a cloud could possibly be: hence the saying *On Cloud Nine*.

My best friend has somehow found a tenth cloud of happiness, and I will do whatever it takes to keep her on it. Even if it means abandoning my position as Social Media Chief Controller President™, because Nat appears to be significantly better at it than I was anyway.

While I was in Byron Bay, she took over all her accounts.

And within minutes, Nat had worked out what I failed to understand after hours of research and a full week of practice: that the random Hamster Wig company is actually Rin's *real* account, she's got 300k Japanese followers all thoroughly obsessed with her manga costumes and animals-in-cute-outfits photos and she's been happily sending them over to Nat from the start.

We now have 15,845 excited followers, all of whom think my best friend's designs are gorgeous, inspiring and visionary.

There's probably a lesson in that somewhere, but I'm not entirely sure what it is.

By five pm, I'm ticking things off today's list like nobody's business. I've studied Yuka's invitation carefully and am clean-faced (tick), hair-washed (tick), wearing denim culottes, my favourite diplodocus T-shirt and underwear that inexplicably makes it look like I'm wearing no underwear when I totally am (tick).

And Nat's in a red dress with what she calls a pink "Peter Pan" collar.

Even though I explained that Peter Pan mostly wore a green tunic made out of leaves so as a description that makes no sense whatsoever.

"Silva's here!" Nat whispers frantically as the doorbell pings. "Oh my God, what if she doesn't like her dress? What if she *hates* it? What if she throws it in my face and—"

"Nat," I say, grabbing her in a hug. "She's going to love it."

And I can feel all of the air whooshing out of Nat like a balloon again: except this time I'm holding her tightly in place.

"You're right," she laughs. "I'm a freaking *sartorial mastermind* and she is going to be *blown away*."

Doing a mini Excited Dance, we jump around the room quietly, bump hips then open the door.

"Hey, babes," Silva says coolly, walking in and looking round. "Nice pad. What's the skinny?"

I hold my hand out, even though her opening gambit seems a bit rude.

"My name's Harriet," I answer politely. "Although I'm actually a B cup now: they measured me recently at John Lewis."

Nat laughs. "She means *what's going on*, H."

"Oh," I flush. "Whoops."

Silva, in the meantime, has headed directly for the dress hanging on the wall. She obviously hasn't been fooled into thinking it's a piece of art, like I was in Paris.

"Oh, *yes*," she says, nodding. "This is *exactly* what I wanted, Natalie. You're so freaking talented, girl."

It's very pale pink with a square neckline.

From a distance the dress looks deceptively simple, but up close there's pale pink embroidery curving up the waist and down the back, and a long, dipped hem with a subtle flash of red in the lining that flickers when you walk.

And I've just realised – with yet another flush of pride – that Nat has coordinated their outfits for the front row. Proving, once again, that not every geek wears glasses, likes trigonometry and uses a calculator.

My best friend is the coolest geek on the entire planet.

Delighted, I wink at Nat and she winks back.

"You might want to put it on slowl—" she starts, but Silva's already in her bra and knickers.

"I need to get there asap," she says briskly, tugging on the dress and zipping it up. "There's a rumour going round that Yuka's retiring tonight, and if I break this news on my blog it could be *huge*."

Nat and I glance at each other.

We both know that Yuka's doing something that involves a *lot* less golf, coffee mornings and long Mediterranean cruises.

"Harriet's actually in the show," Nat says, loyally changing the subject. "She's one of Yuka's ex-models. In fact, she used to be her 'Face'."

Silva looks at me properly for the first time.

"Not Yuka's actual face," I clarify quickly. "She has her own. I just modelled for her brand."

"Yeah?" Silva frowns as Nat laughs again. "Do you know anything?"

I promised I would never lie ever again: but this is not my truth to tell.

So I shake my head.

"Either way it's going to be *mega*," Silva grins, picking up her bag. "Yuka Ito is a legend. She was the one who gave me my first-ever show invite when I had, like, six followers."

The more I hear about Yuka, the more I realise maybe she's not exactly the uncaring Ice Queen she paints herself to be.

"Puddings!" Bunty calls, swishing into the room in a floaty rainbow dress and a vivid blue wool poncho even though it's still twenty-five degrees outside. "I found the *prettiest* flowers in the garden. They're like happy tears on sticks. Look!"

She holds out tiny daisies.

"And it's a full moon, so I can *feel* magic in the air tonight," she beams, tucking one each into our hair. "There's so much we could practically *fly* there."

"We?" I stare at her in surprise. "Are you coming too?"

"Of course I am, darling," she winks. "As if I'd miss my granddaughter doing her swishy pouty thing. Plus there's an old friend I'd very much like to surprise tonight."

It looks like Bunty's not averse to gatecrashing fashion events she's not invited to either.

Maybe some traits aren't passed on genetically after all.

A ripple of excitement bursts through me, and I can see it reflected in the three glowing, expectant faces in front of me. Because if I know Yuka Ito, tonight is going to be something really special.

Magical. Dramatic. Extraordinary.

It's going to be an ending worth waiting for.

59

Sydney Observatory is on top of a hill.

It's an early nineteenth-century astronomical viewing point situated in the very middle of the city, converted into a working museum where visitors can see stars through both a modern forty-centimetre Schmidt–Cassegrain telescope and a historic twenty-nine-centimetre refractor telescope.

And – despite Yuka's attempt to shroud the location of her show in an air of mystery – I've done all my research already.

Just to minimise my chances of doing something wrong.

With increasing delight, I searched the address, pored over the website and memorised as much information as I could before we left.

But I couldn't have foreseen how beautiful it would be.

As we slowly climb the steep slope, all of Sydney unfolds around us like a giant street map: opening square by square.

The air is warm and soft; the light rosy.

Lit by fading sunlight, the harbour expands slowly: glistening and scattered with tiny, faintly beeping boats. The steel bridge looms, and across the water perch a mass of central skyscrapers sitting quietly on the edge of the river like gigantic herons.

The gold turret of Sydney Tower gleams and sparkles.

By the water roost small, quaint orange-and-cream Victorian buildings, and the hill is covered in trees, bright flowers that I still don't know the names of and winding pathways: framing the picture perfectly.

Behind it – like a painted backdrop – the sky is a vivid, forget-me-not blue, flecked with streaks of pale pink and orange.

And I try to breathe it all in happily.

Yuka couldn't have picked anywhere more beautiful or atmospheric in the whole of Sydney, and she *definitely* couldn't have picked anywhere more educational. In fact, if there's time maybe I can slip away and have a look at the—

No, Harriet.

I am here to *model*: *not* to have a look through the oldest functioning telescope in Australia, built in 1874. I'm also not here to enjoy the old time-ball tower, where the ball used to drop at one pm every day to signal to the harbour below.

Or the digital planetarium and 3D space theatre.

And I *definitely* didn't print out a museum map and stick it in my satchel, just in case.

Being professional is so hard, sometimes.

"We must be way too early," Nat frowns as we reach yet another barrier. "There's nobody else here but the bouncer."

She's right: the grounds are spookily empty.

We had to walk round a sign that said CLOSED FOR A PRIVATE EVENT at the bottom of the hill, and there are so many ropes wound round the gardens it looks like somebody's trying to herd humans like obedient sheep.

Which, I would imagine, is Yuka's exact plan.

"Names?" a toweringly tall man in a fluorescent yellow jacket says, standing halfway up the hill with a clipboard held like a bureaucratic Centurion's shield.

"Silva Collins," Silva says, thrusting her invitation at him. "Blogger. Natalie Grey is my guest."

"We're front row!" Nat adds in a burst of unrestrained excitement. "That's the best seats in the house, just in case you didn't already know."

The man looks at the paper, then nods.

"Harriet Manners," I say as stridently as I can, as if any doubt in my voice will render my invitation invalid. "I'm modelling tonight."

The security guard scans through a different page, then nods again.

Then we all turn to Bunty curiously.

"Jadis," she says smoothly, straightening her poncho. "Of Narnia, darling. I should be lurking at the bottom somewhere."

Nat and I burst out laughing, but the security guard obviously isn't a C. S. Lewis fan because he doesn't even blink. "Yep," he says, drawing a line on the page and unclicking the barrier. "In you go, then."

We stop and blink at my grandmother.

"Yuka always adds the White Witch on every event she does," she winks. "It's a little private joke and also means she can get last-minute emergency guests in with a code name."

Then she chuckles loudly. "She's going to be *furious* it's me. Although it *was* my idea in the first place."

Silva already has her mobile phone out. "We've got two hours before it starts. That should give me time to have a sneak around and see what I can find out. Nat, want to come?"

"Umm." Nat glances loyally at me. "I think maybe…"

"Go," I say, nudging her forward. "You won't be allowed backstage anyway. I'll see what I can find out too."

Which – frankly – will be *nothing that I don't know already.*

Because for the first time ever, apparently I know *exactly* what is happening before everyone else does.

I just wish I could enjoy this rare situation more.

"OK," Nat grins. "See you after the show?"

"Let's hunt down the vol-au-vents," Silva says, linking arms with her. "Yuka's catering is the best, although she never eats *any* of it."

"I freaking *love* vol-au-vents," Nat laughs. "Did you know it's actually French for *flight in the wind* because they're supposed to be tiny and light?"

"No way! That's *so* cute. How did you know that?!"

Nat winks at me over her shoulder and then they both wander off round the side of the hill.

I turn to Bunty. "Do you want to come with me?"

"Hmmm?" Bunty's rummaging through her fringed handbag. "Oh, that's OK, darling. I'm going to sit on this bench and watch the sun go down. We only get one sunset a day, after all."

For a second, I deliberate staying with her.

Then I glance at my watch and decide that ON THE DOT – in capitals – is probably not a euphemism for "watch the sunset with your grandma and then just rock up whenever you feel like it".

And it's 6:38, which means I'm eight minutes late already.

Plus it's quite a big hill and I'm not exactly renowned for my speedy hill-climbing prowess.

"I'll see you when the show's over, then?" The sky behind us is turning candy-floss pink and matches Bunty's hair perfectly. "Or will you be in the audience?"

"I'll be there, my sweet girl," Bunty says with a smile, sitting down on the bench and spreading her huge rainbow skirt out. "I promise. Even if you can't see me."

"Great," I say, although that's highly doubtful: there are infinite colours in the universe, and Bunty appears to be wearing all of them. "Although did you know that by the time you see the sun set, it'll actually have already gone?"

Bunty beams at me. "Is that true, darling?"

"Yes, because light takes so long to travel and Earth's atmosphere is so dense it bends the rays, which means by the time the sun hits the horizon we're seeing something that isn't there any more."

I glance at my watch again: 6:41.

Sugar cookies.

When I look up, Bunty is still smiling at me. "But that doesn't make it any less precious," she says softly.

"Actually," I say with another glance up the hill, "it makes it *more* so, because without the Earth's atmosphere the sky wouldn't change colour either."

"Wouldn't it?"

"Even if some of that is unfortunately a result of pollution."

Bunty laughs. "Well, indeed."

I turn to go, then hesitate, lean down and give my grandmother a quick kiss on the cheek. She's velvety and smells sweet: of something smoky, and herb-y.

"I'll see you soon," I say affectionately. "Enjoy."

"Oh, my darling," Bunty sighs, closing her eyes and turning her face towards the orange light. "I always, *always* do."

I look fondly at the glowing face of a grandmother I didn't know that well until a year ago, when she turned up unexpectedly on our doorstep and never really left.

And with a sudden pulse of love, I'm abruptly so glad she didn't.

Even if I wanted her to at the beginning.

None of my stories would have been the same without her.

Then I take a deep breath, pull my satchel on to both my shoulders and start walking to the top of the hill.

60

Obviously, I already know what the observatory looks like, thanks to last night's research.

This show is so important, I basically did everything I could to make sure there would be *no surprises.*

That I couldn't accidentally screw this up.

And – as I finally reach the top of the hill (sticky and sweating behind my knees) – I'm relieved to see it looks exactly as I expected.

It's a large, sandstone building in the Italianate style: pale, blotchy shades of grey, with visible bricks and curved, narrow windows. There's a taller, rectangular tower – four storeys high, with a little yellow pole on top – a few lower buildings and two octagonal domes with rounded, pale green roofs.

There's something kind of regal and austere and Brontë about it: it reminds me of Wuthering Heights or maybe the boarding school in *Jane Eyre.*

So far, so exactly as dictated on the internet.

With one – pretty major – exception.

Because in *none* of the photos I looked at were a huddle of very tall girls collected outside a locked front door, crammed closely together like skinny Emperor penguins. In *none* of my research were these thin, pretty girls grumbling loudly.

And at no point whatsoever did I expect to *already know three of them.*

"I mean," a furious British voice is sniping at full volume, "it *says* six-thirty on the invite. It's *six-fifty-five*. Are we expected to just stand here forever? Does Yuka think we've got nothing better to do?"

"*I'm* not going to just stand here," a brittle Russian accent chimes in angrily. "I'm worth twenty grand an hour. That's like nine hundred dollars a minute."

"It is," another Russian voice agrees. "That's *so* right."

"*And* I didn't even bring SPF," the first voice adds irritably. "The setting sun is damaging my delicate skin. I'm going to get *freckles.*"

"You could sue if that happens."

"I *might,* you know. My new beauty contract is due *any* day now and they'll take it away if I'm covered in ugly brown splodges."

Slowly, I approach the group.

I can't believe that I was so focused on ticking off

everything on the invite that I forgot to focus on what *else* was written on there.

As a previously employed model.

I should have realised that there would be people I already knew on this job. I'd just assumed I'd never see these particular three girls again in my life.

No, a better word is: *hoped.*

"Three hundred and thirty-three dollars and thirty-three cents," I say as I reach the back of the group. "Rounded down, obviously."

One by one, they turn to look at me.

More than a dozen pretty girls I've never seen before, and three I unfortunately have. One, tall and angular with a glossy black bob and big eyebrows; one, smaller and honey-coloured.

And a third: ridiculously beautiful, tall, curvy and blonde with long golden waves of hair, skin like peaches-and-cream and big blue eyes. Like a fairytale princess, except one that wise squirrels and bluebirds don't want to go anywhere near.

"That's how much you should make per minute," I clarify as Shola, Rose and Poppy stare at me blankly. "Although I think we're doing this event for free. It says so on the invite."

"Oh, for the *love* of..." Poppy sighs, looking me up and down with obvious disgust. "You? *Again?*"

I nod. "Me. Again."

"Look, it's the little boy from Moscow," Shola sneers, rolling her eyes. "Still trying to be a proper model. When she's not rolling about on the floor like a little piggy. Ahahaha."

"*Da, ona sovsem malaya dlya etoi raboty!*" Rose laughs in Russian.

"*Eshe i zhirnaya!*"

Calmly, I look at the triumvirate of beautiful girls.

One who befriended me in Tokyo, lied to me, sabotaged my modelling career repeatedly, tried to steal my boyfriend and then – just for kicks – intentionally got me fired. The other two who insulted me and then attempted to ruin my first-ever runway performance.

And finally I have the perfect words for this occasion.

I take a step forward with a bright smile.

"Hello, Poppy," I say, shaking her hand and then the others' in turn. "You're as beautiful and as eloquent as always. And hello, Shola and Rose. I can see you haven't changed in the slightest either."

Because I have, and when in doubt you can *always* avenge yourself with kindness, compassion and forgiveness.

And just a little bit of confidence.

"Did she touch me?" Shola says, staring in horror at her hand. "Like, actually just reach out and touch me?"

For a fraction of a second, I hear another voice in my head.

A familiar voice on a bus, a long time ago.

Ugh. Do you think I might have caught something? Noooooo! I've caught it! I'm... I'm... I'm a geeeeeeeeeeeeek!

And a bubble of laughter pops out of my mouth.

"Yup," I say happily. "I did touch you. You never know, maybe you can magically do maths accurately now too."

Shola blinks at me again. "Huh?"

"Oh, thank *God*," a fourth voice says from the back. "*Harriet*. I thought I was going to be stuck with these idiots for *hours*."

Blinking, I stare as a tall, curly-haired girl with light grey eyes pushes her way through the crowd.

At exactly the same moment, the locked door in front of us clicks open.

"Sorry for the delay," a lady in black says from the doorway, looking at our murmuring group. "We're running behind schedule. Please come in, we're ready for you."

Apparently, on average, humans spend one hour a month hugging.

And as I'm wrapped tightly in long, firm arms, it looks like I'm going to get my allocated ration in one go.

Because grabbing me in the biggest bear hug of my

life is the *other* model I assumed I'd never see again. The very girl I knocked on to the floor of the catwalk in Russia, seventeen months ago.

Fleur.

61

I'm going to correct my earlier statement.

The average British person makes 396 friends in a lifetime, and so far I have made seven and lost just *two* of them.

Because as Fleur and I walk into a large stone room filled with mirrors and lights and make-up and stylists, we can't stop talking.

About what's been happening in the eight months since we saw each other last; about the party in Gotham Hall in New York; about monkeys and snakes and swimming pools and rabbit heads and catacombs and elephants and festivals; about exotic places and people and adventures.

And Fleur has heaps to say. Because the thin, sad, quiet girl I left in America – the girl Kenderall so unkindly called *Blurgh* – has disappeared.

In her place is somebody happy.

Somebody sparky and glowing and healthy; somebody

quite possibly capable of out-talking me completely.

According to statistics, girls use an average of 20,000 words a day, and Fleur's about to hit her limit before we've even sat down at the make-up tables.

"I wanted to get hold of you," she continues as we're plonked in front of bright lights and mirrors, "after the party in New York. But you ran off so abruptly and I couldn't find you on any social media, so it was kind of impossible."

I've now just realised what the *other* purpose of social media is.

"Are you still living in America?" I ask as a make-up artist holds a bottle of pale foundation up to my cheek and then tries with an obvious air of exasperation to find an even lighter one.

"I'm back in London," Fleur enthuses as the face-painting begins. "I managed to get a place through clearing at UCL and I'm studying Architecture. It's the best decision I've ever made."

"Better than dumping Caleb?" I grin.

"Even better than that," Fleur laughs. "Although getting my heart broken by a model-chaser was an all-round low point for me."

"At least we got to hang out together at the bottom."

We both laugh and high-five knowingly.

"Girls," one of our make-up artists sighs. "As touching

as it is that you've found each other after all this time and so on, can you please stop talking so we don't get eyeshadow on your chins?"

Oops.

Yet again, I've momentarily forgotten why we're here.

"*Focus,* Harriet," Fleur whispers. "We're *models,* remember?"

"From the 1600s French word *mode,*" I whisper back. "Which means *fashion or style.*"

"Actually, it's from the Latin *modus,* which means *manners.*"

I blink at Fleur in amazement.

Wait: did she just ace-card my etymological knowledge?

Even more unbelievably, have I just spent the last year and a half of my life ironically living up to my name?

How did I not realise this before now?

"Do you want me to go and get Yuka?" the make-up artist snaps as we both start giggling again. "Because I will."

We both stop laughing, suitably cowed.

But as our faces are slowly made unrecognisable with primer, heavy foundation, powder, blusher, contour, highlighter, sparkling eyeshadows, eyeliner, eyebrow pencil, lip-pencil and lipstick, I find myself glancing to the side.

It's surreal how different Fleur looks.

Her cheeks have filled out, tiny dimples have appeared and her eyes are shiny and clear. The cheeky girl who winked at me behind the stage at the Baylee show in Russia is very much back.

And I can already feel myself trying to work out where an F will go in JRNTH. I could squeeze it on at the end perhaps – JRNTHF – or I could rearrange it all into FRNTHJ and get new hats and badges made: it would be worth the investment.

Oooh – maybe she'll be the perfect girl for Jasp—

No, Harriet.

We learnt our lesson last time, remember? No more *Emma*-ing on your friends.

I'll just invite Fleur to the cafe and see what happens.

Although a *few* bullet points and charts and maybe a scripted introduction wouldn't go amiss. Just, you know, for luck.

"OK," one make-up artist says finally when we're both transformed and our hair has been tied into tight little ballerina-knots. "If you go through to the door on the left, you'll find your outfits. Nametags should be attached. *Next?*"

Two beautiful girls take our places in the chairs.

And together Fleur and I make our way towards a big wooden door at the side of the room: looking pretty ridiculous in full glitter stage make-up, jeans and T-shirts.

Although Fleur's tee is just a plain white V neck and doesn't have a diplodocus on it or anything.

Ooh: maybe I can get her a new one.

"I was thinking," I start as I push the heavy door with both hands. "Art and architecture are quite similar, aren't they? I mean they both start with an A." I push a bit harder. "They both involve pencils." A bit harder. "They both, umm... have lines and... erasers... and..."

The door finally swings open with a squeak.

And my not-very-subtle attempts to force both the door and Jasper and Fleur together disappear with a *pop*.

It feels like my prefrontal cortex has just opened like a trapdoor: as if my temporal lobe has been prodded with an enormous stick.

As if the key to where I keep all my mental souvenirs has just slotted in with a loud click.

Memories are tumbling everywhere.

62

In front of us is a small, round stone room.

And – hanging, perfectly spaced round it – are dresses: shimmering and glistening like large, very organised butterflies.

Blinking, I walk into the middle of the room.

To my left is a fragile, glittering gold column dress with thin straps, covered in tiny fish-type scales and ending in a flurry of gold feathers. *That's my girl,* my dad shouts as I sit down in a velvet-lined theatre in Russia.

Next to it is a resplendent ballet tutu.

And, with a jolt, I'm suddenly covered in handwritten homework stickers: anxiously contorting myself into crazy shapes on the floor.

Swallowing, I keep turning in a circle.

There's a candy-pink, heavily laced and ruffled beaded dress, and it suddenly feels like I'm crouched in a glass box, surrounded by tiny creepy dolls that look exactly like me.

As if a huge cockroach is climbing slowly up my leg.

Getitoffmegetitoffmegetitoffme –

Turning again, I scan past a pretty yellow dress and a short, red glittery one until I reach a long, silky dark blue gown with holes cut into the bottom shaped like stars.

And it abruptly feels as if I'm standing in the centre of a sumo stage in Tokyo: blinking at a crowd of thousands.

Just copy me.

With a lump in my throat, I turn once more.

There's a leopard-skin fake fur coat hanging over a black mini dress with vertiginous red heels dangling from a string, and I'm suddenly entering snowy Red Square: tackling my first-ever fashion shoot.

Blow a raspberry. That's not even a strawberry.

I keep turning.

Next to it is a bright orange, short puffed dress with delicate embroidered tentacles threaded all over it, and I'm covered in blue octopus ink and embarrassment again.

Guess they managed to dry-clean that one after all.

With a small smile, I keep spinning.

Past delicate, incredible dresses I don't recognise: black and lilac and turquoise and ivory; lace and sequinned and feathered and embroidered; starched and floaty, delicate and structured.

Until, finally, at the end of the circumference, my eyes land on a long, white, delicate floor-length dress.

And – just like that – I'm floating in a moonlit lake.

Covered in light and stars.

"*Yesss*," Fleur says happily, running towards the exquisite green dress she wore in Moscow. "Thanks, Yuka! Score!"

Nat says that fashion is history: that clothes aren't just materials we wear, but they become a part of who we are, who we have been and who we will be.

Which always seemed like an exaggeration to me.

I mean, *history* is knowing that 750,000 people died in the American Civil War, the Cuban Missile Crisis happened in 1962 and Joseph Stalin was the dictator of Russia between the years of 1929 and 1953. Then getting an A grade for drawing a coherent timeline.

But as I walk slowly towards my Lake Dress, I think maybe I'm starting to understand what my best friend meant after all.

Because these aren't just *dresses*.

They're *portals*: ways of time-travelling without moving. A little bit of me went into each of them, and it's as if I can see myself in each of them, standing there like a ghost. As if every emotion, every thought, every hope, every memory I had is still drifting visibly through them like smoke.

These are all part of who I am and who I was, and they're also part of who I will be.

My very own historical timeline.

Swallowing, I reach the white dress, hold my breath and close my eyes: *please please please please*. Then I open them and flick the little paper tag over.

Harriet Manners

I don't know how Yuka knew that this was the piece of me I loved the most, but somehow she did. (Or maybe it's the only Horcrux I haven't successfully destroyed yet, like a fashion-world Harry Potter.)

"OK, girls," a lady says, entering the room with three models close behind her. "Get into your dresses *carefully*. This isn't the changing room at Topshop."

Slightly possessively, I watch as a beautiful girl with dark skin and huge eyes takes the Octopus Dress off the wall and holds it against herself and as a girl with pretty blue hair grabs the Sumo Dress with a happy squeak.

Then Poppy unhooks the pink Manga Girl dress and gives me a sharp look of triumph, and I try not to smirk.

It's the least comfortable one of the lot.

Karma clearly works in strange and sometimes very itchy and rash-giving ways.

Carefully, we climb into our outfits.

Then focused, stern stylists wander round us: adjusting, re-pinning and sewing.

"Whoops," Fleur laughs as the stylist starts tugging her crossly into the now slightly-too-small green dress like the corset scene in *Gone With The Wind*. "I'm not modelling any more so I *may* have forgotten to update my measurements."

"Mmmm," the stylist grunts. "I can see that."

"I've been eating a *lot* of Jaffa Cakes," Fleur says proudly. "Like, a *lot*. Boxes and boxes."

"Yes," the stylist snaps, pulling a third time. "I can see that too."

Fleur winks at me conspiratorially and I grin back.

New Best Friend number five: *tick*.

"You've got twenty minutes left, girls!" a woman shouts through the door. "Everybody needs to be ready, perfect and in the main room at eight on the dot! ON. THE. DOT."

Quickly, I look at my watch.

I'm the only model who's now totally ready: the other girls are still being amended, stitched or made-up in the main room.

Which means I've got twenty minutes to spare.

And if my mental map of the entire internal layout of the Sydney Observatory is accurate – which it absolutely is – that should be *plenty* of time.

If not, there's always the printout in my satchel too.

"Soooo…" I say, taking an awkward side step. "Did you know that by the time we reach seventeen years old, most British children will have been driven 80,000 miles by their parents?"

I look round: everyone's chatting, stitching and practising poses without a glance in my direction.

So I take another cautious step.

"And that it would take a garden snail three years and two months to make its way from Land's End to John O'Groats?"

They're all focused intently on the job at hand.

I take one more tiny step. "Or that a raw carrot is still alive when you eat it? Can you believe that?"

Not a single glance in my direction.

And they're three pretty amazing facts: if anyone was listening, they would *definitely* have responded.

My parents certainly did when I told them the first one.

With a surge of excitement, I carefully tuck the daisy Bunty gave me into the back of my bun.

Then I take my final step towards a tiny side door with a piece of paper that says:

TELESCOPE TO THE STARS –
DO NOT ENTER.

Smiling, I hold the skirts of my gown up like Belle in *Beauty and the Beast*.

And then I push it open and flit straight through.

63

I know, I know: I can almost *hear* you judging me.

Because let's be honest, of all the professional things a model should probably do before a big fashion show:

a) *running away in your priceless outfit*
b) *scooting through a forbidden door and*
c) *shuffling down tiny corridors towards a world-famous telescope*

… are not three of them.

I mean, what's wrong with me? Why am I always *asking* for trouble? Haven't I made very similar mistakes before?

Have I actually learnt *nothing*?

Well, I have.

What I've learnt is that you can't just crouch under a table, waiting for life to come and find you.

You have to grab it for yourself.

336

There are eighty-eight official constellations of stars, and each of them has its own story:

- *Cassiopeia: the Greek Goddess placed upside down by Poseidon to punish her for being arrogant.*
- *Ursa Major: a young girl who changed into a bear and killed her seven brothers, who flew into the sky and became the seven stars of The Bear.*
- *Corona Borealis is the crown of Ariadne, who saved Theseus from the Minotaur.*
- *Cygnus turned himself into a swan to save his drowning friend and was rewarded by Zeus with his own constellation.*
- *Delphinus celebrates the dolphins who rescued the poet Arion.*
- *Draco was placed in the northern sky as a dragon to protect Zeus and his treasures.*
- *Leo is a lion defeated by Hercules.*

The whole night sky is a narrative, written by us.

So if our stories are driven by who we *are* and what we *do* – not by the events that happen *to* us – then it also means we get to choose our own adventures.

We decide our own fates.

And we make our *own* luck.

* * *

Quietly, I tiptoe through the corridors with my white dress carefully held off the floor so it doesn't get dusty.

Everything's dark but I don't want to draw attention to myself by switching all the lights of a closed observatory on. So, with a bolt of sudden inspiration, I put my hand to my back.

Smiling, I press a button.

And with a *pop* my entire dress lights up like a candle, just as it did in the lake: brightly enough for me to see a few metres ahead.

Glittering, I reach the bottom of some winding stairs.

Quickly, I check the time: I've got seventeen minutes left to examine the southern hemisphere in detail and be back before anyone notices I'm missing.

Gathering my skirts, I run up the stairs.

Breathing hard, I burst through the door into a small, domed room.

Scientists recently discovered that the flame of a candle creates 1.5 million diamond nanoparticles for every second it burns. But as I stand – glowing – in the doorway I'm forced to wonder if I'm on fire too.

It's pitch-black but I can just see the shadowy outline of a boy, already looking through the telescope.

And I'm suddenly not sure where the tiny diamonds are coming from any more.

My dress, or me.

64

Remember what I told you about ghost words?

Words that officially exist in the English language but don't actually carry any kind of meaning in them?

Well, there's the exact opposite too.

There are approximately 6,500 different languages in the world, and most of them have ways of expressing sensations, experiences, objects and feelings that we forgot to name in English.

In Hawaiian there's *akihi*: the process of listening to directions, walking off and then forgetting them.

In Japanese there's *tsundoku* – the act of buying books and then not reading them – and in German there's *Kabelsalat*: a mess of tangled-up cables, or a "cable salad". *Pisan zapra* in Malay is the time it takes to eat one banana, and *struisvogelpolitiek* in Dutch is the art of sticking your head in the sand (literally, the "politics of the ostrich").

There's also *pochemuchka*: a personal favourite of mine, and Russian for "a person who asks too many questions".

That's how I know these words in the first place.

But as I stare at the boy in front of me – as I glitter all over like the night sky – I realise that there are some experiences that can't be expressed perfectly in any language.

And that this is one of them.

"Nick?" I say, taking a step forward.

I'm the sole source of light in the room: filling it with the bright, eerie glow of an enormous bioluminescent insect, wearing yet *another* white dress.

Honestly, I'm starting to feel like a teenage Miss Havisham.

"Harriet?" Nick says, turning round.

Even in the dark, I can vaguely see the almond outline of his eyes; the halo of his black curls, the curve in the corner of his wide lips. I can see the tiny mole on his left cheek and the slight glimmer of his pointed canine teeth; the slope of his shoulders and the—

Oh, God.

Kilig is a Tagalog word for "butterflies in the stomach".

But mine must have somehow escaped, because they're suddenly everywhere: beating their wings through my whole body. In my chest, in my throat, in my shoulders, in my arms and my legs, through to my fingertips and into my toes.

And I don't know the right word for that.

Honestly, I thought they'd all fallen asleep a long time ago, or at the very least gone on an extended holiday.

You're friends you're friends you're –

"I came to see the catadioptric telescope," I blurt nervously. "It combines a Cassegrain reflector's optical path with a Schmidt corrector plate to make a compact astronomical instrument that uses simple spherical surfaces."

Which is literally, word-for-word, what is written on Wikipedia.

"I know," Nick says with a smile. "It's written on the little sign over there."

Bat poop.

"Does it say that the first-ever large telescope to use that design was the James Gregory Telescope of 1962 at the University of St Andrews?"

Nick's nose twitches. "Nope."

"Oh good. Because I'm all out of facts about this particular telescope now so that would be awkward."

Nick laughs loudly and for just a second the light in the room gets very slightly brighter.

"Do you want to look?" Nick says, taking a step back. "I already know the southern hemisphere pretty well, so…"

Cautiously, I take a few steps forward.

Humans are able to detect one trillion different scents,

but as I put my eye against the viewfinder all I can smell is greenness: limes and wet grass and chewy sweets.

And with a *whoosh* I'm suddenly back under a table again.

"So..." I say, trying to subtly breathe through my mouth. "What exactly am I looking at?"

"You tell me," Nick says with a grin, pressing a button and putting a hand briefly on my shoulder. "You're usually the resident star expert."

With a whirring sound, the roof starts to spin slowly and the night spins with it: a dizzying mass of twinkling lights.

I'm now glowing so hard and my head's spinning so fast it's a wonder I don't just shoot into the sky like a meteor.

Focus, Harriet. You're friends you're friends you're—

Frowning, I peer into the telescope.

"That's Mars," I say, clearing my throat as the telescope focuses. "And right next to it is Saturn."

"No offence, Manners, but for a star expert you aren't pointing out many stars."

I laugh. "I think that's Gemini," I continue, awkwardly pointing. "See? The two brightest stars are Castor and Pollux, and if you trace them down you can see the outline of twins. Which means next to it must be—"

I abruptly stop talking.

Mamihlapinatapai is a Yaghan word that means silent understanding between two people thinking the same thing at the same time, and this is probably the first time I've ever experienced it.

As is well documented, I never normally know what anyone else is thinking at all.

Except right now I do.

Because the telescope is pointing directly at Orion's Belt: Alnitak, Alnilam and Mintaka. The three stars you can see from both the southern and the northern hemisphere: the three stars that held Nick and I together when we were apart.

"A-and th-that's the moon," I stammer quickly, spinning the telescope away. "Not a planet *or* a star, but a satellite. Did you know that you would need 398,110 moons in the sky to equal the luminosity of the sun?"

Nick doesn't say anything.

"Or that a ninety-five per cent illuminated moon is only half as bright as a full moon because of the shadows caused by the craters?"

Still silence.

"Which are… umm… all named after scholars, artists, scientists and explorers?" I swallow, hard. "For instance there's the Copernicus Crater, the Aristotle Crater, the Archimedes Crater, the Calippus Crater, the Descartes Crater…"

"Harriet," Nick says finally.

"The Edison Crater, the Earhart Crater, the Michael Jackson crater..."

"Harriet."

"The Newton Crater, the Marco Polo—"

"Harriet, I need to say something."

Flushing, I slowly lift my head and turn to face him in the dark. There are 300,000 moon craters and frankly I'm so nervous right now there's a good chance I was just going to keep naming them for the rest of the night.

No, Harriet. No no no no no no no –

Because *forelsket* is the Norwegian word for the euphoria you feel when you start falling in love. And I can suddenly feel the beginning of it: tumbling and plummeting and cascading inside me.

Except it's not really the beginning, is it?

All we did was hit *pause*.

"Harriet," Nick says again slowly, and...

I'm watching him sleep under a table;
I'm sitting on the pavement;
   we're running through the snow,
       walking through Manhattan,
          spinning in a circle on a roundabout;
      he's flicking mints at my window;
    we're laughing in my bedroom,
  my sock is wet;
we're standing on a bridge;
   kissing
     kissing
       kissing...
There's a loud *bang*.
And suddenly the room is full of light.

65

We both freeze.

For just a second the light is so blinding, so disorientating, I'm convinced it's coming from me.

I may have a habit of massively overestimating my electric capabilities.

"Harriet," a sharp voice says as Nick and I automatically spin towards the source of light. "When are you going to *do as you are told*."

It's a question but it definitely doesn't have a question mark.

And there – a dark silhouette in the doorway – is the reason we are both here in the first place.

Yuka.

66

Shlimazel.

It's a Yiddish word for somebody who has a lot of bad luck, except – as previously discussed – I almost always bring mine on myself.

We've got an English word for my personalised version.

It's *idiot*.

With a tiny movement, Yuka Ito touches the wall and a neon light flickers on overhead. She looks exactly the same as she did last year: white marble face, long black lace dress, straight black hair, tiny pillbox hat with a net over one eye.

Like an incredibly fashionable, terrifying spider.

Yet again, I get the feeling I'm the fly.

"Nicholas," she says, turning towards him coldly. "I was unaware that you were at this event. I'd ask how you got in, but I suspect it was through a window."

A pulse of fear rockets through me – the truth is all

going to come out now, at the worst possible moment – but Nick just grins.

"Doors are massively overrated," he shrugs.

"Apparently," Yuka says in a clipped voice. "I may have to invest in better security."

Then – as if she's on a pivot – she turns slowly towards me.

Apparently African heart-nosed bats can hear the footsteps of a beetle on sand from two metres away and I *really* wish I had similar audio skills.

At least a *bit* of warning would have been handy.

"And I don't remember my instructions being for every model to congregate at eight pm, apart from Harriet Manners," she adds flatly. "Perhaps you heard them wrong."

I shake my head, even though I've just surreptitiously glanced at my watch and it's nine minutes to eight so I'm not actually late yet.

I'm not going to make that particular observation out loud.

"No," I admit in a tiny voice. "I didn't."

"Then presumably you can explain why you're up here, running down the battery in my dress."

Oops. Quickly, I slip my hand to my back and press the button that turns my lights off. "I…"

"It's my fault," Nick says as I stop glittering in every

sense possible. "I made Harriet meet me up here. There were some stars I wanted to show her."

Blinking, I stare at him. "That's not what—"

"You must be mistaking me for someone who cares," Yuka interrupts. "All I know is that there are five hundred people waiting for a show to start and instead of preparing for it I am searching the building for my missing model."

A wave of guilt rushes through me.

"I'm sorry," I say meekly. "And... I just want to say thank you. For... letting me be part of this..." I glance at Nick. "Special event. With you. Now."

I can't say any more than that without giving it all away.

"You were free," Yuka says bluntly. "I'd rather spend my money on things I can rely on working properly."

Then she turns rigidly towards the stairs.

"I expect you to be downstairs and in position in forty-five seconds, Harriet," she says over her shoulder. "There will not be a next time."

Then she turns the light off over our heads with a *click* and disappears down the stairs.

Just for old times' sake, I guess.

There's a silence while Nick and I stand in the dark.

There will not be a next time.

"Nick," I manage finally into the darkness. "You didn't need to do that. Lie for me, I mean."

"I didn't," he says simply. "Who do you think wrote the sign on the door downstairs in the first place?"

Then with a small smile Nick disappears down the dark stairs too.

Leaving me: transparent like crystal behind him.

67

OK, it's time for me to *focus*.

Because I've done a fair few fashion shows, and so far they have consisted of: walk, walk, walk, walk, make a mistake, get yelled at, regret ever trying to model in the first place.

This time, I'm committed to performing flawlessly.

Partly because this is by far the most important fashion job I've ever done. Partly because humans have been upright and bipedal for 3.7 million years so it's really not that much to ask of me.

But mainly because there are only so many ways you can screw up *walking* and I've already done them all.

As for everything else...

I think we can wait a little while longer.

As calmly as possible, I make my way back into the main room.

Then I blink at the shift in atmosphere.

Just fifteen minutes ago, the room was full of noise and chaos and mess: of hairdryers, make-up, hairbrushes, rollers: models chatting, stylists yelling, Poppy and Shola complaining loudly about their agents in the corner.

But now it's totally silent.

The tables have all been moved and tidied, and there's a line of models queued against the side of the room. All bright, all beautiful; all sparkling and excited.

And all behaving – I have to say it – *perfectly.*

"Harriet!" Fleur hisses across the room, pointing frantically to the space in front of her. "She's coming! Quickly! Get in!"

As fast as possible, I skip over to my position.

"Do we have no shoes?" I whisper, suddenly realising that every single model in the room is barefoot.

"Not for this one," Fleur says with a wry grin. "Although knowing Yuka it may be because this show is going to include walking across burning coals."

Oh, thank *sugar cookies.*

My chances of falling over just decreased by five thousand per cent. I'd happily take third-degree burns over wearing high heels any day.

Poppy glares at me icily from four girls in front, and I smile winningly back.

"If we're all *here* now," a hard voice says as the front door swings open, "I'd like your full attention."

We turn obediently to the front.

Yuka's standing in the doorway. She's now wearing hot pink lipstick, but she still looks tired and pale: fragile and brittle under the thick make-up.

"This show is momentous," she says as I feel another pang of sadness. "It will be the pinnacle of a career that has spanned thirty years and changed the fashion industry as we know it."

From anyone else, this would sound incredibly arrogant: even slightly delusional.

From Yuka, it just sounds true.

"In front of me are nineteen of my best designs," she continues. "This is a lifetime of my work, and I will *not* accept any errors. You are not here to wear my dresses. You are here for my dresses to wear you."

And I suddenly realise that this night might be a tiny part of my own personal history but it represents *all* of Yuka's.

Her entire life, standing in front of her.

Swallowing a lump, I glance at the door behind her: a quiet drumbeat is starting to pulse and, over the top of that, violins, clarinets, oboes, rising softly.

And blimey: is that a *piano*?

"On cue, you will walk through the door, down the aisle, turn and pose for ten seconds at the end," Yuka says sharply. "Then you will wait on the stage, where I will—"

She stops abruptly.

And for just a moment I see an expression flicker across her face: the first real emotion I've ever seen on it.

"Where I will—" she repeats.

Everyone is staring at Yuka with wide eyes: apart from Fleur, who frowns at me in confusion.

What's going on? she signals with her eyebrows.

So I shrug with my best "mystified" expression and turn back to the front with another wave of sadness.

"Where I will join you," Yuka finishes in a clear voice. "At which point you will all applaud me loudly and unreservedly until I tell you to stop."

There's a ripple of relieved laughter, even though I'm absolutely certain that is not a joke.

"I expect nothing but the best," Yuka says firmly, resting her fingertips on the door handle. "I chose you all for a reason."

For a second she pauses and I see it again: something flickers across her face and then flashes away again, like a fish underwater.

A graveness has descended on the room.

Even Poppy, Shola and Rose have apparently been humbled by Yuka's uncharacteristic candour. Nobody else seems to know where it's come from or what to do with it now it's here.

I wish I didn't either.

With a tiny nod Yuka opens the door.

"Models, get out there," she says firmly, turning to look back at all of us. "And I'll see you at the end."

68

One by one, we file out.

First the raven-haired girl in the Octopus Dress, then a brunette in black sequins; then Shola in turquoise lace, the sky-blue-haired girl in the Sumo Dress, Rose in purple feathers…

Slowly, the two lines get shorter.

Swallowing, I watch as Poppy adjusts the pink Manga Girl Dress, lifts her chin, gives her head a quick toss and then swishes through the door: it closes softly behind her.

"No sitting down," Fleur reminds me as we get closer to the front. "I don't think it'll impress them this time."

I smile and shake my head.

Then we both watch as an angular girl in lilac disappears, followed by a brunette in yellow and a blonde in green.

I'm suddenly at the front.

I read somewhere that a red-bellied woodpecker has

a tongue so long that – when retracted – it forks into the throat, goes below the base of the jaw, and wraps round the inside of the bird's skull.

That's exactly how I feel now.

As if I can't speak or swallow; all I can do is hover a few feet off the ground and try to resist the urge to repeatedly bash my head against something.

With infinite slowness, the door begins to swing open and for a split second I can see Nat: sitting next to Silva and leaning forward with an ecstatic, transfixed expression on her lovely face.

Behind her – in the second row – there's a flash of pink hair and smiles.

And then, with a lurch in my chest, I see Nick.

Sitting at the back, dark eyes trained intently on the door I'm about to walk through.

Trembling, I step forward.

A gentle hand pulls me backwards again.

"Harriet," Fleur whispers. "Switch on your dress! Or Yuka will never forgive you." Quickly, she fumbles for the button in the back and presses it. "There you go."

And – with a click – I'm suddenly covered in a thousand glittering stars again. "Thank you," I whisper gratefully, because that was *way* too close for comfort.

I guess there was one mistake I hadn't made yet after all.

Then the door swings open wide.

And everything and everyone on both sides of it disappear completely.

69

In front of me is a garden.

Immediately to my left stands a knotted, ancient oak tree – erupting into a dignified mass of green leaves – and round every branch are wound thousands of tiny white lights on golden wires.

Underneath it sits an orchestra with gold instruments and a grand piano: filling the air with a delicate, lilting, triumphant music.

Around the garden other trees are similarly lit, and yellow and white flowers are strewn everywhere: flowing from huge golden urns, hanging from golden birdcages, sprouting from golden troughs.

Above us is another network of lights, strung like a sparkling cobweb against a black sky dotted with stars and planets, and behind the garden is the whole of Sydney: the glittering bridge arching to the right and the moonlit harbour filled with busy, blinking boats.

In the middle of the garden sit hundreds of ornate

golden metal chairs, on which are perched Yuka's esteemed guests, all wearing rapt expressions.

And directly in front of me is a soft grass aisle.

Edged with flickering golden candles and strewn with yellow petals, leading to the prettiest white bandstand also covered in lights and hung with gold chiffon: on which quietly stand the models who went before me.

I mean, you've got to hand it to Yuka.

When she commits to something, she really goes for it. There are approximately six billion light bulbs in the entire world, and something is telling me she has bought *the majority of them.*

And it was worth every single penny.

Never mind a pot of gold: this is *exactly* what it should look like at the very end of a rainbow.

Taking a deep breath, I wait as the girl in front finishes her pose and carefully sashays up the stairs to the bandstand to join the others.

Then a woman standing silently next to the doorway whispers "Go."

And I suddenly know that this is it.

This is everything my modelling career has been leading up to, from the second it began. Because maybe every mistake I've made – every stumble, every tumble, every crash, every humiliation – I made for a reason.

So I could give the woman who started my career the perfect end to hers.

"*Go*," the woman behind me whispers for a second time, and with a deep breath I nod and lift my chin.

With my face relaxed, I stare straight ahead.

Then I start walking.

And with every step, I can see and feel and hear it all: the soft grass beneath my feet, the soaring fanfare of the orchestra, the glimmering lights of my dress, the proud faces of Nat and Bunty and Nick as I glide past them.

Because I don't always need plans or strategies.

In this moment, I don't need bullet points and maps; I don't need to know where I'm going or where I've been. I don't need to look to the future to try to see what's coming or the past to see what has already happened; I don't need to assess or analyse or theorise or research or dissect anything.

In this precise moment, all I need is *now*.

All I need is *me*.

Face composed, I reach the spot at the end of the aisle.

With more grace than I've ever felt before, I stand very still and twist my head: put my hand on my hip, feel the warmth of the air and smell the countless delicate flowers and feel hundreds of eyes trained in my direction.

Through the door, I can just see Fleur slowly emerging: shimmering green.

Ten, nine, eight...

And I can suddenly feel contentment pouring out of me.

Splashing in a warm light that seems to emanate from my chest and wrap round me: holding me tightly and safely in one place.

Seven, six...

Scientists say that we have approximately $7*10^{27}$ – that's a seven followed by twenty-seven zeroes – atoms in our bodies, consisting predominantly of oxygen, carbon, hydrogen, nitrogen, calcium and phosphorus.

These elements were formed when the universe was created: when the heat and pressure of the Big Bang forced together atoms to create new ones, which slowly – over billions of years – evolved to become us.

Five...

Which is incredible, when you really think about it.

Because it means that ninety-three per cent of every single one of us is made of stardust that has never been combined in this exact order before: it has never been us before and it will never be us again.

But it will always be here somewhere.

Which means we are *all* infinite.

Four, three...

And we are *all* irreplaceable.

Two...

With a joyful smile, I drop my arm.

One.

And, calmly, I walk up the stairs and take my place among the stars.

70

There's just enough room up here.

As the remaining models walk the aisle and join us on the bandstand, it slowly becomes clear that there's exactly the right amount of space for nineteen people, to the nearest centimetre.

Which could be a huge coincidence.

But somehow – knowing Yuka – is a lot more likely to have been strategically planned with a tape measure and our exact hip specifications.

With a wink, Fleur slips in next to me and squeezes my hand.

Then I glance into the audience.

Nick's eyes lock with mine, and – slowly – his face breaks into a wide, bright grin.

I smile proudly back.

Then I turn to the front and watch Yuka walk rigidly down the aisle.

One by one, the crowd rises to its feet.

And – cautiously at first, and then with more vigour – the garden begins to fill with the sound of clapping: rippling through the sky like raindrops.

Slowly, she reaches the end and turns round.

Then as if by some kind of Narnian spell, the clapping slowly halts and the orchestra stops playing.

All that's left is the distant sound of the boats in the harbour and five hundred and twenty hearts.

Beating simultaneously.

"Fashion," Yuka says finally into the silence. "Every single person here tonight has dedicated their life to a love of it."

I blink twice. Not *everyone*, Yuka.

Somewhere in the changing room behind us is a diplodocus T-shirt that would strongly undermine that statement.

"Yet fashion divides. Some see it as frivolous and vain: an elite industry that objectifies and segregates the world into those who have, and those who have not."

There's a murmur in the crowd.

"Some see it as a way to make a frequently ugly world more expressive, more creative, more beautiful."

Now fervent nods.

"Others see it as…" Yuka smiles minutely. "*Just clothes.*"

Abruptly, I flush bright red.

"All are correct, yet without question fashion has the

power to change, unite and inspire. So tonight I have two announcements."

I can literally hear five hundred and twenty breaths drawing in.

Or two thousand, six hundred litres of air being held.

"First," Yuka continues, "these dresses are for sale. Money raised will fund a foundation supporting young people from all backgrounds in design careers, within *Haute couture and* high-street fashion."

The murmurs are starting again.

"It will be called the Yuka Ito Foundation," she adds. "Obviously."

Now a ripple of shocked laughter and claps.

"And secondly…"

Here she pauses, and a wave of panic tightens my throat. *Please not now, Yuka. Don't tell them the truth like this. Not until Nick already knows.* Urgently, I search to meet his eyes in the crowd but he's focused intently on his aunt.

"This will be my final show," Yuka finishes. "I have retired from the fashion industry."

The murmurs are swelling to a frantic chorus, but I only feel relief flooding through me.

At least there's still time.

With a patience I've never seen in her before, Yuka waits until the garden is silent again.

"This show is a celebration of my immense talent," she continues finally, "and of fashion itself. In one way or another, it has changed our lives."

Without warning, there are suddenly tears in my eyes.

Because now I can see a final ghost.

Lying in a pile of broken hats, wearing a green polyester football kit because her clothes had sick on them: wishing she was someone else.

Anyone else, other than herself.

And that girl doesn't exist any more.

Because it turns out they're not *just clothes* at all; they never actually were.

With a glance to the side, Yuka lifts a hand and nods at the orchestra.

Turning, she looks at her models and bows slightly.

Then she clicks her fingers and the sky fills with music and shimmering fireworks – exploding over the garden like metallic flowers – and gold confetti: shooting upwards in a riot of pops around us and raining down in a flurry of glitter.

And as the cheers begin again and the audience rises to its feet once more, Yuka slowly turns and walks stiffly back through the sparkle and chaos to the observatory.

Closing the door behind her.

71

Now, I know a lot about gold.

I know that nearly all the gold on Earth came from meteorites that hit our planet over 200 million years after it was formed.

I know that six ten-billionths of the sun is pure gold, and the most valuable legal tender in the world is a 1,000-kg Australian coin worth forty-five million dollars.

I know that gold has been found in the leaves of Australian Eucalyptus trees and that our own bloodstreams contain about 0.2 milligrams of the element.

And I know that the chemical symbol for gold is *Au*.

But as I stare at the garden of a star observatory in Australia – decorated with gold, coated in gold, filled with people who *are* gold, in a country that literally *starts* with gold – I suddenly realise that Yuka must know all of this too.

Because *nothing* she ever does is by accident.

*   *   *

"Wow," Fleur whispers as we make our way down the aisle towards the backstage. "Did you see that coming? *Retiring?* I thought Yuka was going to keep going forever. I mean, she can't be more than, what – forty-five?"

"Forty-seven," I say quietly.

I know, because during the early stages of our relationship I got Nick to tell me all about his family tree. Then I put the genealogical data into an illustrated chart and gave it to him for Christmas.

I'm *pretty* certain he loved it.

Ears gently ringing from the fireworks, I push open the door to the main room. It's a mess again already: all of the models, including me, are quickly undressing and handing their precious gowns to stylists who immediately cover them in silk and take them out of harm's way.

"Good thing there were no shoes this time, Freckles," Poppy says sweetly, gliding smoothly past me in her non-cartoon bra and knickers with an unsightly red rash rising across her ribcage. "I seem to remember you do *so well* in heels."

So I stick my tongue out at her back.

I know it's not very mature but I'm not seventeen for another five months and it feels *so good.*

"I've got to go," Fleur says, carefully unzipping her dress, handing it to a stylist and then tugging her jeans and T-shirt on. "I have to get the next flight back to London in time for classes on Monday."

She gives me a brief but intense hug.

"Umm," I say nervously, fumbling through my satchel. "Do you want my – uh."

Because frankly the last time I asked Fleur if she wanted my number she literally ran away in the opposite direction.

I'm not sure I want to repeat the experience.

"What the hell is *that*?" she says, widening her grey eyes at the Brick in my hand. "What year is this? Can you time-travel through that thing?"

I laugh. "I'm thinking we should go back to 1876 so we can show this atrocity to Alexander Grahám Bell."

"He'd be outraged."

"Disgusted."

"Maybe you could just leave it with him."

We both laugh, then Fleur puts her number in my phone and I have to stifle an air-punch of triumph. Studies have shown that we may have an average of 155 social-networking friends each, but only turn to *four* of them if we're in trouble.

And now I have five, so take *that,* scientists.

For the first time in my life, I've beaten the friendship odds.

Team FRJNTH, *here we come.*

But before I enter the party, there's something left to do.

And I need a bit of privacy, so after I wave goodbye to Fleur I quietly slip away from the stylists and hubbub.

Then I get a physics textbook out of my bag, sit in a corner chair and quietly study the random nature of radioactive decay until everyone else has left for the party happening outside.

When the room's finally empty, I walk over to a table and sit down in front of the mirror.

Slowly, I pull out a wet, soaped cloth and start wiping at my face.

And, layer by layer, the paint comes off.

Foundation, primer, powder, blusher, lipstick, highlighter, contour, eyeshadow, mascara, eyeliner: covering the white cloth in a thick sludge of muddy colours. With a new wet cloth, I do it again and again: gently wiping my face until it's completely clean.

Then I put the cloth down and stare at my face.

My skin is very pale and densely freckled all over, like the egg of a bird. My cheeks are round, my chin is pointed and my nose is slightly too short for my face: turning up at the end. I have an upturned mouth, and big, almost lashless eyes that are a pale moss green and set far apart, exactly like – as Wilbur once pointed out – a frog or an alien.

One of my front teeth is minutely crooked, my eyebrows are fair and sparse, and there's already a faint line between them from where I scowl when I'm studying hard.

(Which is something I haven't done much of in the last few weeks, come to think of it. I should probably look into drafting a Catch-Up Timetable asap.)

From where I've been scrubbing it, my forehead is rosy and shiny: there's a large, angry spot forming on my chin, and a few more erupting on my cheeks because of all the thick make-up.

Carefully, I untie my hair from its tight bun and it pings out: a riot of frizzy red curls. With a tiny smile, I pull Bunty's slightly wilted daisy off a tendril at the back and put it in my pocket.

There's faint music and laughter coming through the door from the garden, but the room I'm in is totally silent.

But then, with a rush, I can suddenly hear them all: every single unkind word I've ever been called.

Circling in the air above my head like angry flies: buzzing and buzzing, as if they're desperate to find somewhere to land.

Ugly. Freckles. Nobody. Boring. Loser. Spotty. Carrots. GEEK.

But for the first time, they can't seem to settle or stick on me.

There's nowhere for them to go.

Still smiling, I reach a hand up and start batting at

them: hitting the words, one by one, until they're dead on the floor. Empty ghost words that have no meaning, no use, no purpose, no truth in them.

Definitions that aren't in my dictionary any more.

Because from this point onwards, nobody gets to choose the vocabulary I use for myself but *me*.

Smiling, I lean forward and give my beautiful, flawed and irreplaceable face a quick kiss in the mirror. After all, none of those social-networking statistics said that my sixth best friend couldn't be myself.

That's not cheating at all.

Then I stand up and take a deep, brave breath.

Because – as we all know – this is normally the point in my story where everything starts unravelling: where my lies come home to roost.

Except this time I've only told one.

So I guess I'd better make sure I'm there when it does.

72

A salamander can breathe through its skin.

And it's a shame I can't, because the second I step into the garden party I'm being hugged so tightly I'm not sure my lungs will ever be useful again.

"Harriet!" Nat yelps, squeezing me a bit tighter. "Where were you? I've been waiting out here for ages! Oh my God, wasn't that just the most magical, amazing, breathtaking—"

She stops and holds me at arm's length.

"Aww," she says in disappointment, looking me up and down. "Didn't they let you keep that dress, at least for the party? You should have said and I'd have brought another one with me."

I look round at five hundred people, milling around the garden in insanely stylish clothes: holding glasses of champagne and looking a million Australian dollars.

Then I look down at my old, crumpled T-shirt, long, baggy shorts and trusty purple flip-flops.

At a total of about fourteen dollars fifty.

"Nope," I say, beaming and linking my arm through Nat's. "I'm actually a lot more comfortable as I am."

"Even though the diplodocus *is* standing in the wrong position," Nat points out. "Because its neck should be held parallel to the floor and *not* up like a giraffe, right?"

"Right," I laugh. "It's an atrocity. The company didn't even answer my letters."

"How many did you send in the end?"

"Five. Royal Mail sacked Postman Pat in 2000 so I just can't trust them any more."

We both giggle and commence a slow turn around the garden, like recovering ladies in a Victorian convalescence. I'm subtly looking for Yuka and/or Nick, but they're nowhere in the glittering crowd and I'm not exactly sure how to track them down.

Or I *am*, but I've done quite enough of that over the last few days.

Frankly, I've used up my stalking allowance for the decade.

"Where's Silva?" I ask instead, picking a tasty-looking morsel of puffed pastry off a gold platter held by a waitress in a gold waistcoat.

"She went off to write her blog," Nat says, grabbing three cocktail sticks of cheese and olive from another passing waiter and ramming them in her mouth simultaneously. "Newawatospadiseninwau."

I laugh and wipe my face. "You might want to try that again without covering me in dairy-flavoured spit, Natalie."

My best friend swallows with a grimace. "I *said*: Anyway, I want to spend the rest of this evening with you. Although if you're going to be all hoity-toity I might change my mind."

"Well, that phrase comes from the now-defunct verb *hoit*, which meant *to indulge in riotous, noisy mirth*. So maybe I *will*, Natalie. It *is* a party, after all."

"I stand corrected," Nat grins. "As per freaking usual."

Smiling, I stick my hand out to take another pastry *flight in the wind*, then abruptly stop with it hovering in mid-air.

Somewhat — you know, appropriately.

"What?" Nat says as my eyes go very round. "What are we looking at?"

"Over there," I whisper, nodding to a space under the huge oak tree. Bunty and Yuka are standing close together on the other side of it, talking quietly but earnestly. Yuka is rigid in her black lace, and my grandmother is fluttering in rainbow tie-dyed cotton.

The orchestral music is glorious but I wish they'd stop playing for a minute: it's very hard to eavesdrop properly over a grand piano and full accompaniment.

As subtly as we can, Nat and I inch silently towards Yuka and Bunty, like conjoined twin cats.

"Do you think they're making up?" Nat whispers.

"It's hard to tell," I frown, edging closer. Yuka's face is as impassive as always: a perfectly formed piece of carved white granite. Bunty – as usual – is beaming and there are several leaves in her hair.

On the upside, at least Nick remains nowhere to be seen.

Which means there's still time to confess.

"Is she… giving her a daisy?" Nat says doubtfully as Bunty holds out a tiny white flower.

"I don't think that's going to help much," I agree as Yuka stares at the daisy in the exact way my cat Victor regards celery. "I mean, Yuka's not exactly known for—"

"Whoooa," we both say at the same time.

Because in one stiff movement, Yuka has just taken the flower, leant forward and kissed my grandmother firmly on the cheek.

"Blimey," I say as Bunty gives Yuka a warm hug and wanders off down a garden path. "I thought for a second she was going to bite h—"

Then I stop, mid-sentence.

Oh God.

No. No. No no no no no *no* –

Because Nick is striding out of nowhere across the grass directly towards Yuka with a huge, confused frown on his face.

Sugar sugar sugar sugar sugar sugar –

"Quick," I say to Nat, glancing around. "*Hide.*"

And before my best friend can respond, I grab her arm and drag her behind the tree.

73

What can I say?

Tortoise by name, tortoise by nature.

According to an article in *New Scientist* magazine, they're actually much smarter than anyone thought: outwitting rats in a memory-maze-running test, and showing cognitive social skills nobody previously believed they had.

I think they may even outsmart me.

Given that in any emergency I just try to make my surface area as small as possible and hope nobody sees me.

"Harriet?" Nat whispers as I squat on my haunches with my arms wrapped over my head. "Did you lie again?"

I nod, peeking out from under my elbow.

"Oh, *Harriet*," she sighs as we lean out from behind the tree and watch Nick approach, his frown deepening even further. "What are we going to do with you?"

"I don't know," I whisper back honestly, although something tells me we're about to find out.

"Yuka," Nick says urgently, stopping a few metres away from us. "What's going on? None of us knew. The family, I mean. Mum doesn't know. You're retiring early? Why? Is everything OK?"

In a panic, I grab Nat's hand tightly.

Nick's normal laid-back nonchalance has disappeared and his cheeks are flushed: every line in his body is tense, ready to pounce.

"I'm fine, Nicholas," Yuka replies, lifting her eyebrows. "You're being melodramatic. Don't make a scene."

Nick's eyes go very wide. "*I'm* making a scene? *Me?*" He looks around him at the lights and gold confetti and hundreds of people.

I mean, he does have a point.

"This is neither the time nor place," Yuka says firmly. "Please keep your voice down and we will talk about the situation later."

People are starting to stare in their direction.

My hand squeezes Nat's again and – catching up via Best Friend Telepathy – she squeezes silently back.

"Yuka," Nick says, in a much lower voice. "If something's wrong... If you're not... We're your *family*. We should *know.* Is..." He pauses. "Is this why you asked me to be here this evening?"

Oh God. Oh God oh God oh God –

"Excuse me?"

"The apology message you sent through Harriet. Is that what this was about? Do you need to tell me something? Should I call Mum?"

There's a short silence, then Yuka's eyes flicker determinedly round the garden: clearly looking for me.

Quickly, Nat and I pull our heads back behind the tree. *Bat poop.*

"Harriet?" Yuka says with infinite slowness. "Manners?"

For a second I assume she's spotted me, and then I realise she's just clarifying the depths of this round of my eternal fabrications.

"Yes," Nick frowns. "She came all the way to Byron Bay to tell me she'd seen you and that you'd apologised for our fight and asked me to come tonight and it was important… and…"

He draws to a confused halt and I know it's all over.

In one second, Nick's going to know I lied. I'll be the crazy stalker again, and any remaining connection between us is going to burst straight into flames.

Oh God oh God oh God oh –

"Ah," Yuka says, finally. "I asked the girl not to say anything, although I should have realised that was an inherently impossible request. But yes." She pauses. "I apologise, Nicholas. I should have put your happiness

381

above your contractual obligation to me. Sorry."

I blink three times. *What?*

Obviously, I haven't seen Yuka in months. We never bumped into each other or spoke; she didn't pass a message on, or apologise. In fact, this is the first time I've ever heard her apologise to anyone.

So *why did she just lie for me*?

Either this is some kind of weird loyalty, or we actually did have a conversation that I've completely blacked out of my brain: right now I'm so bewildered that either seems perfectly possible.

Nick looks almost as confused now as I do.

Frowning, he stares hard at his aunt – clearly trying to piece it all together – then his face abruptly relaxes with relief.

"I'm sorry too," he says with a wide grin.

And before I can register what's happening, Nick bends down, wraps his strong arms round tiny, pale, fragile Yuka and picks her up in a hug so enthusiastic her feet physically leave the floor.

She winces, and I shoot up in a bolt of horror.

Humans have 0.9 thoughts a second, and I can tell you exactly what my not-quite-complete one is right now.

And not even Nat's hand on my arm is going to stop it.

"Stop!" I yell, jumping out from behind the tree and running towards them both as fast as I can. "Put her down! You're going to *hurt* her! Nick, she's *sick*!"

74

OK: I could have done that *days* ago.

If my Big Plan was to break this sensitive, devastating news to Nick by yelling it at him across a packed garden, I could have saved myself a *whole* lot of meddling, surfing, awkward conversations and uncomfortable bus journeys.

Except... obviously, it wasn't.

Blinking, Nick swiftly puts Yuka down and turns to me. "What?"

I stop on the lawn, breathless.

It's hitting me now what I've just done.

"She's... umm." I swallow as they watch me with wide eyes. "Yuka's not very... I overheard this conversation... It's quite a..."

Nope: it turns out that yelling is the only way I can actually divulge delicate information.

Instead, I turn to Yuka with wide eyes.

"Please," I beg as Nat appears from behind the tree

384

and stands quietly behind me. "Please just tell him. I know I shouldn't have done that, and it wasn't my place, but he needs to know, and… you need someone to be there and look after you."

Nick looks at his aunt, stricken. "What's going on? Yuka?"

But Yuka's still staring directly at me with a look on her face I've never seen before: as if the marble has somehow softened.

Which should be technically impossible as the melting point of calcium carbonate is 825 °C, but maybe the required heat is coming from my face.

"I'm not sick, Harriet," she says quietly.

"You are," I insist, cheeks burning hot enough to melt zirconium (1,852 degrees). "I overheard Bunty saying that she needed to see you…" I swallow. "You know, before you…"

"I'm not sick, Harriet," Yuka says again firmly.

What?

I'm now blinking rapidly, trying to work out what is going on.

Because once more I must have overheard wrong, *again*, constructed an entire narrative in my head that wasn't true, *again*, and jumped to my own ridiculous conclusions.

That were totally wrong, *again*.

"Harriet," Nick says as I stare at them in bewilderment. "Is *that* why you chased me round Byron Bay like a crazy person? Because you thought my aunt was ill?"

I nod, flushing even harder.

Tungsten has the highest melting point of any element at 3,422 °C, and is used in bulb filaments, rocket nozzles and reactor linings. From the heat radiating in my cheeks now I'd *still* be able to destroy it from a hundred metres away.

"I-I just wanted to be there if you were sad."

Nick opens his mouth and shuts it again.

There's a long silence: the kind of silence you could disappear into, if it were possible to make a black hole out of silences.

Then Nat quietly slips her hand in mine.

Because Yuka's still staring at me, and her face is still melting, and her eyes are soft, and her mouth is gentle, and all the heat in my body is beginning to disperse. Slowly dropping from my cheeks, then my stomach; my arms, shoulders, legs and feet; my toes and my fingers.

Back down to thirty-seven degrees – the temperature of a living human body – then plummeting further. To caesium: twenty-nine degrees at freezing point.

To krypton (–157) and argon (–189).

To oxygen (–218) and fluorine (–220) and neon (–249).

Until I'm so cold it's −272 degrees and I'd freeze solid if I was made of helium.

"I'm not sick," Yuka says gently for the third time, and I finally hear it.

I'm not sick.

I'm not sick.

I'm not sick.

"No," I say, taking a step back. "No."

"I'm so sorry, Harriet," Yuka says gently. "She wasn't ready to tell you."

"No," I say again as Nat reaches for me: pulling away and stumbling blindly through the garden.

But it doesn't matter how hard I look: there's no pink hair, no sparkles, no flowers, no floating rainbow clothes, no warm smile, no little chats about daisies.

Just flashing blue and red lights: rounding the corner.

Because it looks like I finally got something right after all.

It just wasn't Yuka I was right about.

It was Bunty.

75

People are like glass.

Some you can see straight through; others shine bright lights and iridescent colours everywhere they go. Some you look at and see parts of yourself reflected, and you look into some and see nothing but darkness.

Some people magnify so that everything around them seems bigger and more beautiful, while others can make even the largest things seem infinitely smaller.

People can be cracked or chipped, fragile or scratched, and still stay in one piece: even more precious and loved for all of their broken parts.

But sometimes... people shatter.

Bunty is released from Sydney Hospital two days later.

We fly straight home.

"I'm sorry, darling," she says blurrily as the air-staff wheel her on to the plane and Nat and I carefully tuck her under three blankets. "I ruined the end of your beautiful

evening." She flickers a smile. "Yuka must be *furious*."

"Yuka's not furious," I say quietly, kissing my grandmother's soft cheek. "She didn't mind at all."

Which is a total lie.

Judging by the way she sat abruptly on a bench and turned so she couldn't see the ambulance, Yuka Ito minded very much indeed.

Just not about the party.

"Naughty cells," Bunty says sleepily as the drugs start to kick in again and she rests her head gently on my shoulder. "Such terrible timing, darling. I did try to tell them that I am on *holiday* but they would not listen."

There's a scientific name for "naughty cells".

They're damaged oncogenes that are encouraging cells to replicate and multiply at an uncontrollable rate: a condition currently affecting one in two people in their lifetime.

Otherwise known as cancer.

I've had plenty of time to think things over during the last forty-eight hours, sitting in the hospital waiting room with Nat still holding my hand.

Bunty's sudden reappearance in my life – moving into our house a fortnight ago; Annabel's stress and exhaustion and forgetfulness, her weepiness and inability to turn off a simple kitchen tap or remember a basic date. The random urgent "spa" trips and "candle shopping" escapades that never made anybody look or feel any better.

All the blankets and tablets; the health foods and crystals; Annabel actually trying to cook; Dad's weird helpfulness and willingness to cover for my dramas.

And I've realised: Moonstone wasn't Bunty's friend.

She was her nurse.

As Bunty falls asleep and the plane takes off with a shudder, I quietly get Annabel's tightly folded KEEP WITH YOU AT ALL TIMES sheet out of my satchel and stare at it for the billionth time since the party.

Underneath her mobile number and Dad's number – below UK doctors and hospitals and insurance and passport details – are three words that would have forced everything else to make a lot more sense.

Sydney Oncology Department.

Except I didn't look at it, did I? I didn't even think to.

And if I had, I'd have seen Wilbur, Annabel, Bunty and Dad sitting round the kitchen table two weeks ago: constructing a plan.

I'd have seen that this was never really a modelling trip at all.

It was *always* about spending time with Bunty.

Dad and Annabel are waiting at the airport.

My grandmother wakes up just enough to give them

a bright smile, and say, "Hello, darlings, I *highly* recommend prescription drugs, that went by in a jiffy," before she drifts off to sleep again.

And I'm abruptly wrapped in parental arms like a jar lid targeted by a very affectionate octopus.

"Oh, my little girl," Annabel whispers into my hair as Dad kisses my forehead. "We're so, so sorry. We thought we'd planned everything so carefully but..."

"Sometimes plans don't work," I say into her bobbly jumper.

Then I blink. Hang on: Annabel's wearing a *jumper*? And *jeans*?

Where did they even come from?

"Sweetheart," my stepmother says, pulling back and holding my face in her hands. There are lines round her eyes I haven't seen before, and it's clear she's been crying hard. "Mum was so determined to have this holiday, she begged us not to say anything. But we thought she had more..."

"Chocolate," Dad finishes, nodding sagely. "We thought she had more chocolate. But we've been through her bags and the boot of her car and everything's made of hemp seed and avocado. A *huge* disappointment and we'll be making our complaints known when your grandmother wakes up."

A gurgle of snot pops out of my nose.

Annabel smiles and gives Nat a hug as well. "Thank you for being there, darling."

Nat nods in silence. We've barely spoken a word to each other for the last two days, but we haven't needed to. Everything I've thought and felt, my best friend has heard and felt too.

Scientists recently discovered that the limpet has teeth composed of thin, tightly packed fibres containing a mineral called goethite. They're the strongest natural material on the planet: so strong, that if they were the size of spaghetti they could hold an adult hippopotamus in the air.

That's what the string between Nat and me is made of.

We can tug and pull at it as much as we like: literally nothing and nobody is ever going to break it.

"Where's Tabby?" I say as we start pushing Bunty's wheelchair out towards the car park.

"*Tabitha!*" Dad says, smacking his head. "I *knew* we'd forgotten something!"

"She's with Toby and Rin," Annabel smiles, opening the car doors. "Dressed as a unicorn complete with a light-up horn, I would imagine."

"I'd like one of those," Bunty says, waking up momentarily. "Is there a spare?"

"We'll find one," Dad confirms. "Unicorn horns for everyone."

Gently, we put Bunty into the car and wait patiently until she falls asleep again.

Then I lean forward. "What happens now?"

"Now," Annabel says gently. "We go home."

76

I give Bunty my bedroom.

I don't need my own bed and my dinosaur posters and my homework and my timetables around me anywhere near as much as I thought I did.

The sofa is fine by me.

Hugo – after his initial flurry of excitement at my return – settles down quietly at my grandmother's feet and refuses to leave for the next five days.

Two researchers at Goldsmiths College in London recently tested eighteen dogs, and discovered that fifteen responded compassionately to a human in trouble: even if they were a stranger.

Victor, on the other hand, sits on Bunty's chest for two minutes, meows at her for food, then gets bored and escapes out of the window.

Which is exactly what you'd expect of a cat.

I'm just glad he was wearing a pink net tutu and a tiny pink bow at the time: as I've said before, karma.

Rin goes to stay with Nat, and – with Jasper and Toby – my friends pop by regularly with hot chocolates and burnt biscuits and information about how flamingos can bend their knees backwards (thanks, Toby).

And my family tiptoe around the house with our shoes off. Whispering and making green juices and trying to stay as calm and as cheerful as we possibly can. Because we know – without even discussing it – that it's what Bunty wants.

That and more crystals, hanging at the windows.

"Rainbows everywhere," she says, leaning back on the pillows with a gentle smile as I open the curtains and string up every wine glass I can find in the house. "Darling, let's fill this room with as many beautiful colours as we possibly can."

And I don't tell her that just by being there, she already does.

Instead, I show it.

Each morning, I ask her what she wants to know and then pull out every poetry book, every textbook, every schoolbook, every fact book.

And – bit by bit – I break the world into pieces and give it to her.

"Harriet?" Bunty says on Sunday as I put a glass of water on the bedside table and try to creep quietly out again. "Sweetheart?"

I turn round and look at her.

She's propped up against a myriad of colourful pillows: my favourite geek-glasses-print duvet pulled up to her chin and a fluffy yellow cashmere blanket over her shoulders. Her face is drawn and pale, her teeth seem a little too big, but her pink hair is still candy-floss bright and the soft smile is there: dimpling the corner of her mouth.

We sleep on average 229,961 hours in a lifetime, and Bunty now seems to be spreading hers out in little hourly bursts.

"Mmm?" I say softly, turning on a small lamp.

The Australian sunshine that briefly came home with us has gone and outside the clouds are dark and heavy: as if they weigh slightly too much for the sky.

Bunty opens her eyes and pats the bed next to her.

"Tell me more about sunrises," she says as I perch and Hugo soundlessly shuffles into my lap and puts his head on my knee. "I'm so very curious."

With a lump in my throat, I nod.

Downstairs I can faintly hear Toby, Nat, Jasper and Rin watching *Kung Fu Panda* for the seventeenth time: Team JRNTH has settled in for the long haul.

Although it's also raining pretty hard so there's a chance they just don't want to go outside and get soaked.

"Ordinary sunlight is made of a spectrum of colours

with wavelengths ranging from .47 micrometres for violet to .64 micrometres for red," I say as my grandmother closes her eyes again and rain hammers at the window. "Air molecules are closer in size to the wavelength of violet light, which means the sky normally appears blue."

I glance out of the window. It's not blue at all: it's a dark, almost metallic grey, and it's getting darker and rainier by the second.

"Although," I add, looking back, "if human eyes were more sensitive it would actually look violet to us."

"A violet sky," she smiles. "Lovely. What else?"

I glance out of the window again, but it's hard to imagine a sun right now: let alone it coming up or going down.

"At sunrise, the light takes a longer path through the atmosphere, and that scatters the blue and violet light so that the light reaches us instead as pink and red."

There's a silence, and for a second I think she's fallen asleep again. In fairness, it wouldn't be the first time somebody's done that during one of my science monologues.

Silently, I watch the rainwater for a few minutes, pouring in rivulets into the garden: filling the whole universe with water.

And I try not to feel like it's filling me too.

Finally Bunty sighs and shifts slightly on the bed. "But the sky is still blue in other places?"

"Yes," I confirm as Hugo softly licks her hand. "The same light can look pink to us while to others it'll look blue. It just depends what part of the world you're standing in."

"Ah. Because the world keeps turning?"

"Exactly." The lump in my throat is getting so big I'm not sure how my voice is getting out, but somehow it is. "For some of us it'll be a sunrise, and for some it'll be a sunset, and for others the sun will be directly overhead."

Bunty smiles. "So it's always there."

I look out of the window at the rain again and it suddenly feels like every bit of love I've ever felt is a bright golden ball, burning warmly in the centre of my chest.

"Yes, the sun's always there."

My grandmother opens her light blue eyes, and there's nothing but happiness: nothing but peace, and love, and contentment, and a life lived gloriously shining out of them.

"Then you can let go, my darling," my grandmother smiles gently. "And know that it always will be."

She dies the next day.

77

Fourteen days later

I've never actually been on a night-time hike through a wood before.

Probably for these three very good reasons:

1. I don't like strenuous physical activity.
2. I'm not very coordinated, even in the daylight.
3. There are a lot of trees.

"You know," Dad says, temporarily blinding me with his head-torch as I smack into yet another large trunk and let out my thirteenth *ow*. "I might get myself one of these for everyday use. They're kind of nifty."

The adult anglerfish is a deep-sea creature with an *esca* at the tip of its dorsal ray: covered in symbiotic bacteria that make the front of its head glow with a bright light.

399

It currently looks like this wood is full of them.

As instructed, each of us is carrying a coloured lantern and wearing a matching camping torch on an elastic band round our head: all you can see are bobbing coloured lights as we stumble and trip over roots and into bushes, grunting loudly.

Everyone apart from Annabel and Nat.

My stepmother refused to wear a head-lamp because she's "not a miner, for God's sake", and Nat has customised her red one with a red headscarf.

"I think Bunty would like it," my best friend asserts for the millionth time, rearranging it carefully and straightening out her red coat.

"I'm certain she would," I grin, looking down at my new leaf-green coat and lantern, then at everybody else: Tabby in white, Dad in blue, Annabel in yellow, Jasper in purple, Rin in pink and Toby in orange.

The list that was left behind was very specific.

And at the very top was written, in her usual beautiful curly writing.

1. ABSOLUTELY NO BLACK. ;)

It had even been underlined, twice.

Annabel and I suspect we're being very gently mocked, even now.

"Did you know," Toby says, flashing his bike helmet light on and off, "that the only anglerfish with a light is actually the *female* of the species? It attracts the tiny male fish, who then *fuses* into the female while his insides melt?"

"Such an appropriate story," Jasper sighs, rolling his eyes over the top of his purple lantern. "Any others you've kept for this occasion, Tobes?"

"Oh, yes," Toby confirms, orange light bobbing up and down. "Manakin birds moonwalk to impress the ladies."

"Like the Michael Jackson Five!" Rin nods, flashing pink.

"I've been known to do a bit of that too," Dad says, walking his blue light backwards straight into a tree stump. "What do you think, Annabel? Am I significantly hotter travelling in the opposite direction?"

Annabel doesn't look up from the compass she's studying.

"Exponentially so," she says, narrowing her eyes in her yellow light. "It's very dark too, so that helps."

"Burn," Dad tells Tabitha soberly. "Baby, burn."

My sister beams under her tiny white flashlight and smacks him gently on the nose.

"Like mother like daughter," he sighs proudly.

"OK," Annabel says, turning the compass again and finally looking up. "It's here. Why Mum couldn't just have left the coordinates so I could use GPS on my phone I have no idea."

Honestly, I think we all know why.

We're lucky we've not been expected to navigate to this precise spot via owl hoots, moonbeams and vague leaf markings done in charcoal. Directions, a map and a compass was actually more technology than any of us could have hoped for.

Blinking, we all flash our torches into the dark.

"What does it say next on the list, Harriet?" Nat says, leaning forward with her red headlight. "Read it out."

It goes without saying that I'm in charge of Bunty's list.

I mean, of all the things I've been training for my entire life, being in charge of other people's lists is right at the top of that list.

Carefully, I take it out of my backpack.

"It says *You will enter a beautiful clearing of trees*," I read slowly, holding my green lantern over the paper. "*One of them is much prettier than the rest.*"

"*Prettier?*" Annabel says in frustration. "How are we supposed to objectively and scientifically quantify, then identify which tree is—"

"It's this one," Dad says, pointing. "Look."

And sure enough: as we hold our lanterns up, the most beautiful tree I've ever seen looms out of the darkness. Huge and knotted and curled and ancient: the roots an intricate network like lace winding across the ground and the branches like a myriad of arms raised to the sky.

Round the bottom of the tree is a blanket of closed night-time daisies.

There's a short silence.

"OK," Annabel agrees with a tiny smile. "Prettiest tree, Mum. Tick. What's next?"

I look at the list. "*Get me out. Try not to drop me, darlings. I'm awfully spilly these days.*"

And I know we're not supposed to laugh right now, but we do.

Something tells me that was kind of the point.

Carefully, Annabel gets an elegant tin pot out of her bag: beautifully engraved with flowers and swirls and elephants, collected on one of Bunty's many journeys through India.

Then she bends down and puts it among the daisies.

"Done," Dad says, putting his arm round Annabel and helping her stand up again. "Now?"

I look at the paper, turn it over and then back again. "Next it says: *Wait.*"

We frown at each other with our rainbow lanterns.

There's a long silence.

"Does it mention for roughly how long?" Dad asks tentatively. "Because it's the middle of the night in a dark wood and I'm no scaredy-cat but..."

In the distance to our left, there's the sound of a twig cracking.

We all jump and spin towards it.

There's a tiny blue light, emerging from the darkness.

"What the—" Annabel says, breathing out.

Then there's another crack to our right, and we jump again: towards the sound of trees rustling and a green light, bobbing closer and closer.

We blink as a shadow emerges from the darkness.

Then behind us, bushes part and a yellow light appears, suspended by a shadow from the air. Followed by a purple one, another blue one, a white one, a yellow one; two red ones, an orange, three pinks, one turquoise.

Slowly more lights emerge from the trees.

People are walking through the darkness, each carrying with them a compass and a different-coloured lantern.

Men and women of every description: an old, white-haired man in a yellowy-orange tunic and orange trousers; a young dark-skinned woman in a long, floaty blue dress; a bald lady with a long green scarf and a small child in her arms.

Each appearing from between the trees, one by one.

"*Annabel*," Dad whispers as the crowd gets bigger. "*We're going to need more sandwiches.*"

We watch in amazement as the clearing slowly fills with dozens of brightly coloured lights and people, standing noiselessly in the dark. Peering with my green lamp, I see Wilbur appear from between two trees in a pink suit: he gives me a little wave and points triumphantly at his silver wellies.

Then Yuka emerges too, clad entirely in white.

She nods with a small smile.

I look back at the list, but there's just one thing left on it.

Say goodbye.

78

*G*oodbye.

We say it every single day, yet not all of us know that it's actually a diminutive of God Be With Ye... *godbwye*.

I don't believe in God, but I do believe in love.

And I think it's kind of saying the same thing. Because when a person leaves us, we instinctively ask them to take all our love with them.

And when we go, we leave as much of it as we can behind.

I don't know how Bunty did it.

Magic, or pigeon-carrier, or (more probably) email.

But she must have known the end was coming for quite a long time, because the wood is filled with people from all over the world: from India, from Bolivia, from Georgia and Russia; from Lithuania and Mongolia; Portugal and Nigeria; Romania and Slovenia, Taiwan and the Philippines; Vietnam and Thailand, Malaysia and

Mexico, Tibet, Peru, Japan and Zimbabwe. All of whom have travelled across the planet to say goodbye.

And as they step forward, they all have a different story for how Bunty touched their lives.

A sofa when they were tired; a hand when they were lost.

A smile or a joke, a wise word or a direction; coconut water when they had explosive diarrhoea.

And as they speak, I realise how much one person can be.

Away from the spotlight, without fame, without riches – without noise and without public attention – there can be so much greatness.

Quietly and gently, one life can be so loud.

Finally, the old man steps forward. He knew Bunty from a three-week trek across the Hebrides, fifteen years ago.

Which was enough to bring him here now.

"I think," he says, standing with his orange lantern under the big tree, "I'd like to say a word about Bunty Brown."

We all wait patiently for a speech.

The kind of long, tragic monologue that will unravel us all.

"Kind," he says, then steps back.

"Generous," a woman in blue with grey hair says, nodding.

"Hilarious," a man in green adds quietly.

"Honest."

"Gentle."

And – one by one – everybody in the group says something: *loving, affectionate, unconventional, adventurous, nomadic, energetic, incredibly unreliable* (there's laughter), *impulsive, inspirational, charming, wise, hippy* (even more laughter)... Words, rising through the treetops.

Finally, it's our turn.

There's a warm silence as we each look for our own individual way of saying goodbye.

"Loyal," Nat says, holding her red lantern higher.

"Interesting." Jasper smiles.

"Sparkly," Rin adds, nodding fervently.

"Bonkers," Toby states matter-of-factly, and there's more laughter.

"Maverick," Dad says with a broad grin, hugging my stepmother a bit tighter. There's a silence, and then Annabel kisses Tabitha gently on the forehead and looks directly at me.

"Mum," she says with a tiny smile.

And that's when I realise.

These aren't just words in the air any more: this is our narrative, and these are the stories we leave behind, written in the sky like stars. Across languages, across countries, across relationships, across years: these are the words that finally find somewhere to land.

And when it's all over, this is how we're read.

These are the words that matter.

Swallowing, I look at the giant tree arching into the darkness and think of my grandmother. Of her compassion and her fearlessness, of her curiosity and courage and wit: of her refusal to ever be anything but herself.

And as the golden sun starts to burn inside me again, I think of all the lessons Bunty taught me: without grades, without exams, without red marker-pens or little gold star stickers.

Without me ever realising I was learning at all.

Smiling, I touch the little dried daisy pinned to my coat.

Then I hold my green lantern higher.

"Brave," I say clearly.

One by one, each person quietly puts their lantern on the ground by the tree, until it's covered in rainbow lights.

Then I look at the list in my hand. There's nothing else written there: just a blank space where Bunty used to be.

So I look up.

At all the places she is now instead.

79

It turns out there are enough sandwiches after all.

From out of nowhere, food begins to appear: baguettes, cakes, camping pots of casserole and curry, fried chicken and fish, crisps and salads, bottles of ginger ale and beer.

Out of bags come guitars, sitars, banjos: triangles and flutes, recorders: pillows and blankets.

Somebody lights a small and frankly dangerous fire.

And, in the forest clearing, people start to chat, then to laugh, then to sing and dance.

Until the wood is full of sound and colour.

"Hello, my Baby-baby-Panda," Wilbur says, awkwardly perching on a tree trunk next to me.

I've found a fluffy blanket and a quiet place to sit, and I'm watching it all happening around me.

Toby and Rin, dancing like robots with a girl from Tibet.

Jasper, chatting to a man from Mexico about intricate art from the pre-Hispanic Mesoamerican era; Nat, asking

a heavily bejewelled woman where the fabric for her beautiful sari came from.

Annabel and Dad, chatting quietly with Yuka by the fire.

My baby sister, fast asleep in Dad's arms.

"Hi, Wilbur," I say, smiling at my agent as he brushes a twig off his twinkly suit with a vague air of confusion: I don't think he spends much time in the great outdoors. "I'm so glad you came."

"Treacle-chip," he says, grinning. "I wouldn't have missed this for the *world*. Especially since the majority of it seems to be here anyway."

We look at the dancing crowd together and I can see what he means.

"I'm not sure I've ever said thank you properly," I say after a short pause, turning back to him. "For... everything."

"You don't need to, my diddle-chop," he laughs. "I've thoroughly enjoyed being your fairy godmother. It's been a *delightification*. And on that note..."

He pauses and looks over at Yuka, who gives an almost imperceptible nod.

"This might not be the right time, poppet, but you should know that I've had a *humongous* amount of calls since the Sydney show. *Gallons* of them. I've been holding on to requests, until you're ready."

I fiddle with the strap on my bag. "Thank you."

"You know that game of Snakes and Ladders?" he says with a swift chuckle. "I don't know how you did it, but that was *exactly* the right ladder, little llama. The big one, that goes all the way to the top."

"Like getting a blank tile in Scrabble?"

"What good would that be, Dingle-bat?" he frowns, wiggling his silver, mirror-encrusted wellies. "Board games are distinctly *unfashionable* but even I know you need letters to play Scrabble."

I smile, then look back at the crowd. "Can I think about it?"

"*Absolutement,*" Wilbur nods. "But just so you know, I'll always be your fairy godmother, Sugar-lump. I am *not* giving up such fabulous wings for *anything.*"

Naz is an Urdu word that means the warm feeling you get from knowing you are loved, unconditionally, by people who will follow you to the end of the Earth.

And as Wilbur and I smile at each other – as I look at my friends and family, glowing in front of the fire – I suddenly know without question that *naz* is what I'm feeling.

Because – if I'd known where to look – it's been there all along.

"Just *one* more teensy thing to think about, chipmunk," Wilbur adds, standing up and shaking his mirrored wellies. "Actually, not so teensy. About six foot two, in fact."

I blink at him.

"Although," he twinkles, winking over my shoulder, "*something* tells me you've been thinking about him already."

There's a loud crackle from the trees behind me.

I spin round.

Walking through the dark, in a black suit, white shirt and black tie – holding a big white torch – is Nick.

80

Sometimes it feels like there aren't enough words in the world.

But at other times, there actually are.

"Nick, you're late."

He glances at the party, then smiles and turns his torch off. "Very, by the looks of it. Sorry. Although this isn't *exactly* what I was expecting." He looks down at his funeral suit. "Obviously."

Then he takes off his tie and jacket and sits down on the blanket next to me.

"Here," I say, handing him a big lime-green fluffy scarf somebody's abandoned during their arm-waving dancing. "There are sartorial rules and colour codes in the forest, and they have to be followed."

Smiling with his head tilted to one side, he wraps the scarf round his neck. "Better?"

"Infinitely."

"Apparently I don't follow instructions properly," he explains wryly. "Or use a compass with any talent. And I'm not very good at navigating woods in the dark either, although there's a shallow pond about a mile away that I know now pretty well."

He lifts his eyebrows and gestures at the thick mud liberally coating the bottom of his suit trousers.

"I did tell you that being a certified Girl Guide was handy for life skills."

"I know," he grins, "but they just wouldn't let me in."

We both laugh.

Then we sit in silence for a few minutes as the orange warmth of the fire flickers on our faces. It's the kind of silence you could nestle under and wrap yourself in, should you ever need to be comforted by silence.

Finally, Nick clears his throat.

"Harriet," he says quietly. "You broke my heart."

I turn to him, blinking in the firelight.

"That's what I wanted to say," he continues as I stare at him. "That night on Brooklyn Bridge – I thought I needed to go home, but when I was home all I could think about was you. And when you didn't respond to my letter I..." He pauses. "I didn't handle it very well."

I open my mouth. "But—"

"Like, at all. I drove my friends and family insane. For six whole months."

Oh. *Ohhhh.* "Is that why they—"

"The diving job was supposed to get me away from all of it," he continues quickly. "But then you showed up, doing disco moves underwater and nearly drowning in front of me."

I flush bright red. He *saw* that? "I wasn't..."

"You were," he says, with a wry grin. "I know a Harriet dance when I see one. And I was scared, and that made me angry, and then I was hurt and confused. But then you told me about Jasper and it all made sense. I realised that you never replied last summer because you'd already moved on."

Glancing up, I look at Jasper on the other side of the fire: still talking to the Mexican man.

And I suddenly remember...

Six months of carrying a box with Nick inside it; of doing everything I could to forget him; of waking up, crying; of going to sleep, crying; of pushing every thought of him I could away, as hard as I could so it wouldn't break me any more.

It never occurred to me that he was breaking too.

"That's not what happened," I say as Jasper looks briefly over, then goes back to talking. "Jasper and I—"

"I know," Nick interrupts. "Nat texted me just before Yuka's show. She also told me that if I ever hurt you again she would rip my head off."

Eyes wide, I glance over to where my best friend is lurking by a huge oak tree, unconvincingly pretending not to watch us.

That wily little monkey.

"But how did she get your—"

"Wilbur," Nick smiles. "Ever the eternal romantic."

I can now see my agent, standing with Rin and Toby. Toby gives me a big thumbs-up, Wilbur doffs an imaginary hat and Rin makes a heart shape with her hands.

"What I'm trying to say," Nick continues quietly. "Is that you were there for me when you thought I needed you. And now... I am here for you."

There's a lump in my throat so big I can't breathe.

After all this time, the truth finally tumbles out of me.

"Nick," I say. "I didn't ignore your letter. I wrote to you. I wrote to you over and over again. But I couldn't send them. I thought you needed me to let you go. So Bunty looked after them for me."

With a tug in the corner of his mouth, Nick reaches into his pocket.

Then he pulls out a wad of envelopes.

And there they are: every single letter I ever wrote to

him. Every word I ran to the post box with, and sent somewhere else instead.

Somewhere that couldn't hurt him.

"I know," he says simply. "I read them at the party. Bunty gave me them all."

81

In 1972, the *Apollo 17* mission was grounded.

Thanks to declining NASA spending, Eugene Cernan officially became the last man in history to ever visit the moon: breaking – with his crew – several records, including the longest moon landing, the longest moonwalks, the largest lunar sample and the longest time in lunar orbit.

Basically, he was up there a long time.

So – while they waited to come back to Earth – Eugene decided to make the most of it, and wrote his daughter's initials (TDC) in the dust with his finger.

He knew that because there's no gravity or wind or atmosphere in space, those letters would stay up there for billions of years: unchanging, unwavering, unshifting.

So when we look at the moon, what we're really seeing is a sign of love.

Engraved into the sky for all eternity.

* * *

"Nick," I say slowly as the golden ball in my chest starts to burn again. "Nothing's changed. The reasons we broke up are still there. We still live in different countries."

"Not for long, Harriet. I just got a place at Plymouth University to study Marine Biology. That's what I was training for on the boat: diving skills come in handy when you want to study plankton."

I stare at him in surprise. "*Plankton?*"

"Well, among other stuff," Nick grins. "I probably won't specialise just yet."

"You know that *plankton* is actually a Greek word that means *wanderer*?" I say automatically, suddenly thinking of the peregrine falcon on Brooklyn Bridge. "It kind of suits you."

"Thanks, Manners. You're a bit like algae that lives near the surface of the ocean too."

We laugh, then I look away: because something's been crystallising in my head for the last two weeks, and this news isn't going to change it.

"I'm... I should probably tell you I'm not going to be in England after school finishes," I say quickly, fiddling with the backpack straps again. "I've decided to go travelling. For a year before Cambridge, so I can see the world."

I'm about to add *Just like Bunty* but as I glance at the daisies under the tree something tells me I don't need to.

Nick's eyes widen in surprise, then he nods.

"OK," he says, visibly thinking it through. "There's more than a whole year until that happens, and then maybe I could just meet you out there? We can check out Vietnam or Cambodia or Peru together."

"Halong Bay has 1,960 limestone islands," I say, excitement starting to build. "We could stay on an authentic Indochina junk, which is a traditional Chinese sailing ship."

"Rich biodiversity in a marine environment," Nick nods. "It would basically be research."

"Four hundred and fifty different types of mollusc and two hundred types of fish. As well as an oceanic and seashore bio-system and a tropical evergreen bio-system."

"All right," he laughs. "You want to do my course for me?"

"No, thanks," I grin. "I'm going to dig up dinosaur bones, thanks very much. It turns out I'm not so skilled in water." I frown. "But, Nick..."

Briefly, I glance at Jasper again.

Then I take a deep breath.

"I'm high-maintenance. I get anxious and insecure, I worry, I try to control everyone and everything..."

"Wait," Nick says, eyes wide. "This is *brand-new infor—*"

"I interrupt people, I talk too much, I tell them facts

they're not interested in. I'm a know-it-all, I'm competitive, I get easily distracted, I analyse *everything*—"

"Just—"

"*Everything*, Nick. Literally everything that happens. I like plans, I like lists, I like schedules. I lie more than I should. I like knowing what's going to happen and I'm not breezy. I've never been laid-back in my life…"

"Harriet."

"I care too much, about everything, all of the time. I'm impatient and I try too hard. I'm bossy. I break a lot of things and fall over. A *lot*. I don't listen—"

"Harriet."

"I'm not even listening now."

"Harriet."

"I'm *hard work*, Nick. And I'm OK with that, but you need to be OK with that too because I'm not going to change."

Finally, I draw to a breathless stop.

"But that's the whole point," he says slowly with a warm smile. "I don't want you to change, Harriet. You're not hard work for *me*."

And that's when I know.

As Nick laces his fingers through mine and the golden sun in my chest starts burning so brightly it feels like it's going to explode, I realise that all that time we were focusing on our three stars, the moon had been there too.

Coming and going – waxing and waning – but never really leaving.

Always there: always shared.

Always reflecting love and light back at me.

"Acceptance," Lion Boy says, kissing me gently. *"Tick."*

82

Every story has an end.

And as Nick and I kiss on a blanket in a rainbow-lantern-lit wood, I realise that this isn't it: not quite yet.

There are two things left that I still have to do.

"Nick," I say, pulling away with my cheeks flushed and my lips tingling. "Would it be OK if I—"

"Course." He stands up. "I reckon there's a Toby Pilgrim conversation going on right now with my name written *all* over it."

I don't know how Nick knows that I want a moment to myself.

But he does.

"Don't let Tobes show you the Batman hankie," I say quickly. "It's been up that jumper sleeve for a *really* long time."

"Noted," Nick laughs loudly, reaching into his pocket. "Here," he adds, pulling out my planet necklace.

"You dropped it on the beach – lucky I found it."

Oh, thank *sugar cookies.*

Then he ambles off to where everyone I love in the world is gathered in a comforting little circle: Nat, Toby, Jasper, Rin, Wilbur, Yuka, Annabel, Dad, Tabby.

Briefly, I see something unspoken pass between him and Jasper, then Jasper nods and moves over so he can sit down.

And Nick takes his rightful place among them.

Still glowing, I put my precious necklace back on, stand up and hoist the candy-pink backpack Bunty gave me on to my shoulders. Frankly, it's *significantly* heavier than my satchel: I may have to do some serious weight training before my travel plans commence next year.

There are supposed to be seventy-seven muscles in the back, but it feels like I only have three or four of them.

On the upside, I have never felt more like a genuine tortoise.

Quietly, I make my way over to the far side of Bunty's prettiest tree.

Then – carefully – I use timeworn niches cut into the trunk to precariously climb up to a tree house, hidden in the branches.

Inside it's small and damp: dark and wooden.

But as I sit with my legs crossed and the precious

backpack tucked snugly in front of me, I can see "BB" carved into the wall with a swirly picture of a daisy.

Exactly where I knew it would be.

Then, I pull the Brick out.

And with a deep breath I make the call that I know is going to change my life once more.

"Howdy, you've reached Wilbur!" the answer machine says chirpily. "With a *bur* not an *iam*. Leave your voice on my digits and I'll tinkle you back if you sound fabulous enough. Ta-ta for now!"

There's a *beep*.

And, in that fraction of a second, I see it all...

Me in bed, covered in lipstick and talcum powder; falling down the coach aisle; smashing into a hat-stall; climbing under a table; thirty hands in the air; spinning under a spotlight; jumping in the snow; a ponytail, cut off; sitting on a catwalk; standing on a doorstep; my first kiss, on a television set.

I see a Japanese fish market and an octopus; a sumo stage; a glass box and a hundred dolls; a shining lake; a zebra crossing; a brand-new sister.

I see New York and a governess; a fairground ride; a planetarium; a party; Brooklyn Bridge. Toilet paper and Icarus; dinosaur biscuits; posters; Marrakesh and a monkey; parties of stars. Picnics and coffee; an advertising agency; a doppelganger; an Indian elephant and firework clouds of paint; a cafe, filled with pink. I see Sydney and diving and a fashion show that glittered with gold.

In short: I see a whole world, opening behind me.

And a new world, opening in front.

A world that I fit into perfectly.

"Hi, Wilbur," I say into his voicemail. "Thank you again. You're the best fairy godmother a polar bear could ask for, and the last year and a half has been a fairy tale. But I'm not going to take any more modelling jobs. I think I'm ready for my next big adventure."

Smiling, I put the phone down and get a red Sharpie out of my pocket. Because if we are all infinite and we are all irreplaceable, then it stands to reason that the narratives we write for ourselves are too.

Each of us, with our own distinct voice and way of looking at the world.

Each of us, a hero.

And every one of us: creating our own plots, selecting our own words and putting them in our own unique order.

Then – one by one – setting them among the stars.

Carefully, I write in big letters on the front of my backpack:

GEEK

Then I put my pen away.

Because these are my words, and this is my story.

Now you get to choose yours.

Acknowledgements

Each of us has a story, and GEEK GIRL is mine.

Not literally. The series is fiction, not autobiography: it has come from reading, from experience and research, from three decades of obsessive scribbling and – most of all – from an "overactive imagination" that has been getting me into trouble since I was three.

But it's the story I needed to tell.

It's also the story I needed to read when I was a teenager: when I was lonely and anxious and unpopular and felt like I would never be good enough, never pretty enough, never confident enough, never cool enough… never *enough*.

And, in telling this story, I think I've found a way to reach her. To slay the dragon, and to climb that tower. It's a fairy tale for the teenager I was, from the adult I turned into.

However, the story also needed help being told.

And – like any good adventure – there have been many magical guides along the way: remarkable people who have supported me, encouraged me, adored me and given me the wisdom I needed to get it done.

My mum, who gave me unlimited access to the local library and an intense love of books before I could even read; my dad, who told me I could be and do anything I wanted. My little sister, Tara, who listened to all my stories and believed them (even when she probably shouldn't have: sorry about that). My English teacher, Mr Bott, who told me at eleven to "always write honestly"; my sixth-form English teacher, Miss Hughes, who didn't punish me for (wrongly) thinking I already knew everything.

Helen, who first encouraged me to write these books and then read *all* of them.

My agent, Kate Shaw, who loved the first three chapters of *Geek Girl* and waited three years for the rest: who tirelessly, passionately and fiercely continues to support my writing and everything I do. Lizzie Clifford, my editor, who found and fought for Harriet and has championed her ever since: helping, beautifully and with great sensitivity, to shape these stories into what they are.

Everybody at HarperCollins, who immediately understood and believed in Team Geek, and has backed me – creatively and with enormous dedication – for years: Ann-Janine, Rachel, Pippa, Ruth, Sam, Abby, Geraldine, Nicola, Hannah, Lily, Kate, Elorine, Mary, Elisabetta, Carla, Paul, Simon, Alison, Sonia, Catherine, Camilla, Jo, Samantha, Rhiannon, Cate, Jessica, Alex and Sarah.

My family who have always loved the (frequently annoying) pilgrim soul in me: Grandma, Grandad, Judith, Lesley, Robin, Lorraine, Caroline, Veronique, Louise, Adrien, Ellen, Freya, Dan and Autumn.

To all these people I owe a huge debt of gratitude, and all these people I thank from the bottom of my heart.

But there's one more person I need to thank: you.

You are the person who has read this book and reminded me over and over again that there is an Army of Geeks already out there: living brilliantly and brightly and uniquely and fearlessly. That we all have the power to be who we want to be, one page at a time.

So, to you, I say thank you.

And I can't wait to tell you another story.